Covert STRENGTH

A *Crush* NOVEL

ELOUISE EAST

Publisher: Elouise East
Cover Design: Maria Vickers
Editor: Maria Vickers
Beta Readers: Emma Brown, Mike Van Eimeren,

CONTENTS

COVERT STRENGTH

DEDICATION

To those who believe they are not enough.
You are.

LIST OF CHARACTERS

(ALPHABETICAL ORDER)

- Analise, Bartender at Crush, Kade's girlfriend, Friends with Crush group
- Asher, Childminder, Sean's boyfriend (Instant Desire), Friends with Crush group
- Ashley, Dane's mother, Zak's ex-wife
- Casey, Paramedic, Luke's boyfriend (Life Support), Friends with Crush group
- Charlie, Bartender at Crush, Josh's boyfriend (First Kiss), Friends with Crush group
- Colton, Woodworker, Ioan's boyfriend (A Crush for Christmas), Friends with Crush group
- Craig, Website designer, Alex's boyfriend (Deep Down), Friends with Casey
- Dane, Zak's son
- David Pick, therapist

- Drake, owner of Distinction Fitness, retired Army
- Emily, Friends with Crush group
- Eric, Actor, Friends with Crush group
- Ethan, Friends with Crush group
- Ginny, Tom's girlfriend
- Ioan, Carer at nursing home, Colton's boyfriend (A Crush for Christmas)
- Jack, Veteran, Kenzo's sounding board
- Josh, Charlie's boyfriend (First Kiss)
- Kade, Police officer, Analise's boyfriend, Friends with Logan and Ava
- **Kenzo, Retired Army, Veteran Centre volunteer, Parents: not around**
- Logan, Detective Sergeant, Casey's brother
- Luke, Personal Trainer, Casey's boyfriend (Life Support), Friends with the Crush group
- Mason, Veteran
- Max, Interior designer, Trent's boyfriend (Primary Seduction)
- Miki/Mikhail, Retired Army, computer expert, Kenzo's roommate
- Miranda, Pete's mother, Kenzo's surrogate mother
- Mr Gant, Distinction Fitness tennis coach
- Mr Truman, Kenzo's former tennis coach
- Noah, Zak's brother
- Pete, Kenzo's best friend, died in explosion

- Rick, ball boy
- Robin, Pete's father, Kenzo's surrogate father
- Sadie, Noah's girlfriend
- Samuel, Zak's Lawyer, Trent and Luke's brother
- Sarah, Receptionist at Veteran Centre
- Sean, Architect, Asher's boyfriend (Instant Desire), Friends with Crush group
- Theo, Baker, (Sweet Truths), Friends with Luke
- Tom, Owner of Crush, Ginny's boyfriend
- Trent, Teacher, Max's boyfriend (Primary Seduction), Luke's brother
- Vince, Carer at Veteran Centre
- **Zak, Woodworker, Son: Dane, Sibling: Noah**

"What are you talking about, Ashley? The only place I've been is in my workshop, trying to earn the money we need." Zak King kept a tight lid on his rage. He refused to become what his parents had been before they divorced. His hands, though, were in tight fists by his side, and he could feel his heart racing.

"Where were you when I was shouting for you to help me with him, eh? I needed you, Zak! And you were off gallivanting somewhere, unwilling to help!" Ashley screamed and threw some plates into the sink, the crash reverberating off the walls. Her shoulder-length curly, blonde hair swung around her as she moved.

Zak reined in his anger, raking his fingers through his hair and gripping the strands that had fallen from his bun. The small bite of pain helped centre him, and he breathed deeply, inhaling the scents of a dinner he, apparently, had missed. "Keep your voice down, Ashley. I'll take him for a walk, and you can get some rest, okay?" He tried to placate her, knowing she wouldn't be too concerned about Dane's wellbeing now that Zak was around.

"Too little, too late, Zak. I needed you hours ago." She crashed and banged the pots as she washed them, and Zak wondered whether there would be any uncracked ones left afterwards.

"You could've come to the workshop. It's not that far away."

"Don't patronise me! You're the one who said you didn't want Dane near the workshop. How was I supposed to come and ask for your help when I can't bring him with me?"

Sighing, his shoulder dropped, and his hands fell to his sides. "You could've come to the door. You didn't need to step inside. I only do it for his—and your—safety. I have tools in there—"

"I don't give a damn, Zak." She grabbed the towel and dried her hands with jerky movements, her eyes glaring daggers at him. She was so pretty, even in her fury, but it hid a lot of unkind characteristics Zak hadn't known about before they got married. The top of Ashley's head came to Zak's nose, and she was slender but curvy, more so since she'd had Dane. Zak wasn't ignorant of her sex appeal, but they'd not touched one another since Dane had been born. Ashley had moved into the spare bedroom as soon as she came home from the hospital without any explanation to Zak.

Ashley waved her hand as if shooing him away and stormed out of the room.

Zak shook his head and wandered into the living room, smiling when he saw Dane sitting in his playpen, surrounded by toys. His son, nearly two already, was pressing the buttons on an electronic caterpillar, making the colours light up and flash. When Zak heard him giggle, his heart expanded with love for the little guy. How anyone could think Dane was a nuisance, he didn't know. But then Ashley had changed since she'd found out she was pregnant. It was not news to him that she hadn't wanted kids because neither of them had, originally. Now, though, Zak couldn't think of a life without the little man.

Dane looked up at Zak, smiled and, using the bars to help him, pulled himself to standing. "Da-da," he said with a wide toothy grin.

"Hey, sweetheart. Have you had a good day?" Zak crouched down next to Dane, smoothing his hand over the top of his soft, blond curls. Dane babbled at him and lifted a hand, trying to grab at Zak. "You want to come out, huh? Come on, then."

Picking Dane up and making a noise like an aeroplane, Zak sat down on the sofa, perching Dane on his knee. As Dane continued to dribble and chatter, Zak tried to figure out what had gone wrong with Ashley.

They had married when Zak was twenty-six and Ashley was twenty, and Dane had come along eighteen months later. The pregnancy had been a surprise, but Zak had been ecstatic about it. Ashley, not so much. Neither of them believed in having an abortion; therefore, the pregnancy went ahead, and Ashley carried and gave birth without issue.

Originally, Zak had thought it was postnatal depression, but after seeing the doctors, they said it wasn't. Zak hadn't been so sure, and it steadily got worse until every word from her mouth towards him was in anger or hatred. He had no idea what he'd done wrong, but she obviously wasn't happy with their situation. He wished she cared more about their son.

Bringing himself back to the present, he tickled Dane, his son's giggles rewarding him. "Would you like to go for a walk?"

Dane babbled back, and Zak took it as an agreement. He stood, propping Dane on his hip, and headed for the hallway, diverting to the changing mat when he realised Dane's nappy needed changing, which it always did when he came home from work.

After cleaning him up, Zak fought to get Dane's coat on him, noticing it was tight and he needed a new one. He decided to head into town to see if he could find one for him—he may as well have a destination to head towards rather than wandering around. When Dane was bundled up, Zak buckled him into the pushchair and retrieved his own coat. Checking he had his wallet, keys and phone, they left the house.

The walk to town was only around twenty-five minutes. Enough time for Zak to be taken back into his thoughts about Ashley. He had no idea what to do, although he was concerned that Dane wasn't being looked after as well as he should be while Zak was working. Several times, he had come back into the house and found Dane in his playpen with a wet or soiled nappy and Ashley bustling around in the kitchen, ignoring him, or sitting on the sofa, watching daytime TV. He couldn't put up with it much longer. Zak hadn't been worried that Ashley would hurt Dane, but her anger seemed to increase every day, and now, he wasn't so sure. He had already asked a family friend Emily to babysit more often so he could have some peace of mind, using the excuse it gave Ashley some time to herself.

He tightened his grip on the handlebars of the pushchair but breathed deeply, willing the anger away; he had a feeling he knew what his next steps were going to be.

As their surroundings changed to shops instead of houses and the noise of traffic increased, he pushed the thoughts to the back of his mind and concentrated on listening to Dane's string of baby-talk as the little guy pointed and kicked when he saw something he liked. The pure innocence of his gestures warmed Zak's heart.

He was heading towards the children's clothing shop when he saw a familiar figure exiting a charity shop with several bags and a grin.

"What's the smile for?" Zak greeted.

The guy glanced over his shoulder, then turned around. "Hey! How're you?" Max bent forward towards Dane. "Hey, buddy. What'cha doing?"

Dane smiled and waved his chubby hands as Zak answered Max's question, "Yeah, we're all right. Just getting some fresh air." He couldn't help the strained note colouring his tone.

Max cocked his head. "What's up?"

Zak blew out a breath. They had been friends for years, but Zak hated airing his dirty laundry for all to see, even his friends. "Having a few issues at home, that's all." He tried for a smile, although he was sure he failed, especially when Max snorted.

"Come on, Zak. You know me better than that. Tell me."

Needing to keep moving, he indicated with his head to walk. "Ashley is…" He shook his head. "I don't know. Her usual self. In all honesty, Max, I'm thinking of leaving." He exhaled heavily, not realising how true his words were until they had been spoken aloud. "And taking Dane with me," he continued quietly.

"Christ, Zak. I didn't realise things were so bad. I must admit, I thought it was a bit strange you had to account for your whereabouts wherever you went, but I didn't realise anything else was wrong. How long has this been going on?"

"Since Ashley found out she was pregnant. I believe she has suffered—quietly—with postnatal depression, but the doctors said she wasn't. She's just angry all the time. Nothing I do appeases her. She gets angry when I work, angry when I'm there, angry when I go out." He shrugged. "I've got no idea what to think."

"Jesus. What's tipped you over the edge for you to make the decision?"

"I haven't made any decision yet, Max. I'm trying to figure out what's best for Dane. The books all say a child develops best being around both parents, but I'm beginning to get concerned for his safety when I'm not there. She takes no interest in him when I'm at home. At all. I'm doing everything for him. I worry she's not looking after him properly when I'm at work because his nappies always need changing and his clothes are dirty. I know kids get dirty, but this is a different kind of dirty. God, Max, I sound like an awful husband."

Zak's voice hitched, and he glanced away, concentrating on the path ahead of them. How the hell could he explain the little things he noticed without sounding shitty? Maybe he needed to cut back on his hours and spend more time with them both instead of thinking of leaving. He doubted he would get custody of Dane if he left since there was no proof of Ashley having done anything wrong. It would be a 'he said, she said' situation.

Zak cleared his throat. "I don't know what the best thing to do is."

"I don't know what…" Max paused. "Hold on. What if you could get some off-the-record advice without anyone finding out?"

Furrowing his brow, he answered, "If it would help me figure out what I needed to do, sure."

He watched as Max pulled out his phone, pressing a few buttons before holding it to his ear. "Hey. I wondered if I could ask a favour. Would you be able to arrange a meeting with your brother for…a friend of mine? Just a chat, if you will. He'd like to know his options." Max paused, glancing at Zak before saying, "A potential custody case." Max listened for a moment. "Sure. And thanks." Max put his phone away. "He's going to speak with his brother and get back to me. I'll let you know what he says."

"Whose brother?"

"Oh, sorry. Trent's brother is a lawyer…Well, actually, two of his brothers are lawyers in different areas. It will be Samuel you'll be speaking to. He'll be discreet."

Zak sighed, some of the tension leaving his body but not all of it when he thought about the upcoming conversation. "Thanks, Max. That'll help a lot."

"No worries. Always here to help." Max chuckled.

After Zak had finished his enlightening conversation

with Max about Max's relationship troubles, which helped distract Zak, he and Dane headed to the clothes shop, bought a new dinosaur coat for Dane and wandered back home. As he had come to expect, the house was empty, Ashley having left to do whatever it was she did when she wasn't with them. So, he carried the sleepy boy to bed, tucking him in before aiming for the kitchen for a drink. His phone rang while he was making a coffee, and he confirmed with Max an appointment for the following day with Trent's brother.

He dropped onto the sofa, sighing heavily. He had no idea what to do, but hopefully, Samuel would be able to help.

Zak decided to take Dane with him when he went to his appointment with Samuel. It would give him peace of mind and make the conversation easier on Zak if he had Dane to concentrate on. His stomach was churning, and his hands were trembling as he pushed Dane towards the large office building where Samuel worked.

It was situated in the city centre, amidst all the other taller buildings, but it didn't appear as unwelcoming as some of the older structures sometimes seemed. The cars whizzing down the street and the fumes from the exhausts were of a higher level than where they lived on the outskirts, but Zak was sure the walls and windows would reduce it a little. That was the problem when he lived so close to nature and worked in it on a daily basis. He was used to the fresh air, the scent of the trees, the sounds of the birds and the taste of sawdust on his lips. Here, all he tasted were fumes, all he smelled was burnt coffee, and all he heard was traffic.

Gratefully closing the external door behind him, he checked in with the receptionist and was quickly taken to Samuel's office.

"Nice to meet you, Zak." Samuel held out his hand, and they shook.

"You, too."

"Take a seat." Samuel sat behind his desk, bringing a notepad and pen closer to him.

Zak sat in the visitor chair and lifted Dane's bag off the back of the pushchair to stop it from tipping over. The little guy was fast asleep, his little snuffles so cute in the quiet office, although he probably wouldn't stay that way.

Samuel smiled at him when he focused on the man. "It was mentioned this was a potential custody case. Can you expand a little?"

Zak sighed, spinning his wedding ring as he gathered his thoughts. "I just want to know where I stand in my situation. My wife has not been herself since she found out she was pregnant with Dane. We had doctors' opinions after he was born, but they denied she had postnatal depression. Her behaviour towards me has become increasingly antagonistic and angry. I don't know how she acts when she's alone with him, and I have no concrete proof to give you that she isn't looking after him properly, only what I've seen with my own eyes."

"What kind of things have you seen?" Samuel picked up his pen.

Zak detailed the different things he'd witnessed, including some bruises Ashley hadn't been able to explain. "I know kids get bruises all the time. I know there are possibly good explanations for things, and as I said, I can't prove anything. My instincts are screaming she's not looking after him properly."

"I think the first thing we could do is get Social Services involved."

Zak's heart stopped for a second, lots of emotions barrelling through him at once. "What!" Zak exploded, waking Dane up. He picked the fussy tot up and cradled him close, soothing him by bouncing his knee up and down and rubbing his back. Turning his focus back to Samuel, he glared at him. He'd thought Samuel was going to help him.

Samuel held out his hands. "It's not because I don't think you're a good father, Zak, on the contrary. I promise you. If we bring them in, they will be able to check up on things when you're not there. They can do unexpected visits and things like that. They will be able to see what's going on, and they are a step away from the situation and will be able to view it through clearer lenses, so to speak."

"But what if she hides it all?"

Samuel pursed his lips, linking his fingers on top of the notepad. "Then we will keep going with the case, if you want to go ahead with it, that is. We would get evidence together to show what's happening. For example, how often you look after Dane, what state he's in when you see him, where she goes when she's not looking after him. You mentioned bringing a babysitter in to help take the pressure off Ashley; well, they can help, too."

Zak closed his eyes and sighed. "This is not going to be an easy fix, is it?" He opened them again and stared at Samuel in resignation.

"No. Though, I will say, it will be worth it."

Several hours later, the doorbell rang while Ashley was screaming at him, "I don't want her here. There's no need for her to be here. I am quite capable of looking after Dane by myself."

"I know you are," Zak placated, "but I thought you wanted a break. I arranged the babysitter because it meant you could have some time to yourself. I was trying to do something nice." He tried to sound soothing, not wanting to get her any more riled up than she already was. Although he was telling a white lie about trying to do something nice for her, he had thought she would appreciate it.

"Fine! I'm going out, then." She stomped out of the room and up the stairs, her footsteps heavy and loud.

Zak's shoulders slumped as he headed for the door, expecting Emily to be there. Instead, Max was, and Zak winced when he realised how loud their argument had been.

"Hey," Max said quietly, coming in and closing the door behind him.

"Come on in." Zak drifted back towards the living room. "Sorry about…" he said in a soft voice and waved his hand. "You probably heard every word."

"No problem."

Zak bobbed his head slowly, gaze on the floor. "We just need to wait for the babysitter to arrive, which will be any time now."

His gaze went to the stairs when Ashley appeared in a tight white dress and black high heels, a sneer on her face. "I'll be home when I'm home." She stalked out of the house, slamming the door behind her.

Zak grimaced, hoping it didn't wake Dane. Seconds later, another knock sounded, and he rose from the sofa, opening the door for Emily.

"Hi." He tried for a smile as he invited her in.

Emily pulled him in for a brief hug, holding him for a second longer than necessary, no doubt because she knew he needed it, then turned to Max. "Hey, Max. I hear happy birthday is in order!" She moved to him and hugged him.

"Hey! I didn't realise you were babysitting now! Although, I bet you've had a lot of practice with Ethan and Eric." Max laughed.

She snorted. "Definitely. If I can sort them out, I can sort anyone out. I don't do it often, but I love little Dane, and it gets me out of the house for a while. If I stare at too many spreadsheets, my eyes will go square." She grinned and shrugged a shoulder. "Gives me to chance to raid someone else's DVD cabinet, too."

Zak managed a laugh. "Which you are more than welcome to do, as you know."

Emily smiled at him. "Yes, I do, and it's much appreciated." She bit her lip. "I saw Ashley leave."

Zak grimaced. "When I told her you were coming, she decided to go out for the night. Not sure if she'll be home before me or not." He smoothed a hand over his hair, trying not to pull any strands out of the bun he'd fixed it in. "Could I ask you to stay here until I get back, even if she is here?"

"I can try. She may not let me, though."

"If she kicks up a stink about it, then leave. I'll pay you now; at least you'll have it."

"No, no. I can wait. Go, have fun, and you can pay me later if I don't see you tonight." She smiled as she shooed them away. "Go!"

Zak wrapped his arms around her again. "Thank you," he whispered.

He spent a pleasant evening with his friends, celebrating Max's birthday, and when he finally got a taxi home, he was feeling mellow and calm. Not drunk because he never drank when he would be in charge of Dane, just relaxed for a change. When he entered the house, he settled further, seeing Emily on the sofa, engrossed in a film.

"Hey. Did you have a nice time?" she asked as she turned off the TV and uncurled from her position.

"Yes, thanks. I needed it."

"You certainly did. I've not heard a peep from him. I checked on him several times, but he was fast off." She smirked. "Does he get his little snuffly snores from you or Ashley?" She stepped over to the hallway, slipping her shoes on.

"Definitely me, unfortunately." Zak smiled.

"Poor boy." Emily pulled her coat on, wrapping a scarf around her neck. She paused, her hands gripping the ends of her scarf. "I've not seen or heard from Ashley at all."

"Thanks." If she wasn't home already, he doubted she would return before tomorrow. He paid Emily and saw her out before climbing the stairs, a nice lethargy to his limbs that would hopefully help him to sleep.

Dane was sleeping on his front with his bum in the air, arms tucked under his tummy and snuffling contentedly, as Emily had said. Zak stared at him for a moment longer, then retreated and trailed to his bedroom. The room was decorated in blues and whites as per Ashley's instruction several years ago. Zak had put a deposit on this house a year before they met with help from some money his father had left him for when he reached eighteen, thinking the three-bedroom house was more than big enough for him and, if he ever found one, a partner, especially as he'd had no plans for kids.

If Zak did leave Ashley, what would they do about the house? He would prefer to have it to help Dane adjust and because his workshop was in the garage. To try and find another place that he would have to rent would be an additional cost he might not be able to afford—yet another thing he needed to speak with Samuel about.

Relaxed as he was, the shower was heavenly, the warmth pounding into his muscles, washing away everything. Falling asleep in the shower was not a good idea. He quickly dried off, pulled on some boxers and climbed under the cold covers. How he wished he could return to the kind of relationship they'd had in the beginning. A time when they would go to bed at the same time, wrapping themselves around each other and falling asleep together.

Even when he'd been in college, he'd been able to have that some nights. Most of his relationships had been short-lived but long enough for him and his partner to sleep over at each other's places and wake up to a leisurely orgasm every once in a while. Be it a blow job, mutual hand jobs, eating the other person out, or receiving or giving a pounding, he hadn't cared. He was indiscriminate about who he was attracted to. He was drawn to people who were nice, end of, and he refused to put a label on himself, both then and now.

The waking up wrapped around someone? That was what he missed most.

His phone beeped from where he'd plugged it in on the bedside table, and he yawned as he reached for it.

Won't be home.

He would've known who it was from even if her name hadn't appeared on it. The abrupt tone came across in the wording, and he could almost hear her saying it. He didn't know when they had stopped adding kisses to the end of their messages, but as he scrolled back through their text conversations, he realised it was a while. The worst thing was, it didn't bother him anymore.

Replacing the phone on the bedside table, he rolled to his other side, staring into the darkness at the empty space next to him, his hands reaching for someone who was not there.

His heart ached.

CHAPTER TWO

KENZO

Mackenzie 'Kenzo' Langley stared at the gym's owner with raised eyebrows. "You want me to do what?"

"It's just for a few sessions until the coach has recovered from his operation. I know you don't work here, but…" Drake pleaded.

"You do realise I have problems with my leg, don't you?"

"I know, but you've always been good with the kids. You don't need to be running around with them, just give them the basics from one position. It's only for a few weeks. Please, Kenzo."

"How can you expect me to teach kids how to play tennis without running around and demonstrating it to them?" Kenzo rubbed his forehead, the tension bleeding into him but already knowing he wouldn't refuse Drake's request.

"I'll give you another member of staff who can do the running around, but they don't know enough about tennis to actually coach them."

Kenzo sighed, shoulders slumping. "Sure. Give me a list of the lesson times. I'll need to make sure they don't clash with the Veterans Centre."

"Thank you!"

"I'm only doing this because you called in the favour."

"And you're saving my ass because of it."

Drake clapped him on the shoulder and walked towards his office, whistling as he went. Kenzo followed behind at a slower rate, his leg twinging as he stepped. It would never get any better than it was now, even with skin grafts and surgery to try and rectify the broken bones and muscle loss. Without clothes, his leg was a hot mess; there was nothing pretty about it at all.

After retiring from the Army and when he'd finally left rehabilitation, he'd started visiting Drake's gym, hoping to regain some muscle mass. Thirteen months later, he was getting there, but his leg would never be as it had been before. The damage from the explosion had left him with a slight limp, which was mostly unnoticeable unless he'd been on it too long when it became more pronounced. He could jog for around five minutes at a sedate speed, but then he was done for. How Drake expected him to keep up with small kids, he had no idea.

"Here you go," Drake said as he entered the office. He handed him a sheet, which Kenzo quickly glanced over.

"The only problem will be the Friday one. Can it be changed?"

"I don't see why not. Let me get in contact with the parents and see. I'll let you know about that one. Are all the others okay?"

Kenzo nodded. "Yeah."

"Thank you. You've saved my ass."

"Don't I always." Kenzo smirked.

They said their goodbyes, and Kenzo headed to his car, glad to be away from the thud and clank of the equipment and the music of the classes. Once he was settled, he said, "Call Miki," as he drove.

"Kenzo."

"Miki. I'm heading back. Do you want takeaway for dinner?"

"Sure. Can we have Indian?"

Kenzo chuckled. "You have a yearning for spicy food, do you?"

"When don't I?"

"True. Your usual order?"

"Of course."

"See you soon."

He rang off, a smile twitching at the corners of his

lips. Miki had been a tough nut to crack when they'd first met, but once they'd figured each other out, they had become fast friends. Mikhail, who went by his middle name after telling Kenzo he hated the thought of being called Armand, lived life in the fast lane, or at least, he used to. Family had always been important to Miki despite his parents having an unhealthy obsession with a certain series of books, and he and his siblings—Claudia, Jesse, Louis and Gabrielle—bearing the brunt of their fascination.

After collecting their dinner and making his way home, Kenzo made sure to make noise as he entered, advertising the fact he'd arrived. It didn't do anything good to surprise Miki. His PTSD could be set off by noises that weren't particularly loud, as well as ones that were. It was one of the reasons why they were roommates. Miki's therapy sessions were going okay, maybe not brilliantly, but he was not nearly far enough through them for it to make the living nightmares non-existent. Kenzo kept an eye on him, and when Miki was suffering, Kenzo was able to stay with him and help him through it.

"I smell food." Miki traipsed into the kitchen, wearing joggers and a t-shirt with more holes than fabric.

"Your dinner is served," Kenzo droned mockingly as he passed the plate over and grabbed one for himself. "How was your day?" he asked, returning to his usual voice. He sat opposite Miki at their dining table with the food between them, the scent of spices filling the air.

Miki grinned. "Good, actually. I finally figured out what the issue was with the computer program and was able to change it to do the job it was supposed to do."

"That's great. Is it finished now, or do you still have some work to do on it?" Kenzo unfolded the foil edges of the cartons and lifted the cardboard lids off, turning them over to avoid a mess on the tabletop.

Miki spooned the food onto his plate as he spoke, "It needs to be checked over to make sure all the links and stuff work, but essentially, yes, it's done. I'll send it back to the company tomorrow."

"I will always say this, but I have no fucking idea how you do all this crap with the computer."

"It's why I was the computer engineer on the team, and you were the brawn."

They swapped a grin and dug into their dinner as they caught each other up on their news. They saw each other every day, sometimes several times a day, but they always had something to say. They had one of those relationships that would never grow old. Even when Miki was struggling and hated being seen that way, they were stronger at the end than they were in the beginning. Each and every time.

"Drake persuaded me to coach some kids at the gym," Kenzo groused.

Miki laughed. "Coach them in what?"

"Tennis."

"Is that wise?" He could hear the worry in Miki's voice.

Kenzo sighed, twirling his fork around in the food but not lifting anything. "He called in his favour."

"'Nuff said, but still…"

When a favour was owed, no one hesitated when it was called in. It was the unwritten rule of the team.

"Are you going to be okay doing it?" Miki leaned his elbows on the table, spearing Kenzo with his gaze, a small crease between his eyebrows. "You know how much trouble you have with your leg sometimes."

"I know. He's giving me an assistant who will do all the running for me. All I need to do is teach them the basics. I can do it standing or sitting if needed." At least, he hoped he could. It had been a while since he'd played tennis due to his recovery time.

"Just take it easy, Kenzo. You're doing enough as it is."

"Pot, meet kettle." Kenzo raised his eyebrows and pointed his fork at Miki. "Who has taken on more jobs than he can handle?"

Miki waved his hand. "I'm at home all day, every day. I have time."

"Hmm."

Standing on the tennis court brought back a lot of memories from when he was younger. He'd had a bright future as a professional tennis player until he'd decided to sign up for the Army instead. His parents had tried to persuade him otherwise, but he'd been determined. Although he didn't regret anything about serving—only how his career ended—standing there was bittersweet.

The feeling of being on the court again: the springiness of the ground, the sound of the net in the soft breeze, the scent of the firm tennis balls, and the soft thwack of the rackets as they hit those balls. It sent him back to when he first started at twelve-years-old. He'd been a late bloomer but had taken to it quickly. Practising every day at the courts at his school and after school on the courts at the leisure centre had increased his skill level swiftly.

Kenzo smiled as he remembered the competitions he'd entered and the wins he'd accrued in such a short time. He'd been told many times he was good enough for Wimbledon and had begun the process of attempting to qualify. He'd achieved passable grades at school, but he couldn't find anything of interest he wanted to pursue except tennis until the school had received a visit from the military for career day. Fascinated by the Army ever since he was a young boy, Kenzo had been amazed by the options of what they offered. He hadn't realised how vast his choices could be within the sector.

That day had been the one to change the course of his life. Pushing tennis aside, despite the protests of his family and coaches, he chose the Army. Twenty-one years after the choice, he was back where it all began.

"Excuse me? Are you Mr Langley?"

Kenzo turned to face the newcomer with a smile. "I am. Nice to meet you." He held out his hand to a brown-haired woman, standing beside a girl of around twelve or thirteen.

"You, too. Thank you for taking over from Mr Gant. We really do appreciate it."

"It's not a problem at all." He scanned the girl, asking, "And what's your name?"

"Felicity. Fliss." The girl flushed and ducked her head.

Kenzo withheld a chuckle. "Nice to meet you, too. Did Mr Gant give you some warm-up exercises to do before each lesson?" Fliss nodded eagerly. "Go ahead and start them while we wait for the other kids."

"Yes, sir."

He watched as she started bouncing the ball on the racket, higher and higher, and then flipping the racket so that the ball bounced on either side. She had good control and hand-eye coordination. The memories of his own beginning repeated in his head. It had been a while since he had last lifted a racket.

"Am I okay to wait by the chairs?" the mother asked.

Kenzo glanced across at the plastic garden chairs against the wall surrounding the court. "Did Mr Gant allow you to watch?"

The woman pursed her lips as her cheeks darkened. "No."

"Then could I ask you to follow his wishes. I understand from personal experience that although you would like to watch how your child is doing, it might not be the best option for the child to have their parent watching their lesson."

"I know. I just like to see how she's doing."

"I understand. Let me see how things go today. If the kids agree, maybe we can set aside a time in the next lesson to showcase their skills. How about that?"

The woman nodded. "Thank you. I'd appreciate it."

She wandered off as another parent approached. When his class was full—four kids—and his assistant, a boy not much older than the kids Kenzo was teaching, arrived, he brought them all together after they had finished their warm-up exercises. As it was his first lesson with them, he did some basic manoeuvres to see where their skill level rested to enable him to plan for the next lesson.

He found he remembered a lot of the drills his old

tennis coach, Mr Truman, had given him to do when he'd been their age, and it was easy to pretend to be that coach. Mr Truman had, unfortunately, passed away before Kenzo turned sixteen and never got to see him try for Wimbledon. He would've loved to have seen it. Kenzo had never regretted his career choices, but sometimes, he wondered whether he had made the right one.

An hour later, he was exhausted, and his shirt was sticking to his skin, despite having not chased after any balls or kids. Luckily, he only had five one-hour lessons a week. Having a ball boy had helped, but it was still strenuous to teach something, especially as he was out of practise himself.

"Remember what advice I've given you individually, and also remember to talk with your parents if you would like them to watch you next week. I would suggest it only be five minutes or so for each of you, but if you don't want to do it, you don't have to. All right, have a good rest of your day, and I will see you next week."

"Bye, Mr Langley!" He watched as the kids trailed into the gym through the back door.

His ball boy, who he found out was called Rick, cleaned up the court for him and bid him goodbye. Kenzo headed to the showers, his limp more pronounced. He had planned to do a gym workout after the lessons, but he knew his leg wouldn't hold up. Next time, he'd do the gym session first.

"How did it go?"

Kenzo whirled around at the voice, dropping to a high crouch, a split second before realising who it was. He stood, wincing and shaking his head. "You should know better, Drake," he said as he rubbed at his thigh.

Hands raised in a calming gesture, Drake replied, "Sorry. I thought you'd heard me coming."

Kenzo shook his head as his heart rate slowed to normal. "It's all right. I'm in my head a bit today. Training never quite leaves you, does it?" He snorted.

"Never."

Kenzo sighed and returned to Drake's previous question, "The lesson went well, although I'm fucking knackered. I forgot tennis uses muscles I don't use as much in daily life. I'm out of practice."

Drake clapped him on the shoulder. "Make sure you soak your muscles, then."

"I will when I get home. But first, I need to get rid of this stench before heading over to the Veteran Centre. I'm sure the guys would find it reminiscent of their time in the forces, but I still don't want to overwhelm them."

They both laughed as they parted ways.

Kenzo washed off in the showers and dressed in khaki trousers and a V-neck jumper before grabbing his belongings from the locker and leaving the gym. Still limping but smelling much fresher, he threw his bag and coat in the boot of his car, climbed in and pointed it towards his next destination.

The St John's Veteran Centre was a large brick building with plenty of windows across the front and fewer windows around the back. The centre had been specifically built for veterans, and there had been a lot of planning put into the layout and what veterans would need or want before it was actually built. The result was a building that catered to the different needs of each individual who walked through the front doors, including residential rooms for those who wanted to stay close to others. The residential side was staffed with nurses and carers who helped those who needed it. The centre also had rooms dedicated to therapy, exercise and a small indoor pool for long-term rehabilitation needs.

He parked, slipped his coat on after retrieving it from the boot and grabbed a few paperback books from the rear seat before entering the building. "Hey, Sarah. How are you?"

Sarah was in her fifties and had been the receptionist at the centre from the minute it had been built seven years ago. She had a decidedly motherly vibe and a definite no-nonsense attitude. Anyone who took her on was hoping for a beat down. "I'm good. Thanks, Kenzo. I see you remembered to bring the books. Jack has been asking about them."

Kenzo chuckled, running his thumb along the edges

of the books. "I bet he has. He's such a fast reader. I can't keep up with him."

"Tell me about it." Sarah hesitated, coming around the desk, her mouth drawn down. "If you have time today, would you mind visiting with Mason for a little while? He had a bad night."

"Sure thing. Is he in his room?"

"Yeah."

"I'll drop these off with Jack, then I'll pop my head in."

"Thanks, Kenzo." She squeezed his arm and returned to her seat.

He waved and headed down the corridor to the recreation room, otherwise known as "The Hub." It was the centre of the building in more ways than one. It looked like a huge living room with lots of comfortable chairs dotted around; shelves upon shelves of books, games and stationery; tables, small and large, for different activities; a record player alongside a cassette and CD player; and a counter for making drinks and grabbing the snacks that had been laid out and regularly replenished by the staff.

Kenzo glanced around the room, noticing the gentle notes of piano music, before zeroing in on Jack, who sat in an armchair by a window with his glasses perched on the end of his nose as he read a book. Kenzo smiled and shook his head. Jack was an avid reader and had already read all the books in The Hub.

Hence the reason Kenzo was lugging a tower of books in his arms.

"Good afternoon, Jack. Onto your second read-through of that book, I see."

Jack blinked up at him, the creases of his face deepening as he smiled and removed his glasses. He placed the book on the little table beside him, dropping his glasses on top. "Kenzo! So good to see you again."

Kenzo narrowed his eyes. "You don't want to see me. You want to see what I brought you," he joked, dropping into the chair next to Jack.

"Well, that may be true, but if I didn't see you, I also wouldn't see the books, so of course, I'm glad to see you." Jack chuckled.

Kenzo huffed, "Here you go, old-timer." He turned the books, allowing Jack to see the spines and read the titles he'd brought him.

Jack's age-lined hand reverently caressed each book as he mouthed the title. "Oh, they're great, Kenzo. Thank you. There are several of these I've never heard of, and only one I've read. Good choices."

"Wow! Not bad for a first try. Bet I won't be able to do it again with how many books you've read. I'm sure you'll enjoy them. I'll pick them up tomorrow, shall I?" Kenzo blinked innocently at the older man.

Jack threw his head back and laughed, the joyous sound turning the heads of several people. "Maybe. Although I think a week or so would be better."

Kenzo narrowed his gaze. "Really? Eight books in one week? Haven't you read like ten books in five days before now?"

"Well, yes. But I need to slow down, Kenzo. There will be no books left in the world if I keep reading so fast."

"That is true, but I bet you can't do it."

Jack grinned, his toothy smile making Kenzo's day brighter. "I bet I can't either."

"Do you want me to put these in your room?"

"Nah, it's okay. Leave them here. I'll get Vince to help me with them later."

Kenzo stood, resting his hand on Jack's slim shoulder. "All right. Have a good day, Jack."

"You, too, Kenzo. Say hi to Mikhail for me."

"Will do."

Kenzo exited the room. Heading further down the corridor, he came to an open door and knocked, poking his head around to make sure Mason was there.

"Hey, Mason," he said quietly. "How're things with you?" Mason's dark-haired head lifted, and his pain-filled gaze met Kenzo's. "Ah, not so good today, huh?"

Kenzo stepped into the room, heading slowly over to the thirty-five-year-old man. His room was immaculate; everything was in its place as it always was with him. Kenzo didn't know the full story, but from what he'd been told and from what Mason had reluctantly disclosed, Mason and his team had been surrounded by gunfire, killing all of his teammates and almost Mason as well. He'd been left for dead and only found when another team had finally stumbled upon them several days later. Dehydrated with a slew of infections thrashing his body, Mason had been given medicine to help him with the pain, but nobody had expected him to live.

Mason had surprised them all, coming through everything that had been thrown at him. Unfortunately, Mason hadn't wanted to because he blamed himself for surviving when his teammates hadn't. His nightmares often happened over the four years he'd been residing there, and no amount of therapy had helped him. It was an awful way to live, but he knew Mason was too strong to end it. A lesser man would've caved to the night-mares and ended their life. Not Mason. He lived because he believed it was what he deserved: to suffer.

Kenzo slid into the chair next to Mason, draping his coat over the back and looking out of the small square window into the rear garden area of the centre. It was a dreary day of grey skies and wet ground, but he knew Mason didn't see any of it. Mason's mind would replay his deployment over and over again if it was anything like what Miki described.

And it broke Kenzo's heart.

Zak couldn't believe Luke had persuaded him to join the gym. He hadn't been particularly close to Luke—he knew Luke's brother Trent better than Luke himself—but he seemed like a nice guy, and when they'd had a chance meeting at the park where Zak often took Dane to feed the ducks, their conversation had somehow turned to talking about the gym and Zak contemplating joining. It had always been something he'd wanted to do but had never made the time to do, especially with the issues surrounding his marriage.

He mentally rolled his eyes as he lay on his back in the weights room, surrounded by the clinks and rhythmic footsteps of the other members working out. Luke supported the bar as Zak rested it on the stand. Sitting upright, he exhaled heavily, sweat dripping down his neck and soaking into his tank top.

"Bloody hell. I'm going to be aching tomorrow."

Luke grinned at him, no repentance showing. "Probably not tomorrow, but the day after, definitely."

"You're a taskmaster when it comes to this." Zak gulped his water, finishing half the bottle in one go.

"Only when the client wants me to be. It's your own fault."

Zak laughed, acknowledging the truth of the statement. "I'm surprised you had room to fit me in. When I spoke to the receptionist, she said you worked more with clients in need of evasive training."

Luke walked around to face him, hands tucked into the pockets of his knee-length shorts. "Yeah, the number of people wanting the training has increased lately. I'm not sure why. But it keeps me busy."

"Have you thought about doing it as a business?" Zak asked, wiping his face with his towel. If Luke had that many clients wanting training, he could make a decent living doing it privately.

"What do you mean?"

Zak rested his forearms on his knees. "Well, here, surely you only get your wages, and the company takes most of the profit." Zak had never been employed, except when he was a teenager and worked at a supermarket to earn some extra cash, so he wasn't on the up and up about employment rules.

"Yeah." Luke's forehead creased.

"Why not open your own business instead. You'd

get a say in where the profits go, and once you make enough, you could donate some to a charity of your choice if you felt bad about reaping all the rewards." It was what Zak planned to do as soon as he was earning enough on top of what he needed to live on.

"It sounds like a lot of hassle."

"I run my own business, and it's not too bad. I know it's not in the same field, but the general business side of things will be the same or similar. I'm happy to go through it with you if you're interested."

"Would people be interested in it when it was being provided at the gym?" Luke asked.

"I bet you'd find a lot of the people are here because *you* train them, not because it's at the gym."

Luke didn't look convinced but said, "I'll have to think about it. Thanks."

"You're welcome. Remember to give me a ring if you need to know anything."

They shook hands, and Zak headed to the showers, the relief of removing sweaty clothes overtaking any embarrassment of showering in a joint shower room. Once he was ready to leave, he grabbed his phone, checking for messages. Seeing a voicemail, he dialled his inbox while exiting the building and wandering to his car.

"Hey, Zak. I have news. Give me a call back, and we'll arrange a time you can come in."

Zak blew out a breath, slumped against the side of

his car and stared at the wintery sky. The tone of Samuel's voice hadn't indicated whether the news was good or bad, and Zak wasn't sure if he wanted to know. He'd been fighting his case for nine months now, and he was tired of it.

Ashley had refused to move out when Zak made it clear their relationship was over, and he was applying for custody. Whenever they had visitors, be it friends, family or Social Services, Ashley was all sweet and innocent, but the moment it was him and her, she screamed and shouted, even when Dane was in the room. It was getting to the stage Dane didn't want to go anywhere with her, which angered Ashley more. Zak refused to let her take him when she was in one of her moods. It was one thing he wouldn't budge on.

Samuel had cautioned him with refusing her access to Dane but agreed if she was showing signs of irrational behaviour to keep Dane from being alone with her. Thus far, Zak had been able to do so by bringing friends or family around whenever she was in one of her agitated moods. He couldn't keep doing it. Every day had become full of worry that he would arrive home to find Ashley and Dane gone with no clue of their whereabouts, and he didn't have a leg to stand on if it happened because as it stood at the moment, she had every right to take him anywhere she wanted to without his permission.

Sighing, he climbed into his car and switched the

engine on, letting the heater do its job before he dialled the lawyer's office, asking to be put through to Samuel.

"Hi, Zak. Thanks for calling me back."

"No problem. What's up?" His voice was strained, and his stomach churned as he gripped the cold steering wheel.

"Ashley has changed lawyers again."

Zak frowned. "What? Why?"

"The lawyer quit, same as the previous one. He cited she was too difficult to work for."

Exhaling, Zak dropped his forehead into his free hand, noticing his palm was damp. "Does this mean things are going to be delayed again?"

"Nope."

Zak's head came up, and he stared out of the front windscreen, not seeing anything. "Why? Surely if a new lawyer has to get up to speed on the case, it will slow things down?"

"Maybe by a day or two, but Ashley isn't doing herself any favours here. Every time this happens, it's showing the lawyers, the judges and everyone else that she is difficult, manipulative and a general pain in the ass."

"You don't need to tell me that," Zak mumbled. "What's the plan, then?" He pinched his bottom lip between his fingers.

"We're continuing as we were. I have managed to get a date for the hearing."

Zak sucked in a breath, not sure if he wanted to know. "When?" he whispered.

"Three weeks today."

Silence reigned as the words sunk in. Three weeks until he'd have an answer to whether someone else thought he was capable of looking after his son better than his mother. Three weeks until his life would change, one way or another. Three weeks until either the best day of his life or the worst.

"Are you all right?" Samuel's voice broke through his thoughts.

He cleared his throat. "Yeah," he croaked, his mouth as dry as a desert.

"I shouldn't say this, Zak, but I will. I have high hopes. Really high hopes."

He should've felt relief at his lawyer's words, but he didn't. Instead, he felt empty, worn out, drained. "Thanks, Samuel."

"Have a good day, Zak. I'll be in touch in a couple of days to let you know how the new lawyer is holding up."

"Okay, thanks."

Zak stared out of the window as he hung up, the sound of the engine running the only noise he could hear. Having a set date made everything more real. The reality he could lose his son because he knew if Ashley got custody of Dane, she'd leave the city to spite him. Then Zak would have to make the decision to start fresh wherever she went or stay and have limited visitation. He knew what his choice would be, and the rest of his life would be spent at her whim.

His phone's old-fashioned ringtone pealed through the silence, making him jump. He answered, conjuring up a small smile, even though the caller couldn't see him. "Hey, Sean."

"Hey, you. We're heading out tonight. Do you want to come?"

"God, yes!"

Sean's laughter was loud through the phone. "Great. We'll see you there."

Neither had to confirm where "there" was. As usual, they would be meeting at Crush, their home away from home whenever they went out together. The bar had become integral to their lives as many of their friends either worked or frequented there, and Sean and Max had been part of the crew who had helped make the Garden Bar area what it had become. The space had been transformed from a wasteland to a haven for those who loved the outdoors. Trellises and vines enclosed the space from the sides and top but still allowed the air to circulate through the gaps. Waterproof chairs and tables had been added for those wanting to brave the weather, and when it was obliging, heaters were placed in the corners to allow customers to sit there and watch the activities on the River Cam or stare up at the stars, depending on the time of day or night.

Zak had taken Dane there in the early evening once, and he had been fascinated by the twinkling lights hanging from the trellis above them. Dane had happily sat in his pushchair with the back laid flat, so he could stare at the small, flickering globes, giggling softly. Zak would have to take him again nearer Christmas when they swapped the white lights for Christmas colours. Dane was sure to love those.

When Zak arrived home, his muscles were complaining despite what Luke had said about it not hurting for a couple of days. He needed a soak in a bath before he went out that evening. He'd sent a message to Emily earlier, asking if she could babysit, which she agreed with several high-five emojis and a celebration gif. He was so lucky to have her, and if either of them had been interested in the other, maybe they could've had a relationship, but Emily was more like his sister, which made thoughts like that weird.

"Hey, buddy!" Zak crouched down next to the playpen, relief running through him when he saw him, and ruffled the top of his son's head, receiving a toothy smile in return. Dane crawled over to the bars and pulled himself to standing, holding out his arms. Zak grinned and picked him up, cradling him close and inhaling his scent. He couldn't leave him; even if she took him away, Zak would have no choice but to follow.

"Shall we go see what's for dinner?" he asked the little guy who was busily chomping on a toy he'd brought out with him. Zak drifted towards the kitchen, hesitating when he heard Ashley's raised voice.

"What do you mean? For God's sake, Brian! I took you on because you said you could do this. I'm paying your wage. You damn well better do your job. No one is taking Dane away from me. Not even his father." She stopped, possibly listening to the other person, though Zak couldn't see from where he was standing. "Fucking hell, Brian! Whatever they're claiming, make it go away. No one can prove anything. Whenever we have visitors, I am the epitome of nice. Whoever says differently is wrong." The venom in her voice no longer surprised him.

Zak heard a pot being slammed on the hard surface and winced, flicking his gaze to Dane. He shouldn't be hearing this, although how often did he? How often did she shout and scream like this when Zak wasn't present? Or did she only do it when he was there? No, it couldn't be because, unless she'd heard his car or the front door, she didn't know he was here. If she did, he doubted she would be talking this way.

"Do you fucking job, Brian, or I will find someone else who can."

Something skidded across a surface, and Zak assumed she had thrown her phone down.

He quietly stepped back towards the living room, then started forward again, ensuring his footsteps were heavier and easier to hear. When he entered the kitchen, he gave a small smile towards his soon-to-be ex-wife.

"Emily is babysitting tonight if you want to go out."

Ashley huffed in reply. Zak set Dane into his chair, buckling him in before heading to the fridge to retrieve the food he'd made for Dane the previous day. He usually batch-cooked a lot of food, dividing it into small portions that were frozen for Dane to have whenever he was hungry. Ashley wouldn't spend the time doing it, citing it was a waste of time; therefore, Zak had taken the job on himself as soon as Dane started weaning. Popping it in the microwave for a minute, he turned to remove his coat, hooking it on the back of the chair next to Dane.

He tried to pretend Ashley wasn't present, though it wasn't easy with her banging and crashing unnecessarily. When the microwave pinged, he retrieved the spaghetti bolognese, poured it into a bowl and mixed it around, blowing on it until it was the correct temperature.

Dane was happily tucking into his food, a tomato-based moustache and beard covering him when Ashley walked towards them. Zak tensed, wondering what she was going to do. When all she did was lift her hand to Dane's head, Zak exhaled quietly but narrowed his eyes when Dane pulled his head away from Ashley's hand with a flinch.

Ashley huffed again and left the room, saying, "I'll be back tomorrow."

Zak made a note of Dane's reaction, deciding to check whether Dane had an injury on his head he didn't know about or whether Dane just didn't want Ashley to touch him. Either way, it was something he would mention to Samuel and Social Services.

Once Dane was sufficiently covered in food to Zak's humour, he picked him up and headed to the bathroom. "Come on, buddy. You desperately need a bath."

As Zak washed Dane, he checked him over from head to toe. He hated not being able to trust Ashley, but he had to be certain. Finding no unusual bruises or injuries settled him down.

An hour later, Dane was clean and dressed in his pyjamas, ready for bed. Zak took him downstairs and turned on the TV, flicking to the children's channel for the bedtime story. Their nightly routine had not wavered since he'd been born, except for adding a TV bedtime story in before a story read by Zak. He remembered his father always read them a story before bed. Didn't matter how late or early it was, a story before bed helped them sleep, his dad said. Naturally, it stopped when his parents divorced, and his dad left them. It was something Zak had insisted on when Dane was born. It also gave him more time to spend with his son.

When the little guy was finally sleeping deeply, Zak

shuffled to his own room to get ready. He didn't go out as often as Ashley thought he did. Once a week at the most, unless there was a special occasion, but sometimes he needed to let go, and it was one of those nights.

Zak found Samuel waiting on the courthouse steps for him, three weeks later. After letting the usher know they were both present, they sat and waited. Samuel had explained the family court worked slightly differently from other courts in that there was a designated timeframe in which several cases were to be heard, and all cases were heard in a specific order not known to the lawyers. The clients and their lawyers had to be present during the whole timeframe to ensure they didn't miss their timeslot, which could be any time, hence the need to be early.

Having not seen Ashley anywhere, he'd checked with Samuel, who confirmed she was present; therefore, as soon as their case was called, they would be ready. Zak knew the procedure after that, as Samuel had explained it a few days before.

It was an awful time to be going to court with a

family issue because it was only a week until Christmas. Zak sat, wringing his hands together. He would've twisted his ring, but he no longer wore the wedding band. He used his time to think about Dane, who was currently in Emily's care again. She had been an absolute godsend since all this began and had been regularly caring for Dane throughout the months to alleviate some of his concerns.

When they were called into the courtroom, Zak and Samuel took a seat at a table to the left, and Ashley and her lawyer sat to the right. As Zak had begun the proceedings, his side of the case was heard first. Samuel stood to address the judge, laying out the facts and reasons behind the case. After he had finished, Samuel sat, and Ashley's lawyer stood, repeating the process but explaining why they were contesting the case.

"Mr King, in your own words, why should I accept you would be a better choice as your son's primary carer?" the judge asked after all the statements had been made.

Zak's pulse jumped, and he paused to gain his bearings, inhaling the slightly stale smell of the room. "I know what I've seen, although it will forever be a case of 'he said, she said.' I know my son's reactions to his mother, the way he flinches away from her, how some of his basic needs have not been met when I arrive back from work. Family means everything to me, and Dane's needs always come first with me, always have, always will."

The judge nodded and turned to Ashley. "Mrs King, same question, please."

"Dane is my baby. He is a gift I've been given, and I would do everything in my power to keep him safe. I would never hurt him."

Zak saw the judge raise his eyebrows when Ashley didn't say anything more.

"This case is difficult, and I will not be giving an answer today." Zak's heart dropped. "We have one week until Christmas." The judge met Zak's gaze, then looked over to Ashley, probably piercing her with his bright blue eyes, too. "I'm offering a slightly unorthodox ruling for now. What I am going to say is this: you have three weeks from this day to spend Christmas and New Year with your son, with your family and with your extended families. When we meet back here on 7 January, I want photographic evidence you have tried to give Dane the best Christmas that little man deserves." He held up his hand as Ashley protested. "If you have tried your hardest and things are still unsalvageable, I will reconsider this case. Now, let me say this as well. I'm not expecting you both," he pointed at them in turn, "to reconcile. I can see a divorce in the works without the paperwork that says so, but what I do expect is for you to put aside your differences, hatred, anger, whatever you want to call it.

Put it aside for Christmas, give that boy a Christmas miracle, then we will figure out the custody. Case postponed until 7 January." His gavel hit the table, and he left the room.

Zak blew out a breath and dropped his head into his hands.

"Hey. We knew we were unlikely to get an answer today. Granted, the judge was a little untraditional with his ruling, but we can work with it. All you need to do is concentrate on Dane. Do what you would normally do, get family and friends to take photos at random intervals without asking. They can all be admitted as evidence. The less staged they are, the better. Come on. Let's head to the office and have a chat."

Zak had wanted to get an answer so he could spend Christmas either celebrating or commiserating, but now he was going to have to spend it with Ashley. Samuel was right. He needed to concentrate on what was best for Dane as he always did. Dane was only two. Christmas was still magical for him, and Zak was determined that year would be no different.

CHAPTER FOUR

KENZO

Kenzo drew his elbows together in front of his chest, then slowly fought against the machine as he pulled them open again to get the best workout. He repeated the action, working his inner biceps over and over. His gaze was not on his reflection. It was on a long-haired, blond man sitting on a bench halfway across the room. The guy had been at the gym several times with one of the trainers and alone, but it was the first time Kenzo had noticed his posture was wrong for the exercise he was doing. He mentally acknowledged he'd been watching the guy before that moment. Although it was none of his business, he couldn't, in all good conscience, leave him to potentially hurt himself.

Stepping away from the machine, he wrapped his towel around his neck, grabbed his bottle and strode over to the other man. The closer he got, the more detail he saw. The strain in the guy's face, deepening lines that had nothing to do with his current strenuous activity. The clenched jaw spoke of anger or frustration. The man's hair was tied back in a bun, which, although Kenzo had seen on men before and not particularly liked the look, appeared to suit the guy in front of him.

"You need to correct your posture, or you'll hurt yourself," Kenzo said, crouching down.

The man repeatedly blinked before halting his lifting and sitting straighter. "Sorry?"

Kenzo quirked the corner of his mouth. Apparently, the man was also away with the fairies. "Your posture. You need to concentrate when working those muscles, or you'll end up doing more harm than good."

Looking down at his hands, the guy's forehead creased as he huffed. "I can't remember starting these exercises," he mumbled.

Kenzo narrowed his gaze, then cleared his face. "Hey. How about we grab a drink and have a break?"

The man nodded distractedly, putting the weight in its proper place with a clunk before turning back to Kenzo, who led the way to the little break room the gym had put in for those who wanted to refuel but not necessarily go home. It wasn't the staff's room; this was for members.

Kenzo strode to the water cooler and filled two cups before taking them back to where the guy had sat near the window he was currently staring out of. Kenzo placed the cup in front of him and sat opposite.

"I know you don't know me from Adam, but are you okay?"

The guy huffed a laugh and rubbed his palm across his forehead several times before resting his chin on his hand. "Not at the moment, but hopefully, soon I will be."

Kenzo didn't know how to reply to that, so he kept quiet, the muted sounds of the weight room and exercise classes surrounding them.

The man gave a small smile and held out his hand. "Zak."

Kenzo shook it. "Kenzo." Zak raised his eyebrows, and he explained, "Mackenzie, therefore, Kenzo."

Zak grinned, showcasing a gorgeous smile, making him look years younger. "Understood."

"I don't mean to get on you about it, but you shouldn't workout when you're distracted. I've seen more accidents than I care to when it happens." Kenzo swallowed some water.

"You're right. I needed to get out of the house."

Kenzo nodded slowly. When Zak didn't appear stressed, he was good looking, handsome even. It had been a while since Kenzo had found someone remotely appealing, but it seemed this chance meeting was a reminder he needed to take care of himself sometimes, too.

"How about I spot you for a while? That way, you can get a bit of stress relief, and I can have a clear conscience." Kenzo didn't know where the offer came from, but if it meant he could spend some time with the guy, he might be able to figure out whether Zak liked men or not. There was no point asking him out if he didn't. That could end up with a fist to the face, although Zak didn't seem like the type to become physical in that way.

"No, don't worry about me. You have your own routine to get through." Zak gulped the water down and stood. "I'll head home."

"Honestly, I don't mind at all."

Zak scratched at his neatly trimmed beard as he studied Kenzo like a target through a sniper lens, then his shoulders slumped, and he nodded. "That'd be great. Thanks."

Kenzo exhaled his relief quietly, following Zak back to the weights room. If his gaze dropped to Zak's ass, he wasn't admitting it. "What do you want to work on?"

"Luke had me starting on the barbell bench press the other week. I've done it a few times with him. Would that be all right?"

"Sure."

They headed that way, and luckily, no one was using it. Zak slid into place on his back, while Kenzo adjusted the weights to the correct size, according to what Zak told him. The noise around them receded as he stood at Zak's head, checking his posture was correct before helping him lift the bar off the stand. Zak kept his arms straight, and Kenzo kept hold of some of the weight until Zak nodded to say he was ready. Releasing his hands, Kenzo held them in front of him, ready to take the weight should Zak need him to.

Zak managed ten reps, then Kenzo helped him set it back on the stand. "Jesus. I think Luke is trying to kill me."

"It probably feels that way because you're tense. It's not easy, but if you try to relax into it, it might feel more comfortable."

Kenzo spoke while Zak was still lying on the bench, far too close to his groin for Kenzo's liking, especially as he was interested in the guy.

"Okay, I'll give it a try."

Kenzo watched as Zak's gaze flicked to Kenzo's waist—or below, he couldn't tell—then licked his lips and refocused on the bar. As before, Kenzo helped, and when Zak's arms began to shake at five, they returned the bar once more.

"It felt a bit easier, but I definitely need more practice," Zak said when he sat upright.

"You'll get there. These guys make it look easy because they've been doing it for years. You've only just started."

"I know." Zak blew out a breath.

"Look, you seem like you have a lot on your plate at the moment. Why not visit somewhere you enjoy and just relax? It does wonders for stress levels." Kenzo knew the words to be true because he had to do it several times a month. With how busy he could get, especially with the tennis coaching, which had become a regular thing for him while the previous coach was in recovery longer than they had planned, he needed the respite. It could be difficult to find the best place for it.

"Like where?"

Kenzo crouched in front of him, his hands hanging between his legs. "I don't know. What do you do to relax? What do you enjoy listening to? Ask yourself what lifts your spirits, then go do it."

"Other than being with my son, I have no idea. As much as I love him, he would remind me of the stress I was trying to avoid." Zak got to his feet, shaking his head at the floor.

Kenzo's heart missed a beat when Zak mentioned a child. It could mean several things, but he assumed it meant Zak was in a relationship, and he needed to back off. Not that he had been trying for anything, anyway. He stood. "I don't know… could you spend some time by the river, or people-watching in a café, or listening to music." Kenzo shrugged a shoulder. "Only you can decide what will help."

"Thanks, Kenzo. Sorry to be such a downer. I appreciate you spotting for me, but I think you're right... I need to get out of here." Zak held out a hand.

Kenzo clasped it. "It's fine. I know I'm pretty much a stranger, but I'm here if you need anything."

Zak met his gaze, and something passed between them as Zak narrowed his eyes. "What if I need your company?" Zak mumbled.

Kenzo realised they were still holding hands, and he brushed his thumb on the back of Zak's hand before releasing him, considering his answer. "Then as long as both parties were free and single, I'd enjoy your...company."

The word "company" had never had a different connotation to Kenzo before, but he knew what Zak was asking. If Kenzo had been unsure about Zak's sexual orientation, it had been made clear what he wanted.

"I'm free and single."

Kenzo nodded slowly. "When?"

"Now?"

He almost smiled at the eagerness in Zak's voice but thought it might come across as insensitive and withheld it. "Sure. I need to get showered and changed, and I'm free."

"Me, too." Zak flicked his focus away, then back. "I'll see you in a few minutes."

Kenzo nodded and gave him a small smile before Zak left the weights room. Kenzo realised their whole conversation had been in hearing and viewing distance of everyone. He cleared his throat and glanced around, noticing a few smirks thrown in his direction.

"Fuck off all of you," he said without heat and strode away to the background noise of chuckles.

"Enjoy your company!" one of the assholes shouted.

Kenzo answered with his middle finger. He needed this potential release as much as Zak probably did. The last time he'd been with a guy was seven months ago when a friend had come in from Devon. They'd gone out for the evening, and both ended up with a partner for the night. It felt... safer, almost. Having a friend close by when you let yourself be vulnerable with a stranger made the experience more relaxed in some ways. With Zak, though, he didn't feel the need to have someone nearby. Although if they ended up at Kenzo's place, which was likely with Zak having a child, Miki would be there.

A quick shower and change later, and he was ready. He hitched his bag on his shoulder and headed to the exit. They hadn't agreed where they were going to meet, but a good guess would be the car park.

As he thought, Zak was stood under the overhang of the building, shielding himself from the light drizzle that had started while Kenzo had been inside. He stopped in front of Zak.

"Mine's the black tank over there." Kenzo smirked slightly at his description of his huge black car. It was a family car, really, but with the number of people he ferried to and from places sometimes, he'd wanted something spacious enough for them. He didn't care what it looked like. It needed to be useful. "You okay to follow me to my house?"

He watched Zak's Adam's apple bob as he swallowed, then he nodded.

"Which is your car?"

Zak coughed slightly. "The blue compact one."

"Okay." Kenzo turned then pivoted back again, taking Zak's chin between his thumb and finger, the softness of the beard surprising him. Moving slowly so Zak had a chance to deny him should he wish to, Kenzo dropped his lips until they brushed against Zak's, sealing their deal. He pulled away immediately after, rubbing his thumb along Zak's glistening lower lip. "Follow me."

Moving to his car was hard because he wanted to stay with Zak, but Kenzo had to be patient. Zak would be in his bed soon enough.

Climbing into his car and throwing his bag on the passenger seat, Kenzo turned the engine on and waited for Zak to get to his car. Once he was sure Zak had enough time to get ready, he flicked on his wipers, reversed out of his space and headed for the exit, slowing enough that Zak could catch up.

"Call Miki," he told the car.

"Hey."

"I'm bringing home a…guest," Kenzo said, unsure of how to describe Zak. Usually, he would've had no qualms about using the word "fuck buddy" or "conquest," but neither of those seemed to fit the situation for some reason.

"Okay. I'll put my headphones on."

"I wanted to let you know. I didn't want you surprised if you saw him, that's all."

"It's fine, Kenzo. I'll catch up with you later or tomorrow, depending on if I see you."

Miki was smirking if his tone of voice was anything to go by. "Hopefully tomorrow, if I do my job right."

He hung up to Miki's laughter and concentrated on the road ahead of him as much as he did the car behind him. Zak was stressed about something involving his kid, as he'd admitted. Kenzo couldn't begin to think of the stresses in general involved in raising a child. He would love to have children in the future, but right now, he had other things to think about. Nothing could be done about his current situation until he came out the other side of it; a family and kids would have to wait.

Brief flings or de-stressing sessions were great; neither needed commitment.

As he pulled into the car park of the building, the heater finally throwing out some heat—a little too late —he tried to see his home as if viewing it from a stranger's point of view. It was a standard brick four-storey building with several parking spaces for residents and guests. The previous owners were an elderly couple who had passed away a few years prior, and the family had only put the apartment on the market the day before Kenzo had started looking for places to buy. As soon as he'd seen the advert for it, he'd made an offer before even viewing it.

Zak pulled into another spot as Kenzo climbed out, swinging his bag to his shoulder again. He waited on the path for Zak to decide if he was staying or leaving, and their eyes locked through his rain-splattered window. He watched Zak exit the car and wander over to where Kenzo stood.

"Second thoughts?" he asked the younger-looking man, staying still despite the rain drenching them.

"And third and fourth and fifth." Zak grinned, his focus dropping to the keys in his noticeably trembling hands.

Kenzo licked his bottom lip, allowing his smile free. "Understood. Decision?"

Zak's gaze lifted to his, blinking away raindrops. "I'm here, aren't I?"

Kenzo studied the man for a moment before holding out his hand, allowing Zak to make the final choice. When Zak slid a hand into his, Kenzo felt a tingling sensation along the nerves of his palm and fingers. Ignoring it, he walked them up to the front door, unlocking it and closing them in after they entered.

Climbing two flights of stairs, he let them into the three-bedroom apartment, then let go of Zak's hand so they could take their coats and shoes off.

"I do have a roommate, but you're unlikely to see him as he works in the office at the back of the apartment, and my room is at the front. I will say, though, if you do happen to come across him, please make a little noise. He doesn't do well being startled, but he wouldn't hurt you."

Zak nodded, his expression taut, his Adam's apple bobbing.

Kenzo lowered his voice. "Come here."

Zak stepped closer until they were only a breath away from each other, a flush beginning to colour his pale cheeks. The little crease between his eyebrows was pronounced, likely from the stress of his life, but also the stress from their proximity. If Kenzo were to guess, he'd say Zak didn't do hook-ups often. Kenzo slowly lifted a hand, not wanting to startle Zak, and rubbed at the frown lines, Zak's eyes closing as he did. Zak's lips parted, and a soft sigh came out.

Smoothing that single finger over an eyebrow, down his cheekbone and along his jaw where two other fingers joined in, skimming their way down Zak's neck. Zak tilted his head slightly, allowing Kenzo greater access. Kenzo's focus was on the soft hair and skin underneath his fingertips, and he licked his lips, breath increasing, even though he'd hardly touched the guy.

Knowing he needed Zak in his bedroom now, he pulled back, Zak's eyes fluttering open to show barely banked heat. Grabbing his hand, Kenzo dragged Zak to his room. He kicked the door shut behind him, the soft-closer stopping any loud bang, then slowed his movements. As much as he wanted to fuck Zak, he wanted to treasure him, slow things down until they had no choice except to explode. He had no idea where the need came from, but he was unable to stop it.

"Kenzo?" Zak's voice was barely a whisper.

"Yes, sweetheart." The nickname rolled off his tongue too easily.

"It's…" Zak cleared his throat. "It's been a while…" he trailed off, his eyes conveying his meaning.

Kenzo tilted his head. "A while since sex, or a while since sex with a guy?"

"Both, but mainly the last one."

Kenzo lifted his hands, cupping Zak's jaw, his eyes devouring every blemish, every line, every dimple of his face. "I'll make it all better."

Zak's eyes drifted closed as Kenzo narrowed the distance. He pressed their lips together in a chaste kiss before swiping his tongue over the full mounds, requesting entry. Zak's hands gripped Kenzo's biceps as his mouth opened, and Kenzo's tongue swooped inside.

The taste of Zak exploded into his mouth, and he couldn't help but moan as he deepened their kiss. Zak's hands slid from his arms to his back, gripping at his t-shirt while Kenzo's fingers tunnelled through Zak's hair, pulling it from the band holding it back. He held a handful of hair and pulled slightly, Zak dropping his head back and releasing from the kiss, allowing Kenzo to nip at the hair covering his jawline.

Zak's hands slid under his t-shirt, lifting it higher as his fingers skimmed over his spine, leaving goosebumps in his wake. Kenzo let go briefly to yank his t-shirt off and repeated it with Zak's, groaning as their warmed, naked skin pressed together.

With a hand cupping the back of Zak's head, Kenzo kissed him again, his other hand holding Zak's ass and pulling him closer. Their cocks were hard, and Kenzo's nostrils flared as he tried to go slow for Zak's sake. Skimming his fingers up and down Zak's back, he relished the sounds he was tearing from the man. When Kenzo's fingers brushed against his nipples, Zak arched into the caress, the kiss pausing as he breathed heavily through the sensations.

Kenzo continued his ministrations, pressing little kisses along his collarbone, his free hand flicking at the nubs alternately. Then he fluttered his tongue over them, and Zak cried out, grabbing Kenzo's head. While Zak was distracted, Kenzo slid a hand around his back again to slide under the waistband of his joggers and briefs, cupping his bare ass cheek and squeezing gently.

Wanting a little more, he pulled away and spun Zak around, holding Zak tight to stop him from falling.

With a groan from deep in his throat, Kenzo pressed his front against Zak's back, gliding a hand up to wrap around the base of Zak's neck—not tightly, just enough to show he was there. Kenzo's mouth found the place where Zak's neck met his shoulder, and he licked along the skin, tasting the sweat beading there. Zak dropped his head back against Kenzo's shoulder, one hand lifting to wrap around Kenzo's neck.

Kenzo's free hand slipped down Zak's body to massage his cock through the material. The noises coming from Zak's mouth were arousing him enough to press his shaft against Zak's ass, his own moans joining in as his eyes crossed from the friction.

Kenzo's mouth found its way to Zak's jaw, and he turned Zak's head enough to join their lips again. His tongue entered Zak's mouth, his hand ground down on Zak's cock, and his hips thrust against his ass, his arousal heightening with each movement.

"Oh, fuck," Zak breathed as he pulled away, air noisily escaping his mouth.

Kenzo dipped his hand under Zak's joggers, wrapping his fingers around his warm, solid shaft and giving it a few strokes.

"Oh! Oh!"

"Yeah, that's it. Let go for me," Kenzo whispered. He sensed Zak was near and wanted to get his first orgasm out of the way to have time for more afterwards.

He pulled the joggers over his shaft and returned to grip Zak's cock tighter, stroking faster, releasing his hold on Zak's neck to flick at his nubs.

"Oh, yes! Fuck!"

Zak's grip on Kenzo's head indicated he was close, but Kenzo wanted to see it. He *needed* to see him lose it.

He took Zak's earlobe in between his teeth, tugging slightly as he mumbled, "Come on, baby. You're so fucking gorgeous. Come for me."

Zak tensed and growled his release, his abs contracting as his cock spurted over Kenzo's hand. Kenzo continued smoothing his free hand over Zak's skin to help him come down a little, though not too far because Kenzo wanted to work him up again. Zak trembled when Kenzo stroked once more, and Kenzo finally let go, sensing Zak was raw.

"Watch," Kenzo commanded as he lifted his hand to his mouth. When Zak's gaze fell on him, he licked the release from his hand. He should've been more worried about the possible implications of not having had "the talk," but he couldn't find it in him to care at that moment.

CHAPTER FIVE

ZAK

Watching as Kenzo licked his hand clean shouldn't have been as hot as it had been. Zak was sensitive to every touch, but the release had been exquisite and much needed.

He turned in Kenzo's arms and fused their lips, wrapping his arms around Kenzo's head to get as close as he could. He wanted more. He needed more. It had been years since he'd felt like this. Kenzo's dick in his mouth was what he wanted.

Kenzo pushed them backwards—towards the bed hopefully—and when the back of Zak's knees hit something, he allowed it to topple him backwards. Kenzo let him go, and Zak found himself staring up at the gorgeous, built specimen who had agreed to his half-assed request.

Watching, Zak saw Kenzo's eyes narrow as his gaze

roamed Zak's half-naked body. Kenzo's hands lifted to his own joggers, and he pulled his cock into view, hooking the waistband under his balls. His hand encircled it, stroking as he licked his lips. Zak was transfixed by the thick, dark red shaft. His tongue ran along his own lips, wanting nothing more than to wrap them around the dick and take every inch inside him. It had been years, but he'd be happy to try.

With the thought, Zak sat upright, scooting forward, and batted Kenzo's hands away. Stroking the heated flesh, he wet his lips again and pressed a kiss to the head. Sticking his tongue out, he licked around, taking the leaking fluid in and closing his eyes as the flavour exploded in his mouth. He covered his teeth with his lips and sank down slowly, stopping when he gagged and wrapping his hand around as a marker.

Then he sucked and withdrew, never once stopping for breath because he was in heaven.

"Fucking hell! Shit, yeah. It feels... Ah!" Kenzo's groans and growls were music to his ears and a declaration he was doing it right.

More fluid released into his mouth, and he hungrily swallowed it down. His ass clenched, and he felt the need coursing through him. He wanted this cock in his ass. Now!

Pulling off, he glanced up at Kenzo, seeing flushed cheeks, an open mouth and perspiration dripping down his forehead.

"Please fuck me," Zak whispered.

Kenzo bobbed his head once and pulled away. He grabbed Zak's hands and helped him to stand, then pushed Zak's joggers to the floor. Zak kicked them away, and Kenzo sank onto the bed, reaching for the lube from the bedside table, and sat with his legs outstretched and his back against the headboard.

"Climb on."

Zak hesitated but waved a hand at Kenzo. "Don't you want to take your joggers off?"

A brief expression, which Zak couldn't decipher, crossed Kenzo's face.

"No. Come here."

Zak saw the barely banked arousal in Kenzo's eyes, and he crawled from the bottom of the bed, up Kenzo's legs and straddled him, Kenzo's cock nestling nicely between his ass cheeks.

He paused, staring in Kenzo's eyes, then dropped his mouth, licking into Kenzo's as Zak began to rock his hips. Kenzo's hands disappeared from his back, and Zak heard the rip of a wrapper.

"Do you want to fuck me? Or do you want me to fuck you?"

Zak hesitated, but he didn't know why. He had already decided he needed Kenzo's cock in his ass, especially after so many years without it. "You in me," he grated out. "Please."

Kenzo smirked and reached around the back of Zak

to cover his cock. The click of a tube followed, and seconds later, he felt a finger press against his hole. Zak's mouth dropped open as he relaxed and allowed it to penetrate him. It felt fucking amazing. He had forgotten the feeling of being opened slowly, forgotten the sensation of having something inside him that way, but it had not changed how good it felt.

Kenzo prepared him slowly, increasing the number of fingers until Zak could easily take three of them. By that point, Zak was going out of his mind and begging repeatedly.

"Ready for me?"

"Fuck, yes! Please!"

"Tell me if it's too much."

Before the final syllable had left his mouth, Kenzo was pushing into him. Zak's breath was suspended as his ass was spread further than he'd been before. The burn was sore, but it was wanted. He panted as Kenzo lifted and lowered Zak until he was fully seated. Then they paused, Kenzo's hand smoothing across Zak's back, sides and legs as he became accustomed to the intrusion.

When Zak was ready, he experimented by lifting himself a little; the burn had gone, but the fullness remained. He dropped his head back as pleasure tingled throughout his body. Holding onto Kenzo's shoulders, he worked himself on the shaft, taking and giving pleasure if Kenzo's moans were anything to go by.

He had needed this so badly. After realising what he'd been missing, he didn't think he'd be able to give it up for a while, but short hook-ups would be all he could do.

"Fuck! I'm close, Zak. You're working me so good."

Zak's thighs were burning with the effort, but Kenzo slipped his hands underneath his ass and helped hold him while Kenzo took over, pounding from below. Zak's head dropped back as he held onto Kenzo's neck, his fingers linked behind to stop them from slipping free.

"God, yeah. Fuck!" Zak's second release came from nowhere, and he coated both their stomachs with his come.

He rested his head against Kenzo's shoulder while Kenzo used him until he climaxed a minute or so later. The growl that reverberated through his chest as he came lit a spark in Zak again, but he was too exhausted.

They lay sated for a while before Kenzo's cock slipped free, and he patted Zak's leg to get him to move. Zak's legs protested the shift, but he sank onto the bed. Kenzo got up and came back with a cloth, cleaning Zak before tucking him under the covers.

Zak bit his lip, knowing he wouldn't be staying, but he didn't want to upset Kenzo after sharing something so intimate. They hadn't discussed how the afternoon would end. It was probably past dinner time now.

Zak kept his eyes closed and breathing even as Kenzo wrapped his arm around his waist, the heat of the man spreading along his back. He tried not to tense. As much as he had enjoyed their time together, Zak had to get back to Dane. Emily was babysitting, and he didn't want to leave her there all night without letting her know, and he hadn't told her what he was doing after leaving the gym. If he didn't return soon, she would get worried.

He stayed as still and relaxed as possible until he heard the deep, even breathing that usually indicated someone was asleep, then he waited a little longer before trying to slowly extricate himself from Kenzo's embrace. As much as he wanted to burrow deeper into Kenzo's arms, he couldn't.

Zak had forgotten what it was like having sex with a man. Having been with Ashley for five years, he had forgotten how strong and rough a male could be, and he relished it. Zak was vers—he didn't mind whether he fucked or was fucked—but there was something about Kenzo's strength and tenderness that hit all of Zak's buttons.

Picking his clothes from the floor and listening for signs Kenzo was waking, he slid into his briefs, joggers and t-shirt with barely a whisper, and taking one more glance at the man who could've meant more to him, Zak left, closing the bedroom door quietly behind him. Slipping on his shoes and coat, Zak exited into the cool January air, carefully clicking the front door shut before striding down the path to his car. With one last look at the window where he knew Kenzo was sleeping, Zak sighed, started the engine and aimed the car towards home.

One hand on the wheel, his other rubbed across his chest, trying to relieve the tension as he fought back the emotions bombarding him. Kenzo had been right in one respect…relaxing had been the best way to de-stress. It was a shame that as soon as he went back to his life, the stress would come back, especially because, in two days, he would be back in court.

Ashley had been more distant and disappeared more often since Christmas had ended. She hardly spent any time with Dane, and Zak wondered why she was even trying for custody when it didn't seem like she wanted to spend any time with their son, anyway. That was the worst thing for Zak. She was fighting him tooth and nail for custody but didn't seem to want it. He felt the bitterness festering inside him at the thought she was doing it to spite him.

He pulled up to the house, seeing the lights on in the living room. Taking a moment to collect himself before he faced Emily, Zak stared out of the window, seeing nothing except Kenzo asleep in bed. How he was going to face seeing him at the gym from then on, he had no idea.

Clearing his throat and rubbing his hands over his face, he climbed out of the car and entered his home, the warmth from the heating seeping into his chilled bones as soon as he closed out the cold air.

"Hey, sorry I'm later than planned," he said as Emily stood from the sofa.

"Hey, you're back. No worries. Did you have a good time?"

Zak's heart jumped at her question. How did she know about what he'd been doing? He'd only met Kenzo today and… She didn't. She was asking about the gym. "Yeah. Um, it was good."

Emily cocked her head at him, narrowing her gaze. "Are you okay?"

"I'm all right." He gave a half-hearted smile, but she raised her eyebrow at him. "God! No wonder Ethan and Eric behave for you. You have that stare down perfect." He exhaled heavily and felt his cheeks flush as he looked away. "I let off a little steam after the gym," he mumbled.

"Good for you. Is it a bad thing?" she asked after a second of silence.

"No, not bad, just…" Zak shook his head. He didn't know how to explain it to her.

"You felt guilty for not being with Dane."

Zak raised his eyebrows and stared at her as her words reverberated around his mind. "How did you figure it out when I didn't know what I was feeling?"

"Because I'm me." She grinned. "Dane is fine. He's being looked after while you relax and recuperate.

There is nothing wrong with that. Now, if you had left him alone or with someone who wouldn't look after him, then it's a different matter." She placed a hand on his arm. "You always make sure he's safe before you do your thing, Zak. Nobody will ever be able to fault you for putting Dane first."

Zak closed his eyes and breathed deeply, trying to withhold the emotion. "Thank you," he croaked, finally.

"You're welcome. Now, have you eaten?" He shook his head. "Well, it's a good thing we have leftovers from dinner, then. Come on."

"You don't have to look after me as well, Emily."

"I know I don't, but I choose to, especially when you're hanging by a thread."

Zak followed her into the kitchen and dropped into a seat when she told him to. As she bustled around his kitchen, his thoughts turned, once more, to Kenzo. He hadn't said goodbye or anything to him, which he now regretted. Sneaking out while he was sleeping was an asshole move. Not that they had made any promises or anything, but still…after everything Kenzo had done for him…not cool.

A plate was placed in front of him, making him flinch. He glanced up at Emily, noticing her concerned expression. "Thanks. I'm all right, Emily. It'll be over soon."

She squeezed his shoulder. "It will. Dane went out like a light, no issues. I gave him a bath before bed, too.

Unless you need me tomorrow for anything, I will see you on Thursday."

"No, we should be good tomorrow. Thank you for everything. You go above and beyond for us."

"You're very welcome, Zak. I wouldn't have it any other way." She pressed a kiss to his cheek and left.

He heard the front door click shut as he dug into the heavenly-smelling shepherd's pie she had cooked for their dinner. Zak was not paying her enough for everything she did for him. She refused to take any kind of payment for the times Zak needed, except for night's out when he was out later, and that was only because he'd insisted.

As he lay in bed later that night, listening to the snuffles of Dane through the monitor, his thoughts turned to his whole situation: Ashley, Dane, Kenzo, work, Emily, his friends, the gym. He was being pulled in too many directions. Something had to give, and Zak wasn't sure what it would be.

He knew what he hoped would happen: Ashley would give up on trying for custody and leave them alone. Well, actually, he hoped she'd give up on the case, but for Dane's sake, he hoped she would still be around. He had a feeling if she lost the case, she would disappear for good. While that would be Zak's preference, he wasn't certain it the best option for Dane.

As for Kenzo, nothing would happen there. Zak was in no position to introduce someone new into Dane's life at the moment, especially with everything that was happening with Ashley. Dane was clingy enough as it was. Apart from him and Emily, Dane refused to go to anyone else, even Zak's brother or friends. It went to show how kids could pick up on people's emotions.

As far as he was concerned, Thursday couldn't come fast enough, regardless of the outcome.

Zak sat in the same seat he'd been sitting in for the previous court hearing, his hands twisting beneath the polished oak table as his leg bounced. They were waiting for the judge to arrive, and Samuel was quietly flicking through the paperwork beside him.

"What happens if he goes in her favour?" Zak asked the same question he had asked several times over the course of the case.

"Then we contest it. I have a good feeling about this. Emily, your family and your friends have all given statements about what they've seen, though it might not help, and we have the photos the judge asked for from Christmas. Those who took the photos did a good job. I have faith."

Zak wasn't so sure. He rolled his shoulders and

peeked at the clock, wishing the judge would hurry up. He wanted it over and done with.

The judge entered and went through the usual court procedures before addressing them. "You have provided the information I asked for and more." He paused. "This is a difficult decision because as Mr King so rightly pointed out at the last hearing, much of this is his word against Mrs King's." He sighed. "My job is never an easy one because someone will always be unhappy with my decision, but after taking into consideration all the evidence provided, I have decided to award full custody to Mr King."

"What?" Ashley's voice ripped through the courtroom. "Why the hell is he being given my son when he's hardly ever there? I'm the one who has been looking after him all day while he works," she said, holding her fingers up as air quotes. Her lawyer pulled on her arm, trying to get her to sit down. She batted him away. "I demand you reconsider!"

The judge stared at Ashley, linking his fingers on top of his table and leaned forward. "Mrs King, firstly, do not raise your voice in this courtroom. Secondly, do not raise your voice at me. Finally, you have proven why my decision is the correct one. Mr Boon, please ensure your client remains silent for the remainder of the hearing."

Zak's eyes widened as he stared at the judge, unable to believe his words. He tried to listen to what the judge was saying, but his brain had misfired, and everything was buzzing.

"Zak?" Samuel's voice pierced his bubble.

"Sorry." He refocused on the hearing, realising the judge had been speaking to him. "I apologise, Judge."

The judge nodded with a small smile. "There are some considerations you need to take into account, Mr King. If Mrs King wishes, she will be allowed supervised visits every week with someone from Social Services present. I was originally going to say unsupervised, but after that outburst, I have changed my mind." He flicked a frown at Ashley. "Also, I will be expecting you to have regular contact with Social Services to let them check on Dane's wellbeing and ensure this decision was in his best interests. I believe it to be true, but I will insist on those visits until all parties are happy. Do you agree to these terms, Mr King?"

"Yes, I do." He'd agree to anything as long as he got to take care of Dane.

"Very well. Full custody is awarded to Mr King with immediate effect." He banged the gavel.

Zak sank into the chair, unable to believe it. He dropped his head into his hands, trying to stop the tears. All the tension from the last year or more lifted with the knowledge Dane was safe from her. Now, he needed to get her out of the house, which reminded him…

He lifted his head. "Samuel? How do I get her out of

the house? Or would it be easier to move us out?" Zak asked.

Samuel smiled. "I will speak with her lawyer and get him to break the news. She doesn't have to leave as the house is in both your names, but—"

"Actually, it's not."

"It's not what?"

"The house is not in her name."

Samuel frowned at him. "I thought it was a joint purchase?"

"No, I bought the house before we got together, and we never added her details to it. She'll still expect half in the divorce, won't she?"

"Probably. Let me see what I can do. But in the meantime, I will speak with her lawyer. See if we can't come to a compromise."

"Thanks, Samuel. For everything."

"You're welcome. Now, go home and see your son."

Zak grinned and ran out of the courthouse as if his ass was on fire. He didn't ring anyone on the way, just sped home and parked out front, hopping out and racing to the house. Bursting through the door, he made Emily and Dane jump.

Zak did nothing but smile as he reached Dane and picked him up, swinging him around in his arms, the toddler's giggles filling the air.

"You did it?" Emily asked.

Zak stopped, held Dane close and closed his eyes,

breathing in Dane's scent, one of the only scents that helped him settle. "Yeah, we did it."

"Awesome! Your daddy is going to look after you so good, little man." Emily came close and drew a finger down Dane's cheek. She cupped Zak's jaw. "Well done."

"I don't know what to do with myself." Zak felt like a little puppy full of energy, wanting to bounce around and play. His insides were jittery and buzzing.

"What you need to do is relax and enjoy your son's company as usual. Nothing has to change for you, Zak, because you were already an amazing father. The only thing you need to concern yourself with is being with your son. Everything else can wait for a day or two."

"Well, reality might come calling sooner rather than later because Samuel is trying to figure out about the house and what it means since Ashley still lives here at the moment."

"Does she?" Emily frowned.

Zak raised his eyebrows. "Of course, she does. We might not be in the same bedroom any longer, but she still uses the spare room."

"I've not seen her for days, Zak. Every time I've been here, I've never seen her. Are you sure she hasn't already taken her stuff?"

Zak frowned and, still holding Dane, headed up the stairs to the room Ashley had been using since they'd split. When he opened the door, he saw the emptiness straight away. Apart from the bed being a mess, there were no clothes in the drawers or wardrobe, no toiletries cluttering the units or shelves, no personal effects of any kind visible in the room. The air was stale as if the room had not been used for days or weeks. It appeared Emily was right; Ashley had left ages ago. How did he not know? Ever since the last custody hearing, he had asked Emily to take care of Dane whenever he wasn't around, so he knew Dane had been cared for, but he'd assumed Ashley was still around but was avoiding him.

He pulled out his phone and dialled Samuel's office. After being put through, he said, "Hey, I thought I'd let you know that I think Ashley might have already moved out. None of her stuff is here anymore."

"When did that happen?"

"I can honestly say I have no idea. I thought she was still popping in now and then but Emily mentioned she hadn't seen her. I've checked her room, and it's empty of belongings."

"That makes things easier. It appears she's made her choice. It won't stop her trying for half the value, but we'll see."

He rang off again after a few more words and headed back downstairs to where Emily was tidying up the living room. "Leave it. You don't need to tidy up after us."

"I don't mind. Unless you need me, I'm going to head off after."

"No, you're fine. Thank you, Emily. You're right. She's taken everything with her."

"I thought so." Emily smiled. "Now, get yourselves settled, and when Dane is in bed tonight, have a think about what you want to do about work and my babysitting. I'm happy to do it, and I can work my job around it. Having my own accounting business has its perks." She grinned.

"Thanks."

He saw Emily to the door, hugging her tightly before letting her go.

"Well, little man, shall we get some kids' TV on?"

Dane babbled incoherently at him, which he took as an agreement, and settled them both on the floor in front of the big screen, surrounding them with toys and books. He was determined to do exactly as Emily said… what he normally did with his son.

CHAPTER SIX
KENZO

Kenzo sat with Miki on the sofa, the blinds in the room lowered, lights off apart from one. Day three of Miki's latest PTSD episode had dawned with a little less trembling, crying and anger from the man—it was called hyperarousal from what Kenzo's research had turned up. It had been a stressful few days for them both, but mainly for Miki. Despite receiving therapy, which helped him a great deal, there was nothing to do for these dark moments until they had passed. Miki was taking some medication that helped, but it still didn't stop them completely.

All Kenzo could do was make sure Miki didn't hurt himself or others, sit with him when he wanted company and make food and drink to persuade him to keep fuelled. It didn't always work. This session hadn't lasted as long as the previous one, but it was still taking its toll on both of them.

Kenzo was glad Miki hadn't resorted to drug or alcohol misuse in the two years since the incident, but the depression and anxiety were wearing the man down.

Miki was booked into a session with his therapist late that afternoon, and all being well, he would be able to go without issue. He was already climbing his way back from the abyss of his nightmares.

After making a carb-loaded pasta and chicken salad for lunch and watching as Miki picked at it, Kenzo deemed him on the mend, at least this time. Kenzo always thought he was one lucky son of a bitch to not have developed PTSD despite everything he'd been through. He would've loved to know why some people were more susceptible to it, and others weren't. One of these days, he'd research it more. Maybe when it wasn't so close to home.

To distract himself a bit, he thought about Zak. He'd not seen or heard from him in the two weeks since they'd slept together, and it annoyed him a little. Either Zak was completely ignoring him, or something had happened. He wondered whether whatever stressful thing Zak had been dealing with had been sorted or not. He'd hated seeing the defeated expression on his face.

When Miki went off to his therapy session, stating

he wanted to drive himself, not have Kenzo do it, Kenzo decided to head to the gym. After three days of inactivity, he needed the burn in his muscles to help clear his head. He wasn't needed for tennis coaching until the next day. He was glad the sessions were spread over three days instead of one on each day.

Dropping his things in his locker, he grabbed his water bottle and towel and headed down the corridor to the weights room. He saw Drake coming out of his office.

"Hey, Drake. How're things going?"

"Good, thanks. The coach should be back in three weeks if you're okay to cover until then?"

Kenzo nodded. "Yeah, it'll be fine."

Drake narrowed his eyes. "You look like crap."

"Gee, thanks."

"You know what I mean. Everything okay?"

"Yeah." Kenzo exhaled. "Miki had a bad few days."

"Ah." Drake squeezed his shoulders. "Anything I can do?"

Kenzo shrugged and shook his head. "Nothing, either of us, can do apart from being there for him."

"Well, let me know if there is."

"Will do." He nodded, then continued on his way. He entered the weights room, the overpowering scent of sweat making his eyes water, and immediately aimed for a treadmill. He couldn't race away from his problems like he wanted to, but he could do a steady walk to warm up. Then he would get his muscles burning.

Keeping his hands on the rails to stop him from losing his balance, Kenzo strolled his way through his warm-up sequence, eyes on the floor. It wasn't until he heard a voice that he looked up.

"That's it. One more. Perfect. You're doing really well, Zak," Luke said.

Kenzo, tightening his hands on the rail, glanced across the room, watching as Zak stood from the barbell bench press, sweat making his top stick to his body. The soft yet hard body Kenzo had worshipped and touched all over.

"It doesn't feel like I've made much progress."

The voice, tinged with heavy breathing, shot straight to Kenzo's cock, the reminder of how Zak sounded when he was aroused.

"Give it time. It isn't something that happens overnight, and you've been under a lot of stress. Hopefully, now that it's all sorted, you can start concentrating on yourself and little Dane," Luke said with a wink.

Zak smiled before gulping some water. "Yeah. It's crazy, but I never thought I'd actually get custody of him."

"They would've been fools to be blind to what she was like. No one in their right mind would ignore it."

"Thankfully, the judge saw it, too."

They walked towards Kenzo, who slowed the tread-mill speed a little as he kept his eyes on Zak. He wasn't sure if he wanted any reaction or not. Who was he kidding? Of course, he wanted some kind of acknowl-edgement. After the few hours they spent together, he wanted more, but Zak obviously hadn't if his sneaking out while thinking Kenzo was asleep was any indication.

No, Kenzo reminded himself. He didn't want more. He couldn't.

"Come on, let's get the training part of this session completed," Luke said as they exited the room.

Zak's gaze met his, widening slightly, before flicking away to follow Luke. Kenzo's heart pounded, and he clenched his jaw and stopped the treadmill, more than ready for his workout.

He didn't know why it annoyed him as much as it did. He supposed it was more that he was the recipient of a "wham, bam, thank you, man" instead of the other way around. Having never had it happen to him, he hadn't realised what a prick he'd been to his previous hook-ups. That would be changing from now on.

Kenzo decided to forget about Zak. Zak obviously wanted an itch scratched, especially as it had been a while since he'd been with a guy. It can't have meant much to him. It didn't mean anything to Kenzo either— at least it was what he tried to tell himself. He had far too much going on to add anything else to the balls he was juggling above his head. Which reminded him, he needed to head to the Veteran Centre that afternoon as well. Jack was probably finished with the third lot of books Kenzo had sent.

After spending an hour or so taking himself to the edge with his workout, his body felt sweaty but great. No doubt the endorphins from working out were flowing through his body, and he'd regret pushing himself so hard later. He strode down the corridor to the showers, wiping his face with his towel after he'd thrown his bottle in the bin on the way. When he got there, he was dumbfounded to find Zak still there.

He pursed his lips and approached his locker, his heart racing, making enough noise he didn't startle Zak. He ignored the temptation to glance in the direction of the showers until he had no option except to enter.

The furthest shower away was Kenzo's destination. It was pettiness, but he felt the overwhelming need to reach out to Zak, and he refused to do so when it was obviously not wanted.

"I'm sorry."

The words were whispered into the small area, barely heard over the spray of the showers. Kenzo paused in the act of spreading shower gel over his body, and despite the talking to he had given himself, looked over his shoulder, seeing Zak stood with his hand braced against the tile, facing away from him. His demeanour screamed defeat: hunched shoulders, head lowered and rigid posture.

"Don't worry about it." Kenzo hadn't planned on saying anything, but he couldn't let Zak feel like it was his fault. They hadn't exactly expressed their intentions for it being more than one night. He resumed cleaning, rinsing off the suds, starting when something touched his upper back. Glancing over his shoulder again, he saw a mop of wet, blond hair against his back and felt hot breath on his spine. Hands slid around his waist until they rested against his stomach.

"I'm sorry," Zak mumbled. "So sorry."

Kenzo closed his eyes, took a breath and covered Zak's hands with his own. "It's okay, Zak," he muttered. "Everything is okay."

"Oh, sorry!" the voice squeaked, and Zak moved away, Kenzo immediately feeling the loss in the coldness that seeped back where Zak had been pressed.

They finished their showers, drying off in silence. Once they were both dressed, Kenzo stopped next to Zak, who was staring into a locker. When Zak didn't make any move to look at him, Kenzo cupped his jaw and turned Zak to face him.

"Look at me." Zak lifted his gaze. "My house or yours?"

Zak swallowed hard, and never breaking eye contact, replied, "Mine. My son will be asleep, though."

Kenzo smirked. "That's fine. I'll gag you if I have to."

Zak smiled and ducked his head. "I'll keep it in mind."

Kenzo asked for Zak's address, explaining he had to nip home before he headed over, and Zak complied before nodding and leaving the changing room. Shaking his head, Kenzo grinned as he collected his belongings and dropped by Drake's office before he left.

"Hey, Drake? Could you do me a favour?"

"Is this a normal favour, or one I can collect on at a later date?" Drake joked.

Kenzo rolled his eyes. "I need to go out tonight. Would you mind keeping an eye on Miki for me? You don't necessarily have to be there unless he wants you to or you want to be but be at the end of the phone if nothing else."

"Of course! I've not caught up with him for a while. Maybe I can grab some takeaway and a movie and make a night of it." Drake's grin turned to a smirk. "That way, if you need to stay over, you can."

Kenzo flipped his middle finger—a regular occurrence with Drake—and left the man laughing his ass off. It was nice to not have to think about anything. As much as he loved Miki, he was always drained after an episode and needed time to recoup himself.

He entered their apartment, dropping his bag to the floor with a bump—the easiest way to make his presence known sometimes. Wandering towards the kitchen, where he heard movement, he called out Miki's name.

"I'm about to start cooking. Do you want some?"

"How about you put that on hold. Drake said he might be nipping over with takeaway for you both."

"Are you heading out?" Nothing got past Miki. It was why he had been the team's communications expert, but Kenzo also didn't miss the slight smile and blush on Miki's face at the mention of Drake.

"Yeah."

"Good, you need a breather. Plus, I'm sick of the sight of you." Miki turned to face him with a grin.

"Ah, there he is. The cheeky bastard is alive and kicking again."

"You said Drake's bringing takeaway?"

"Well, he said he'd bring a movie, too. Sounds like date night if you ask me." Miki spun back to the oven, switching it off, but not before Kenzo saw the blush darkening his cheeks further. "Seriously? You two? That's great!"

"Shut up! It's nothing at the minute. Just an itch we scratch."

Kenzo checked his watch; he needed to get going. "Well, you go ahead and scratch whatever itch you both have for as long as you both want it." Kenzo chuckled. "I'll leave you to it. I'm going to run and get changed, then I'll head out."

He did just that and found himself outside Zak's house quicker than he imagined. In the darkening sky, he could see it was a nice family-sized house, which was perfect considering Zak had a child—a son if he recalled correctly. Kenzo needed to make sure he was out of the house before the kid woke up in the morning. He didn't want either of them to have to answer any questions. He didn't even know how old the kid was.

Shaking his head, he locked his car and strode to the door, knocking softly. The door opened slowly, Zak's head peeking around the edge until he saw who it was. Opening it fully, Zak gestured for him to enter and shut it again behind him.

"Hi," Zak said.

"Hey."

"Would you like a drink?"

"Sure. Whatever you're having."

They walked into the kitchen, Kenzo having followed slightly behind, and Zak went to the kettle, setting it boiling. "Tea?"

It wasn't his cup of choice, but he didn't hate it. "Thanks."

As Zak made the drink, Kenzo took in the kitchen. It was a spacious room with a small, highly polished, wooden, four-person table in the centre. The cupboards were pristine white with a dark wood counter, and there were several bright lights overhead that shone on a grey slate tiled floor.

"Nice place."

"Thanks." Zak ducked his head.

Kenzo couldn't see his face, but he was certain a flush stained his cheeks. He wondered what could have caused it. He hardly knew anything about Zak, except his body...he knew plenty about that.

The brew was placed in front of him on the table, and Zak sat, cradling his cup.

"Thank you." Kenzo took a sip of scalding tea, the surprised look on Zak's face making him grin when he swallowed. "I have a steel mouth, I'm told."

Zak rested both his elbows on the table and blew across the top of his cup. "I definitely haven't."

A hint of...reluctance? No, maybe shyness? He wasn't sure what it was, but Zak wouldn't meet his gaze. He needed to be certain this was what Zak wanted because Kenzo didn't want to have any issues with Zak's son being here.

"Would you like me to leave?"

"No! Sorry, no. I'm...I...This is all new to me. I've recently gained full custody of my son, and things are a bit all over the place. But I want you here. I really do." The last sentence was whispered.

"What's your son's name?" Kenzo thought the subject might calm Zak down a bit.

Sure enough, Zak smiled. "Dane." He shook his head. "It's been a long year for us, but, hopefully, it's over now." He replaced his cup on the table and stared at Kenzo. "I want you." This time it was said with more force as if he needed the reminder himself.

"Then you shall have me."

Zak hesitated and stood, leaving the cups where they were as he grabbed Kenzo's hand and pulled him towards the stairs. They ascended in silence until they entered a room where Zak flicked on the light.

"I'm just going to…" He rushed over to the bedside table and switched on the lamp. "Would you mind…" He pointed to the main light switch, and Kenzo turned it back off again, bathing the room in a softer, more intimate glow. "Thanks." Zak pulled something from his belt and rested it on the bedside table.

The room had a king-size, Japanese-style bed, low to the floor as well as a chest of drawers and wardrobe, all made from a darker wood with exquisite design features. Every item matched as if it had been specially made to order.

"I love these pieces. Did you have them commissioned?"

"Um…yeah, kind of."

"They're fantastic. Such attention to detail." Kenzo slid his hand along the drawers, fingering the pattern set deeply into the wood. "So smooth."

"Thank you."

Kenzo could tell Zak was uncomfortable for some reason. He changed direction and headed straight for the man who had moved to the end of the bed, thinking he probably wanted to get to the reason why Kenzo was there rather than having small talk. Though he was intrigued by what he'd seen of Zak's home.

Locking gazes, Kenzo stopped in front of Zak and lifted a hand to his beard, slightly tugging on the hairs. "You're gorgeous," he whispered. As a faint blush tinted Zak's cheeks, Kenzo slid his hands into Zak's hair, pulling the band from it, setting it free. "Your hair is..." He couldn't think of an appropriate description but grinned instead, holding some of the strands as he pulled Zak closer. "I'm gonna kiss you now."

"Please..."

Their lips met in a soft brush. Kenzo nipped at each lip in turn, barely grazing the skin with his teeth. Zak's hand gripped at his shirt, and he stepped closer, his tongue slipping out to catch Kenzo's lips. Returning the motion, Kenzo licked along Zak's full mouth, waiting until he opened before delving in. He cupped Zak's jaw, tilting his head to get closer. Spearing into the wet heat, he retreated just as quickly, repeating the motion several times, mimicking the act they would hopefully get to later.

When Zak moaned, Kenzo wrapped his arms around Zak and deepened the kiss, swirling his tongue around Zak's before retreating once more. He slid one hand to the top of the curve of Zak's still covered ass, the other moved up to the base of Zak's neck. Pulling back, he pressed some gentle kisses to Zak's mouth, then ran his tongue along Zak's lips before plundering once again.

Zak draped his arms around Kenzo's neck and held him tight, refusing to submit when Kenzo tried to move away. "More," Zak mumbled, fusing their mouths once again.

Their cocks were rigid rods between them as their bodies pressed tight against each other. Kenzo cupped Zak's ass, pulling him harder, then releasing, then pulling again. Zak understood his actions and began thrusting his hips against Kenzo. The friction was divine, and their kiss spun out of control. Their breathing increased, air noisily channelling through their noses when their mouths declined to part.

Kenzo broke Zak's hold on his neck and dragged their mouths away, gasping. His lips felt bruised and tingly, and peering at Zak's, they appeared swollen and red. Debauched looked good on him.

"I want you."

Kenzo wasn't sure which one of them said it, but it lit a fire beneath them. He gripped the hem of Zak's shirt and ripped it over his head, bearing his body to him. Zak unbuttoned Kenzo's shirt and did the same, throwing it away before clashing their mouths together in a fierce, passionate kiss, his nails raking Kenzo's back.

Hands dropping to Zak's jeans, Kenzo swiftly unzipped them and pushed them down, Zak's cock straining forward, making Kenzo realise he hadn't worn underwear. Unable to resist, Kenzo pushed Zak backwards, sending him sprawling across the low bed with a yelp, then grabbed the jeans and yanked them off. He dropped to his knees in front of Zak, careful of his bad one, and encircled the man's dick, feeling the steel beneath the softness. A pearl of precum bubbled to the tip, and Kenzo lapped it up, closing his eyes at the bitter but addictive taste. He swirled his tongue around the head and sucked on it, trying to bring more of the cream from him. He inhaled deeply, taking in the clean scent.

"Ah, fuck," Zak mumbled as Kenzo opened his mouth and sank down on his shaft. Zak's hand rested against the back of Kenzo's head, not pressing, not pushing, just present. Zak's hips thrust up when Kenzo pressed a finger against his taint. "Oh, god!"

Kenzo glanced up at him from under his eyelashes and saw Zak's fingers gripping his own hair as the tendons stood proud in his neck from the strain of holding back. As he worshipped Zak's cock, he watched Zak reach for the covers beneath him, fisting them as his stomach contracted. Knowing he was close, Kenzo pulled off, not wanting the night to end so soon.

"Turn over," Kenzo ordered.

CHAPTER SEVEN

ZAK

Zak inhaled through his clenched teeth and rolled onto his stomach, his knees coming underneath him to prop him up higher. He glanced over his shoulder, watching as Kenzo's eyes darkened further at the sight before him. Usually, Zak would be embarrassed by the exposed position, but he couldn't be. Not with the look in Kenzo's eye. A look that told Zak exactly what he thought of the view.

Swallowing hard against the lump that rose in his throat, he rested his forehead on his warm hands, cupped around each other as they were, and closed his eyes. His other senses awoke when his vision was cut off. A rustle behind him had goosebumps flowing down his spine, and his breathing increased, sweat beading on his skin. He startled when fingers touched his back.

"Steady," Kenzo whispered from above him, and Zak surmised he now stood.

All the air rushed out of his lungs when Kenzo reached Zak's ass, gently sliding a finger between his cheeks until he reached his sack. The hand returned to his ass along with the other, squeezing the firm mounds before pulling them apart. Without warning, hot breath fanned against his entrance, and smooth, hot skin pressed against his most intimate place. His hole clenched in response, and Zak licked his dry lips, trying to get moisture back into his mouth.

"Fuck," Zak breathed.

Kenzo licked around his opening, pressing and retreating until Zak relaxed enough for him to enter. The feeling of his tongue spearing into him was something he had never experienced but had always wanted to. Ashley hadn't been into it, giving or receiving; therefore, Zak had never had the chance. And as for his teenage experiments, it wasn't something he'd come across. Porn, however, had shown him a lot of new things.

Unable to help himself, Zak pressed his hips back, requesting more without words. He heard and felt Kenzo chuckle against his sensitive skin, and he shivered, resting the side of his head on the cool covers and cupping his head, fisting his hair as the emotion and arousal overwhelmed him.

Kenzo's mouth left Zak's ass, and his hands slid up

Zak's back until they were braced on either side of Zak, and Kenzo was covering him.

"Where's the lube and condoms?" Kenzo slid Zak's hair away from his face, kissing beneath his ear, his cheek and jaw while waiting for Zak's answer.

Zak cleared his throat and pointed to the bedside table to the right. "Drawer."

Cool air replaced the warm body when Kenzo moved, but Zak was frozen in place, head burrowed into the bed. His body tingled.

Kenzo gripped his hips, startling him. He hadn't heard the drawer open or close, but it must have.

"This is the perfect height for me to stand. I want you to stay on your knees near the end of the bed."

Zak blinked as he lifted his head, letting the words sink in. Checking over his shoulder, he saw Kenzo nod, and he slid down the bed until he could kneel on the edge with his upper body lowered to the mattress.

"Perfect. Let me know if your knees begin to hurt."

Zak nodded absentmindedly. He didn't think he'd last long when Kenzo entered him. Shivering again, he closed his eyes, resting his head and submitting to whatever Kenzo wanted because it was also what he wanted. What he had not had for many years—someone else taking care of him.

He felt Kenzo behind him, his hands smoothing across Zak's skin, gentling him. If he hadn't been so aroused, it would be soothing enough to fall asleep. As it was, his skin pebbled to meet Kenzo's fingers, and his body trembled.

"Please…" he whispered.

The click of a lid twice, then a small thump as the bottle bounced on the bed advertised the next move. Zak waited for Kenzo. A fingertip rubbed against his hole, and Zak instinctively clenched before purposefully relaxing, allowing the tip to push past his rim. He gasped at the feel. Although they had fucked once before, Zak was still tight, and the entry burned a little. Breathing through it and the two other fingers joining the first, Zak humped at nothing, finding no friction for his cock.

His hands gripped the sheets on either side of his head as Kenzo scissored his fingers, stretching Zak to be able to take the girth of Kenzo's cock. The fingers retreated, and Kenzo's cock pressed against his opening. Zak had no idea when Kenzo had removed his jeans or when he had rolled on the condom, but he didn't care any longer. His nerves were alight with need.

"Yes, please."

Zak pushed back, but Kenzo gripped his hips, holding him steady.

"I refuse to hurt you. Be patient."

Gritting his teeth, Zak froze, allowing Kenzo to thrust and withdraw several times, breaching further with every move. When he was fully seated, Kenzo braced himself on his hands over Zak's back, pressing a kiss to his shoulder blade.

"You feel fucking good, Zak."

Kenzo pulled his hips back slightly and pushed forward, the motion rubbing Zak's nipples against the bed.

"Ah!" He hadn't realised how sensitive his nubs became when he was aroused.

The small, short movements were nice but not what Zak needed. "Please! Harder!" he whimpered, trying to remember to keep his voice low.

"Is that what you need from me, sweetheart? Hard thrusts to get you there?"

"Yes! Oh, god, yes!"

"As you wish." Kenzo lifted his upper body and took hold of Zak's hips. "Brace yourself." Then he plunged forward.

"Oh, fuck, yes!"

Zak could do nothing except hold on as Kenzo rammed his ass, repeatedly slamming into him in fast thrusts. Zak was right—he was not going to last long at all. "Right there! Please! I'm gonna come!"

Any other time, he would be mortified by how quickly he came, but he'd been on the edge for what felt like hours. As his climax screamed through him and he clenched around Kenzo's cock, he heard a muted groan from behind him and a stuttering in the movements. After that, Zak relaxed against the bed, his muscles weak and trembling. He winced when Kenzo withdrew but didn't move from his position.

A warm washcloth against his ass made him jump, but he sighed as the heat eased some of his soreness. "Thank you," he mumbled.

"Turn over," Kenzo said.

"I don't know if I can move," Zak admitted.

An arm slid under his chest, lifting him upright, his knees protesting with having been in the position for so long. Kenzo helped him to stand and, when Zak was steady, washed his spent cock.

Zak wasn't sure what Kenzo would do now that they'd fucked, but it didn't take long to find out. Once he'd disposed of the washcloth, he guided Zak into bed, pulling the covers over him, then walked around the other side and slid in. Zak swallowed, not sure if he wanted Kenzo staying over or not, but Kenzo's words stopped the thought.

"I'll head home in a bit, and you won't have to introduce me to your son tomorrow. Let's take a breather." He lifted his arm in invitation, and Zak immediately stuck himself to Kenzo's side, breathing deeply of his musky scent. Resting his head on Kenzo's chest, he placed his hand over his heart, feeling the steady thrum beneath his palm.

He knew there could be nothing more than what they'd already shared, but it was nice to be held.

Dane's babbling chatter woke him, and Zak stretched his arms above his head and yawned before swinging his legs over the edge of the bed. In the beginning, it had taken him a while to get used to a bed that was lower to the floor than usual, but in one of Ashley's good moments, she said it would be easier for Dane to climb onto when he was older. She was right, and it wasn't something he said lightly.

He stood and stretched again before turning to make his bed, eyes widening when he saw Kenzo staring back at him.

The man cleared his throat. "Sorry. I fell asleep. I'll creep out when you go downstairs." Kenzo's expression was full of apology. "I really am sorry. I know this wasn't what you wanted. I only woke when I heard your son call you; otherwise, I would've been gone already."

He could tell Kenzo wanted to say more, but he sat upright and turned away. Zak wasn't worried as much about Dane—he was, after all, only two—but Zak hadn't had anyone stay over before, which was a stupid thing to think about when he'd been married for the last four years. Refusing to acknowledge the way his heart missed a beat when Kenzo said he would've already left, Zak swallowed hard.

"It's fine."

He realised he was stark naked and strode to the en-suite, closing the door behind him and leaning against it, the coldness seeping onto his warm skin. His feelings were all mixed up, and he couldn't tell up from down. Kenzo's being there was unexpected but not… unwelcome. Zak frowned and shook his head.

Pushing the thought aside, he quickly did his business, knowing Dane would begin to shout for him real soon. It was only as he went to leave, he realised he'd forgotten to bring any clothes with him—which meant he was going to have to walk out there naked again. Knocking his head against the door, he inhaled and opened the door.

Kenzo stood, fully dressed, with his back to the bathroom door, looking at the picture on the wall. Zak's heart stuttered at the thoughtfulness of the gesture, and he quickly rummaged through his drawers for some joggers and a t-shirt.

"Da-da," Dane called, followed by a lot of babble and a banging noise, which he knew to be the sound of his son banging a toy against the cot.

"I didn't realise how young your son was." Kenzo's voice was quiet.

"I… never thought to tell you," Zak admitted. "I'm dressed," he added quietly.

Kenzo turned to him and gave a small smile. "You didn't need to tell me anything. I'm sorry, again, for still being here. I must've been more tired than I thought."

"It's okay." Dane called him again. "I have to go get him." He hesitated at the door. "Kenzo…"

"It's all right."

Zak didn't say anything further, drifting across the landing to Dane's bedroom. "Hey, buddy. Did you sleep well?" Dane grinned at him and lifted his arms, babbling constantly. "Let's go get some breakfast." He exited Dane's room and paused, glancing across at his bedroom door, which was only slightly ajar, no doubt so Dane didn't see Kenzo. "Hey, buddy. We have a guest for breakfast. How cool is that?"

His heart raced as he said the words. This was not what he'd planned on happening, but once it had, he was loathed to stop it. He could've easily ignored Kenzo being there and allowed him to sneak out, but for some reason, he couldn't do it. His stomach was in knots as he raised his voice and said, "Kenzo? We're going to get some breakfast if you want to join us."

Zak didn't wait to see if Kenzo would come; he jogged down the stairs, bumping Dane up and down like the little boy loved until he got into the kitchen. Fastening his son in his little chair, he swept his own hair into a ponytail, grabbed the cups they'd left from last night and turned to the counter to begin making some porridge. It was Dane's favourite breakfast food. Zak didn't mind it, but he had to have a little sugar with it. He had no idea how Kenzo took it, so he placed a few items on the table: honey, milk, sugar and chocolate sauce—blame Noah for that one. Ever since they'd been kids, his brother had loved adding the ice cream sauce to his porridge.

He knew when Kenzo entered the kitchen because Dane went quiet, then started babbling faster and banging on his tray. Zak added the milk to the pan and glanced over his shoulder with a small smile, his gaze going to Dane rather than Kenzo.

"Is porridge okay for you?" he asked, returning his focus to their breakfast.

Kenzo cleared his throat. "Yes, thanks." His voice was hesitant, and he didn't venture any further into the kitchen.

"Come on in. We won't bite. Well, I won't. I can't make guarantees for Dane." Zak chuckled, though it sounded a little forced. He turned the cooker on. "Do you drink tea or coffee in the morning because I have both?"

"Coffee would be great."

"Can you do me a favour, then, please? Could you flick the kettle on, and I'll make the drinks once the porridge is done?" He held the pan's handle and stirred the mixture with a wooden spoon, the scent of porridge filling the kitchen.

"I'll do it. You're okay. Do you want coffee?" Kenzo stepped over to the kettle and switched it on.

"Yes, please. Mugs are above your head, granules are in the container there," he pointed before resuming stirring, "and spoons are in the drawer to your right."

They worked in companionable silence, bar the nonsensical musings of Dane, and Zak couldn't get over how domestic it seemed. He was not used to feeling so at ease—well, except for the butterflies in his stomach—in his own home when someone else was present. Usually, it meant Ashley was there, and the tension between them was unbearable. It felt amazing to not have to worry about whether his words or behaviour would set her off.

It was a bit weird having Kenzo, who he'd only known a couple of weeks, in his kitchen with him and his son. A good sense of weird. Zak inwardly rolled his eyes. He was talking himself in circles.

"Okay, all ready."

He had never got out of the habit of talking to himself, which made his life easier when Dane had come along because it meant he had someone to focus his words on instead of an empty room. People had often given him funny looks because he was chatting away to no one in particular.

Pouring the porridge into three bowls—two larger, one smaller—he carried them to the table. He set the two larger bowls opposite each other and the smaller one next to his place. Turning to grab some spoons, he stopped when he saw Kenzo holding them out.

"Thanks." He ducked his head, the flutter becoming a swarm instead.

Zak stirred and blew on Dane's food, cooling it down, while Kenzo placed the full coffee mugs in front of each of them, which Zak acknowledged with a nod of thanks. There was no conversation as Zak made sure the food wasn't too hot for his son. He secured a bib around Dane's neck and gave him the bowl and spoon.

"Have at it, champ."

"You're letting him feed himself?"

Kenzo's eyebrows were raised, eyes wide as he stared at Dane. Zak took in the vision of Dane dropping the food from his spoon directly onto his bib, not much getting into his mouth. Zak smiled. "He has to learn. Plus, it allows me to eat a warm breakfast instead of a cold one. Cold porridge is not pleasant."

"True."

They ate in almost silence, just the clink of spoons against bowls and Dane's babbling.

When he'd finished, he bit his lip and asked, "What do you do? As a job, I mean."

Kenzo sat back in his chair, a hand wrapped around his mug. "I'm retired from the Army."

Zak raised his eyebrows but realised it fit him like a glove. "Yeah, I can see it now you've said that. Did you enjoy it?"

Kenzo huffed. "I wouldn't say I *enjoyed* it as such, but I was happy with what needed to be done."

Zak sensed his reluctance to talk about it and changed the subject. "And you work out for fun."

"Most of the time." Kenzo grinned. "Sometimes, I just ogle the guys there." He winked.

Zak sputtered his coffee, coughing slightly.

Kenzo laughed. "Sorry."

"No, you're not," Zak complained once he'd recovered.

"Okay, I'm not." Kenzo drained his mug. "I'm going to go and leave you. Thank you for breakfast." He stood, picking up his bowl and mug and rinsing them out in the sink without asking if he should.

When Kenzo walked past to leave, Zak stood and placed his hand on Kenzo's forearm, pulling him to a stop. Gaze finally connecting with Kenzo and roaming his face, Zak said, "Thank you."

"You're welcome." They stared at each other for a moment, an expression Zak couldn't decipher on the other man's face before Kenzo leaned forward and placed a kiss on Zak's cheek. "Take care."

Zak swallowed hard against the need to call Kenzo back as he walked away. He didn't need him here; he was fine alone.

"And who might you be?" He heard from the hallway.

"Damn it! Noah!" He rubbed a hand across his face. This was the last thing he needed.

"What? I'm saying hi," his brother shouted back.

"Leave him alone!"

"He can't leave now. I've only just met him."

"Noah! If he wants to leave, let him!" Zak sat again, using Dane's spoon to collect all the bits he'd missed his mouth with. "Meddling brothers are not pleasant. Be grateful you're an only child," he muttered to his son.

Noah entered the kitchen with a smug expression on his face. His brother looked a lot like him, except with short, spiky hair and a clean-shaven jaw. They had the same slender build, although Noah had more muscles than Zak did—at least for now, he thought smugly. Though he was only five years younger than Zak, he appeared even younger, especially when wearing skinny jeans and a tight black t-shirt like he was.

Zak rolled his eyes, only stopping when Kenzo joined them with a pinched expression on his face.

"I see you've met my annoying little brother. Kenzo, Noah. Noah, Kenzo."

At those words, Kenzo's face relaxed, the tension releasing from his body. Zak realised he must've thought they were a couple, which he thought was a strange assumption as there was no denying they were related. To each their own, of course. The two men nodded at each other.

"Mmm, coffee." Noah helped himself to a mug, leaning back against the counter as he cupped it. "Have you seen or heard anything from Ashley?"

Zak glanced across at Kenzo before returning to Noah, shaking his head. "Nothing. I don't know why she bothered when we all know she didn't want him in the first place."

"Probably to mess with you."

"Probably. You have a girlfriend yet?" Zak wanted off the topic and distracted Noah with his relationship issues.

"Nah." Noah's demeanour showed he was hiding something, but Zak would get it out of him later.

"Better hurry up, or you'll be a spinster in no time." Zak grinned.

"Shut up, asshole."

"Hey!" Zak indicated Dane.

"Sorry, but it's true. You are."

"What are you doing here, anyway?" Zak asked as he cleaned Dane up.

"Mum isn't coming. She sent me in her stead."

Zak shook his head and briefly closed his eyes. He knew better than to rely on his mother. At least she'd sent reinforcements this time, instead of just not turning up. When Zak needed to get some work done, he asked for either his mother, his brother or Emily to watch after Dane for him. So far, it was usually Emily or Noah because his mother had a tendency to want to be elsewhere. She loved her grandson, but she had little time for him. For any of them.

"Have you got many orders to complete?"

"A few, but there's no rush on them. I'd like to get them done as soon as I can, though. The delivery dates on future orders will be months down the line if I don't get some finished."

"What have you got to do?" Noah rinsed out his mug and came over to Dane, lifting him from the highchair.

"A child's wardrobe and chest of drawers set, a table and chairs, and a large tree ornament, would you believe? The rest of the orders don't have to be completed for another few months."

"You made the furniture upstairs?"

Kenzo's deep voice sounded through the kitchen, making Zak jump; firstly, because he'd forgotten Kenzo was still there, and secondly, because he'd confirmed what Noah had only hinted at. That they'd slept together.

CHAPTER EIGHT

KENZO

Kenzo realised his mistake as soon as he opened his mouth. "Sorry," he muttered. "I'll head out." Sighing at how much of an idiot he was, he strode towards the front door.

"Kenzo, wait!"

He stopped and waited for Zak.

"I'm really sorry. I didn't mean to blurt that out."

Zak flushed and studied the floor. "It's all right. It's not as if he didn't know."

They were silent for a moment before Kenzo couldn't help but acknowledge, "You made the furniture upstairs?"

Zak caught his eye and glanced down again as he nodded.

Kenzo tucked his finger under Zak's chin, lifting his gaze. "It's amazing. You're amazing. So fucking talented," he mumbled. Leaning forward, Kenzo advertised what he was intending, and Zak allowed him to join their lips in a soft kiss. "I'll see you soon. Say bye to Noah and Dane for me."

Zak nodded, his eyes a little unfocused.

He let himself out of the house, clicking the door closed behind him. He needed to shower before he started his day properly. This had been such a strange morning…and one that was weirdly appealing.

When the…incident happened, and his leg had been mangled, he realised he didn't want to put his life on someone else's shoulders. He decided to stay single and help others where he could. Unfortunately, seeing the domestic scene that morning had his heart swelling for something he had thought he'd put to bed.

Zak wasn't scared to be himself in front of his son or his brother. When faced with a surprise visit, Zak adapted. It had happened twice that morning: once when he'd still been there, and again when Noah had turned up. Both times, Zak barely blinked an eye before carrying on as if it was how things were supposed to be. It was the kind of thing they did in the Army.

As for Zak's son, he was bloody adorable.

It didn't change anything. Kenzo would be too much hassle for someone to live with, and from what he gathered from Zak and Noah's conversation and the one he overheard with Luke the previous day, Zak had been going through a custody battle. That must've been the stressful thing relating to his son that he'd mentioned before.

Kenzo parked his car and entered the building, wanting to get a shower as soon as possible. Life had other ideas.

"Oh my god! Couldn't you guys be doing that in the bedroom!" He shielded his eyes and wandered down the hallway, the vision of Drake and Miki naked seared onto his retinas. "Jesus, guys!"

"Sorry!" Miki shouted.

"I'm going for a shower. Hurry up and finish before I come down. And don't make a mess on the sofa!"

Huffing a laugh, Kenzo entered his bedroom and stripped as he walked to the en-suite. His bathroom had a large shower with two shower heads—his one extravagance when he'd bought the apartment. As soon as he was under the spray, he groaned as the heat pounded his well-used muscles. Memories from the previous night invaded his thoughts, and he felt himself getting hard.

Zak was not muscular like Kenzo was, but he was developing some definition since he'd started working out. He had strong shoulders and thighs, which was a good thing as far as Kenzo was concerned. Comparing him to his brother, Zak was the slimmer of the two, Noah being closer to Kenzo's physicality. There was no comparison in other aspects. Zak lit a fire in him. Noah did not.

Kenzo ignored that his cock was hard, hissing at the sensitivity of it as he washed himself. Visions of Zak on his knees tormented him until he couldn't resist any longer. He wrapped his hand around his dick, the heat of it searing his palm. Resting a hand against the tiles, he dropped his head, allowing the water to pelt his shoulders as he slowly stroked. Closing his eyes, he envisioned Zak as he had been the previous night, on his knees, hands fisted in the sheets, moans filling the air as Kenzo's cock speared into him. The heat of Zak's tight channel surrounding him had sent him higher a lot faster than he'd thought it would, and despite it only being a memory, it was seared into his brain.

His balls lifted as he drew closer to his climax. He remembered the feel of Zak's lips on his, their tongues duelling, the heated kiss which kicked his libido into overdrive. Kenzo clenched his teeth, his hand tightening around his cock as his hips thrust in reaction. As his abs contracted with the first wave of his orgasm, he threw his head back, groaning his release to the ceiling as the water washed away the evidence.

When his legs felt they could hold him without the need for his knees to be locked, he stepped out of the shower. The arousal had been banked, but he could feel the little buzz at the base of his spine that said it could easily return given the right circumstances.

He sat, naked, on his bed and grabbed the tub of cream the doctor had given him. After every shower—

or anytime he got wet—he needed to rehydrate the skin on his leg to stop it from becoming dry and itchy. He'd suffered with it for a short while, and it had been torturous, never-ending itchiness that wouldn't abate. After he'd spoken to the doctor and been prescribed the cream, he'd never had a problem, only if he missed applying it.

Throwing on some joggers and a t-shirt when he finished, he tentatively wandered down the stairs, averting his gaze from the living room in case Miki and Drake had not finished their…get together. He entered the kitchen to the scent of coffee, finding the pair of them at the table, nursing mugs of the hot brew.

"I see you had a good night and morning," Kenzo deadpanned with a raised eyebrow.

Miki grinned. "You betcha. So did you, if I'm right, and you've only just arrived home."

"It was a good night." He turned to the kettle. "I should've been home," he mumbled, shaking his head.

"Why?"

"I hadn't planned on staying over. The guy has a kid and asked me not to, but we fell asleep."

"Ah, this morning was a bit awkward, then?"

"Yeah, a little. Especially when his brother walked in as I was leaving."

Drake groaned, ending with a laugh. "How did *that* work out?"

Kenzo wrinkled his nose. "Could've been worse."

"At least you got out before the kid saw you. It's a bonus in my book." Drake pointed at him. "That would've been worse."

"Actually…" Kenzo blew out a breath, thinking back to breakfast that morning. Dane had not seemed at all bothered that there was an unknown man in his house. He knew he was only two years old, but even at that age, he knew some kids didn't like strangers. "I had breakfast with them both before I left." Kenzo frowned. He didn't know why he'd accepted when he could have easily declined and left before the awkwardness between them increased.

"Seriously?" Miki's mouth dropped open.

Kenzo turned back to the kettle to finish making his drink. He knew why Miki was surprised. He'd never had any remote interest in interacting with people outside of the necessary social niceties. As Kenzo had always said, he had too many things to do to be distracted by something other than a one-night fling.

Grabbing his mug, he leaned back against the counter and changed the subject, "How are you doing, Miki?"

Miki nodded with a small smile. "Better, thanks."

"Glad to hear it. So…" He raised his eyebrows at them. "How long has this been going on?" He waved a hand between the two of them. "I knew it had potential, but…" He waited for them to fill in the blanks while he sipped at the hot liquid.

He had no issues at all with their relationship; he only wanted what was best for Miki...and for Drake. When Miki had his bad days, things were difficult. He wanted to make sure whoever Miki ended up with understood and could handle what he went through. Kenzo knew Drake enough to believe he could. Drake had been in one of the other teams that had sometimes worked with them on assignments.

"We're taking things easy. I've explained to Drake... some of what happens, but I'd like it if...you could speak to him, too."

Kenzo knew how hard it was for Miki to say. His mug clunked as he put it down, and he grabbed Miki, pulling him into a bear hug, slapping him on the back. "Will do." He couldn't say more because his emotions were too close to the edge.

"Thanks." Miki coughed. "We've been seeing each other for..." He looked at Drake. "Five weeks? Is that right?" Drake nodded.

"I knew something was going to happen between you, but I didn't realise it already had. Congrats. Take care of each other."

They moved onto other topics to stop the emotional bullshit they knew they didn't want to air. Drake ducked out shortly after, having to get to the gym, and Miki headed to his office to start work. Kenzo felt a little out of sorts. He had nothing arranged except for coaching at four that afternoon and had planned on researching some books for Jack. He'd expressed a wish to read some biographies, and Kenzo wanted to find someone who he thought Jack might have an interest in. Unfortunately, he wasn't in the mood, and he felt uneasy being at a loss.

He ran a finger along a crack that had been on the table for as long as he could remember, and it brought his thoughts back around to Zak. The pieces of furniture in his bedroom were amazingly detailed, and he realised what he wanted to do. Refilling his coffee, he strode to his bedroom to grab his laptop and settled in the living room. He pulled up the internet and searched for Zak's name along with some other search terms. It took him a few minutes, but he finally found Zak's website.

Woodwork King was his company name, which Kenzo thought was a good play on words, though a little cheesy. He clicked on the gallery to see the type of things he made. There were pictures of several larger pieces, including a four-poster, king-size bed, which was extremely extravagant. He hoped Zak had charged an arm and a leg for that piece. There were plenty more pieces that were as good if not better.

He checked out the catalogue page, seeing what he currently had available and what he was able to make. Surprisingly, there was a page for smaller items, too. It had a big 'Coming Soon' banner across the top and stated the name Colton Jenkins underneath. From what he could gather, Zak was gaining a partner or an employee.

Many years ago, he and his best friend, Pete, had been contemplating joining forces to create a security business when they finally left the Army. Pete's family was already in security, his dad a partner in a company that provided bodyguards. Pete's brother and sister were also part of the same company, although in different areas. It had seemed like the perfect fit for them, and they'd had Pete's father's backing, too.

They had met at secondary school at age eleven and had become firm friends, spending time at each other's houses throughout their teens, playing tennis together. Both their parents had expected them to go pro with tennis, but when they were of age, there had been no doubt they were signing up. Being assigned to the same team was a bonus neither had expected, but they both brought different things to the table: Kenzo was the sniper, Pete was the explosives expert.

A hobby-turned-job that ended up killing several innocent men.

Kenzo pushed the laptop aside, rubbing a hand over his face and closing his eyes as the memories resurfaced. He hadn't seen it coming, although if he'd paid more attention to Pete, maybe he would have. There was nothing to be done about it now.

Pete had walked into the ammunitions building on their base and blew the place up. Later, it was revealed

Pete had been suffering from PTSD after their latest visit abroad but had hidden it from everyone except their immediate superior. Their superior had put in for him to begin therapy, but something—no one knew what—had set it off, and it seemed like Pete had enough.

Unfortunately, several of them had been mingling around, waiting for their boss to arrive for an impromptu meeting. Kenzo, Miki and seven other soldiers were injured, but Pete and three men died. That was two years ago.

Kenzo blew out a breath, shaking his head. His stomach churned, his chest was tight, and his skin itched as the guilt reminded him he had been responsible for his teammates, and he should've recognised the symptoms, despite being told there was nothing he could've done about it. It was the reason he'd been determined to see Miki through his PTSD. He refused to allow it to happen again. Drake knew about the incident with Pete, but he hadn't seen Miki on his bad days yet. He wasn't sure if Miki *wanted* Drake to see him like that. It was a conversation they needed to have and soon.

Drifting back to the kitchen, he tried to decide what to do as he washed his cup. He was too restless to do any paperwork, and with his memories so close to the surface, he also didn't want to go to the Veteran Centre.

The gym it was, then.

Several hours later, sweat dripped off him, even though he had wiped himself with his towel. Kenzo had pushed himself too hard, and now his knee was killing him. He had no idea how he was going to coach the tennis kids that afternoon, but he wouldn't let Drake down. There were only three more weeks left.

He took a shower in the changing rooms. To begin with, he'd been reluctant to use public showers because the chance someone would see his leg bothered him, but he'd figured out how to keep it from happening. All the mess was around the front of the leg; therefore, as long as he held a towel in front of him as he entered and wrapped it around him when he left, no one could see the disfigurement from the back.

Driving home was a painful experience, but when he got there, he took some paracetamol and got started on a late lunch. No doubt Miki hadn't eaten yet either.

Kenzo's day carried on as if nothing was amiss. The tennis lesson was a success despite him having to sit down to teach it. He couldn't shake the unsettled feeling that had followed him around the whole day, as if he had to get things done before everything went wrong. It was weird. He decided to ignore it and get some sleep, hoping the following morning was better.

Three days later, he bumped into Zak at the gym. They had not communicated at all since Kenzo walked out the other morning, and he'd thought Zak might have been avoiding him. It seemed he wasn't or, at least, wasn't any longer because there he was, working out with Luke again.

The sounds receded in the background as he watched—which sounded a bit less creepy than stared —the man he'd dragged his fingers over several times, salivating at the way his muscles bunched and strained as he lifted the weights. Kenzo could see the difference in Zak from when he'd first started weightlifting, despite what Zak had said.

When Zak and Luke shook hands, Kenzo had no choice but to walk over to him; his feet just started moving.

"Hey," he said, inwardly rolling his eyes at the mundane greeting.

Zak glanced at him. "Hi."

The silence lasted for a second too long, and Kenzo blurted out the first thing that came to mind. "Would you come for a coffee with me?"

Eyebrows raised, Zak checked his watch before nodding slowly. "Okay. Where?"

"Pop's?"

Zak grinned. "Definitely."

"Do you need a lift?"

"No. I'll meet you there."

Kenzo nodded, biting his lip, then pivoted and exited the weights room. As he passed Drake's office, the man's voice called his name. Retracing a few steps, Kenzo peered his head around the door.

"What's up?"

"That was a quick workout," Drake said, his forehead creasing as he paused with his fingers hovering over the keyboard of his laptop. "Everything okay?"

"Yeah. I decided to give it a rest today." Although it hadn't been the reason, it was the truth to a degree. He'd been pushing himself too hard lately.

Drake's gaze bored into him, and Kenzo fought not to move. It was like being back in the team and having to avoid any reaction to their superior's words or actions. He hoped his expression was neutral.

"Nothing to do with a certain somebody?" Drake drawled, resting his elbows on the table and leaning forward.

"I changed my mind." He needed to stick with his story, or Drake would never let him hear the end of it.

Drake smirked. "If you say so. Mr Gant has been in

touch to say he will be back next week instead. You only have this week to finish out if that's okay."

"Thanks for letting me know. I'm going to head out." Kenzo thumbed over his shoulder. "See you later."

He didn't wait to see if Drake said anything further because he hot-footed it—as much as his leg would allow anyway—to the changing rooms and redressed in his street clothes. Pop's wasn't far away, and they had amazing home-cooked food and delicious coffee and equalled the popularity of Sweet Tooth and Crush. He hoped they'd be able to get a table, especially since it was close to lunch.

The car park was busy but not packed yet; therefore, he and Zak would be able to get a space. A table was another matter. Luckily, when he entered, Maria, the owner's daughter, saw him and pointed to a table in the far back corner, near the kitchen door. It was the darkest of the tables and the most intimate, but he didn't care as long as he got coffee and maybe some food after.

Dropping into the chair sideways, he rubbed his leg, focusing on the knee joint both front and back. His kneecap had been shattered from the impact of Kenzo meeting the ground when he was thrown in the blast, and he often had trouble. Sometimes, excess movement exacerbated it; sometimes, it helped, which was why he spent so much time working out, but he was also supposed to rest it. Keeping the joint moving was his goal because it was worse when it was kept in the same position for too long. When that happened, it took him several long minutes to massage away the stiffness.

"Are you okay?"

Zak's voice had his head swinging around to see him. He stood with a backpack over his shoulder and hair dripping onto his jacket, leaving wet patches along his shoulders. He looked stunning.

"Kenzo?"

———

CHAPTER NINE

———

ZAK

Zak stood there, staring at Kenzo, who stared back at him. It was a little unnerving being under such scrutiny, but he didn't avoid his gaze. After Zak had said his name, Kenzo blinked as if coming out of a daze and smiled.

"Sorry, yeah, I'm okay. My knee's twinging a little. Will you join me?"

"That was the idea, wasn't it?" Zak pursed his lips, hiding his smile and sat opposite the man he hadn't been able to get out of his head. The café was loud because of the number of people in the place, but their table was more secluded, meaning they were able to talk without having to shout.

"Would you like your usual drinks, gentlemen?"

Kenzo checked with Zak, who nodded, and then he answered, "Yes, please, Maria."

"I'll be back soon."

Zak fidgeted in his seat, focusing on the table and running his fingers over the sugar packets.

"Are we good?"

The small voice sounded so unsure, Zak couldn't help flicking his gaze up, seeing Kenzo staring at his hands and biting his lip. The hunched demeanour had Zak relaxing, not happy Kenzo was uncomfortable, but that they both were hesitant with each other. "We are as far as I'm concerned," Zak replied.

He watched Kenzo's shoulders lower and his head lift a little. The knowledge that his words had helped relax him made Zak's stomach flutter. He had no idea why it was Kenzo that elicited these responses from him, but he couldn't do anything about it. Their shared breakfast the other day had been a mistake, especially when Noah had walked in—the shit he got from his brother when Kenzo had left.

His family knew he was into men and women, so it hadn't come as a surprise to Noah that Kenzo had been there. What had surprised him, Noah had said after, was Kenzo had still been there for breakfast. After Zak had confided in Noah several months ago that if he ever found someone he wanted to get to know, there would be no introducing him to Dane until after several months of seeing where their relationship was going. Noah hadn't agreed with him at the time, but Zak had put his foot down. His argument had been that Dane was being put through enough with what was happening with him and Ashley. Now, though, things were different. Although he wouldn't admit it to Noah.

He hadn't planned on introducing Kenzo to Dane, but when Kenzo had said he would leave while Zak was busy with Dane, Zak couldn't allow him to. It felt... wrong, somehow. He couldn't figure out why, but his instant reaction to invite him for breakfast had been a surprise. He'd kept an eye on Dane while they were eating, but he hadn't seemed bothered by a new arrival at their table.

It bothered Zak more that it felt so natural, so right for Kenzo to be joining them when they'd only fooled around twice. It seemed too fast.

Zak brushed the thought away, bringing his focus back to the present. "How are you?"

The question was innocuous enough but proved how much they didn't know about each other. When Kenzo had first asked about having a coffee, Zak hadn't been sure, but his instinct told him to say yes. He had plenty of time before he had to be home for Dane. He wasn't sure what they were trying to get from their interactions, but Zak couldn't say no.

"I'm good. Busy but good."

"What is it you do now you're retired?"

"Well, at the moment, I'm helping cover the tennis lessons for the kids as the coach has been off sick, but I finish at the end of this weekend, which I'm glad about."

"Do you not like tennis?"

"Oh, I love tennis, but my…knee prevents me from doing much running or heavy landing. I have to be careful about what I do."

"How come this guy asked you to do it, then? Couldn't he have asked someone else?" Zak frowned. He had seen from the way Kenzo had been rubbing his knee how much pain he was in. Why had he agreed?

"Drake is the owner of the gym, and yes, he could have, but I owed him a favour."

"That doesn't mean you should hurt yourself to pay him back." He felt like slapping the guy upside the head, and that reaction had him focusing on his watch and fiddling with the strap, his eyes wide, his heart racing.

Kenzo was silent for a moment. "I know, and he wouldn't make me hurt myself. He gave me a ball boy, so to speak, to chase after the balls and fetch stuff for me. All I have to do is stand there and use my arms to show or put the kids in the right positions." He paused, and Zak glanced up. "I'm not putting pressure on myself."

Zak bit back his reply, which would have been that he obviously was because he was in pain. It wasn't up to him to decide what Kenzo did or didn't do.

"You said you love tennis. Was it something you used to do? Before your knee started hurting, that is."

Maria returned with their drinks and two plates with a cookie on each. "From me to you guys. Can I get you any food?"

"Not for me, thank you," Zak said. He glanced over at Kenzo. "I have to get back to Dane soon."

Kenzo nodded, his expression softening. "Not for me, either, Maria. Thanks, though."

"No problem. Enjoy."

"Thank you for the cookie, Maria," he called after her. She waved her hand above her head as she walked away.

Zak wrapped his hands around his mug, lifting it to his face. He closed his eyes and inhaled the freshly brewed aroma, slurping at the extremely hot liquid. His mouth wasn't made of steel like Kenzo's, and he could only take small sips, but the warmth began to spread through him. Opening his eyes, he saw Kenzo staring at him, mouth parted, hand clenched on the table. The balm that flowed through him was a different kind of heat. It soothed him, relaxed him, made him want to be closer to Kenzo.

Clearing his throat, he focused on his coffee, trying to cool his libido. They were particularly compatible in bed, as had been shown, but Zak needed to be able to walk out of the café without his cock leading the way.

"So, you're a woodworker."

Zak was glad for the reprieve. He thought they had been discussing something else but couldn't remember what. "Yes, I am. I build furniture mainly, large and small pieces. Although last year, I did a friend's hallway, replacing the bannister with a more intricate handmade one. I enjoyed it, but I haven't had the chance to test those skills since."

"What do you enjoy making the most?" Kenzo lifted his coffee to his lips, licking them before they were hidden by the cup.

Zak paused at the realisation few others had asked him that question. "I like making furniture for kids. You know, like small tables and chairs, toy boxes, small bed frames and such." He peered at Kenzo from under his eyelashes, wanting to see his reaction to his words.

"They sound like they wouldn't take as long, but I have a feeling they're a lot more fiddly."

Zak's head lifted at his words. "Exactly! That's the problem I have. Sometimes, I think children should make the pieces because their hands are smaller."

They shared a laugh at the thought.

"I don't think Dane is quite capable enough yet," Kenzo said, smiling.

Zak was floored by the fact Kenzo had brought his son into the conversation. He had imagined Kenzo not wanting a reminder of the fact Zak had kids, but he seemed genuinely interested. "Give him a couple more years." Zak smiled, not just at the idea of Dane helping him, but at the spark of hope flickering inside him. He needed to quench it. There was no way he could invite someone into their lives full time.

Their conversation flowed until their cups were empty, and Zak apologised for needing to leave.

"Don't ever apologise for needing to leave to look after your son," Kenzo said. "He's your priority."

Zak swallowed hard against the lump in his throat. On impulse, he leaned in and kissed Kenzo on the lips before pulling back quickly. "Thanks."

"You get going. I'll pay for the coffees."

"You sure?"

Kenzo nodded. "I invited you. I pay."

Zak stared at him for a second longer and walked to the exit. He wanted to look over his shoulder but didn't want to appear sappy, so he continued to his car, avoiding the puddles from the rain shower they'd had earlier. He dropped the backpack to the passenger seat and walked around to the other side. As his hand wrapped around the handle to open the driver's door, he was whirled around, his back pressing against the car. He briefly noticed it was Kenzo before lips covered his, and his attention narrowed down to where they were touching.

Hands slid around his back, pulling him closer until there was no space between them. Zak cupped the back of Kenzo's head, his other arm wrapping around his neck. Their mouths took on a life of their own, tongues tangling, pursuing and retreating. Before long, Zak had to pull away, eyes blinking open as he gasped for breath. They rested their foreheads together, sharing the air.

When the splash of cars driving through the puddles finally registered again, Zak said, "Wow. Nice goodbye."

Kenzo quirked the corner of his mouth. "Couldn't resist such a tempting sight."

Zak pulled back fully, Kenzo understanding and stepping back. "Thank you for the coffee."

"You're welcome." Zak could see Kenzo wanted to say something else, and he waited. "Can I see you again?"

Zak's stomach fluttered its agreement, but his head cautioned him. He'd only just been granted custody of Dane. He didn't want anything to mess with that or with Dane; therefore, he knew what he needed to do.

"I don't think it's a good idea." His voice cracked at the end, and he closed his eyes briefly at the pain those words sent through him.

Kenzo lowered his head and nodded at the ground. "Okay." He audibly inhaled and returned his gaze to Zak. "Take care of yourself. And of Dane."

Zak couldn't speak, but he bobbed his head. Kenzo leaned forward, pressed a chaste kiss to his lips and pivoted away. He stopped breathing as he watched Kenzo climb into his car, trying not to react until he'd driven out of sight. Then he slumped against his car, head silent, heart galloping, soul pining.

He knew he'd done the right thing, but why did it feel like Kenzo had taken part of Zak with him?

"No, Mum. Dane will be coming with me to the wedding. They want him there."

Zak swallowed hard, trying to keep his cool as his mother wandered around her living room, unable to sit still. He'd visited because she'd left a message for him asking him to come and see her. Dane was busy on the floor at Zak's feet, chewing on one of the plastic toys he'd brought with them and didn't seem bothered about where he was. It wasn't like they visited often, but it must be enough for Dane to feel comfortable there.

His childhood home had not changed much over the years. The décor was still outdated, and the furniture more threadbare than it had been when he was younger. His mother never cared about the state of the house. The only thing she insisted upon was there was nothing out of place. She didn't want to be tripping over anything; therefore, except for their bedrooms, the house was clutter-free. Shame she didn't care about the cleanliness of it, what with the sheet of dust that had only thickened over the years.

Zak and Noah had taken it upon themselves to clean the house when they were thirteen and eight, respectively. They would come home from school, clean the house, and Zak would make dinner while Noah did his homework. Then when Noah was settled into bed, Zak would do his own homework before crashing and repeating the process the following day. After a while, they had given up trying to clean the house. Their mother didn't care for their attempts; therefore, they stopped. Nothing was said either way.

"You don't want him around all those other… people. He'll be fine with me here."

Zak couldn't figure out why she was so adamant about having Dane stay with her while Zak went to Max and Trent's wedding. He listened to his instincts and declined once more, "No, thank you. He's coming with me." He cleared his throat. "Was that what you wanted to talk to me about?"

His mother paused, staring out the window, rotating the ring on her right hand. It made Zak more unsettled to see the nervous tic of hers. Suddenly, her breath caught, and she beamed, heading towards the door at a fast clip. Uneasy, Zak picked Dane up and settled him on his hip, turning to the entryway.

"Sweetheart! You came!"

"Evelyn."

A man entered with light grey, almost white hair with matching moustache and beard, making him look a little like Santa Claus. His fitted black suit with a grey tie was so clean, Zak wanted to warn him not to brush against any of the furniture in case of dust transfer, but he refrained. As the man pressed a kiss to each of his mother's cheeks, he realised the reason for his requested presence.

"Zak, I'd like to introduce you to Clive. Clive, this is my eldest son, Zak."

"Nice to meet you, Zak. Your mother has told me a lot about you." Clive held out the opposite hand to what his mother had wrapped her arm around. They shook awkwardly.

"Nice to meet you, too." He bit his lip against any other comment, especially as this was the first time he'd heard anything about Clive. He wasn't surprised. His mother rarely remembered to tell them anything until it suited her interest. Why she was introducing them now was beyond him. They had no birthdays or anniversaries coming up.

"Clive is an investment banker," Evelyn said proudly, staring up at Clive as if he hung the moon.

"Was. I've not been for a few years now, but I was good, even if I do say so myself." Clive quirked the corner of his mouth as he peered down at Zak's mother.

Zak rolled his eyes and hitched Dane higher on his hip. "Well, it was nice to meet you, Clive, but I'm afraid we have to go. We have a wedding to prepare for." The corners of his mouth lifted in an attempt to smile, but he didn't know if he managed it. Picking up the bag full of Dane's things that he took everywhere with him, he sidestepped to the front door. "See you soon, Mum."

He didn't look back but instinctively knew she had flinched at the word "Mum." She always hated them calling her that when she had men around—she said it made her sound old.

After he'd fastened Dane into his seat, Zak pointed the car towards home. The wedding wasn't until tomorrow, but he wanted to make sure the present he'd made for them was perfect. It was too late to do anything about it if it wasn't, but he needed to check. He wasn't as good with smaller objects as Colton was, but he held his own. If Colton hadn't been busy with his new relationship with Ioan, he would've asked him for his help, but as the guy had recently moved three thousand miles from New York to live with Ioan there in Cambridge, Zak hadn't wanted to throw anything at him before he was settled.

Soon, Colton would be joining his team, and they could offer a wider variety of skills and products to their business. Zak couldn't wait. He often found his work to be lonely, despite him loving what he did. He'd never stop doing it, but having someone he could work alongside and talk to as well as bounce ideas off and share the workload with was going to be great.

His phone rang as he was lifting Dane from the car, and he quickly settled Dane into place on his hip before fishing his phone out of his pocket.

"Hey. What's up?"

"Mum wants us to meet Clive properly," Noah said without preamble.

"I've only just found out about the guy! When did you find out?"

"This morning."

"Seriously? What's the point? I met him just now. What more does she want?" Zak shuffled into the house, holding the phone between his shoulder and ear while he locked the door behind him—more out of habit than any other reason. It was one of the things Ashley had insisted on when they got together. She'd said she hated the idea anyone could walk in whenever they wanted to. Zak hadn't cared one way or the other, but after so many years, it was second nature.

"Come on. We have to at least try."

Zak huffed, "Why? This one will last as long as all the rest."

Placing Dane into the playpen, so he could get organised without having to worry about Dane's whereabouts, he strode to the kitchen, gripping the phone again and stretching out the new kink in his neck.

"You know she'll keep ringing and bothering us unless we make it to dinner." He could hear the resignation in Noah's voice and knew he was right. Still, it didn't mean Zak had to like it.

"How often did we get attached to her boyfriends when we were younger, and when we came home from school, they'd left without a word? Because I've lost count." He opened the fridge, grabbing lunch for Dane and putting it in the microwave.

"We're not kids anymore, Zak."

"Doesn't matter. I don't want the same thing for Dane. In fact, I refuse to allow it to happen." It was the reason he'd pushed Kenzo away after all.

"Shall I tell her no, then?"

Zak sighed, watching the bowl spin through the glass door of the microwave. "I'm not bringing Dane, but if you can't get her to change her mind, I'll find a babysitter for him."

"She wants it to be tomorrow."

"No." Zak clenched his jaw, knowing the reason why she was insistent upon it being the following day—the wedding. For some reason, she was dead set against it, and she didn't even know Max and Trent. "She knows it's the wedding. I can do it next week, but no sooner." He needed time to prepare.

"All right." Noah paused, then continued, "I don't want you to go through this any more than you do, you know."

Zak dropped his head back and stared at the ceiling as he exhaled hard. The beep of the microwave pulled him from the past. "I know, Noah. I suppose we should be grateful for the happiness she does get, even if it makes our lives harder. I..." He didn't need to say anymore. Noah knew exactly how he felt.

He hated that he'd put Dane through a similar situation to what they'd been dragged through as kids. Their parents had fought over taking one child each in the divorce settlement, which Zak, at only nine years old, had screamed and rallied against. Luckily, in some ways, their mother had won full custody of him and Noah, and they weren't split up, but looking back on their mother's treatment of them...he wasn't sure if it was a win or not. Especially as their dad had up and disappeared, never to be seen again.

He was happy things with Ashley had happened now, when Dane was only two, rather than when he was older and could understand more of what was happening. If he had stuck with the marriage...he didn't want to think about what life would've been like.

CHAPTER TEN

KENZO

It had been another shitty few days. Miki had been struggling again, and as per usual, when he did, he pushed everyone away apart from Kenzo. Two days of no sleep and not enough food was wearing on them both, but Miki was on the mend. Kenzo was worried. He'd decided to approach Miki about his episodes in a couple of days, once Miki's head was back on straight. The nightmares and flashbacks appeared to be worsening, and Miki needed to speak with his therapist about them if he hadn't already. There was no point in hiding things from her if they were getting worse.

Kenzo didn't know anything about how to deal with PTSD except what he'd learned so he could help Miki, and that was by trial and error over the years. Maybe his therapist would be able to suggest better alternatives to what they'd already tried.

Resting his head back against the headboard as he sat on his bed, he tried to energise himself into getting up and grabbing some food, but he couldn't. What he needed was sleep, but after the screams of fear from Miki, he didn't think he'd be able to sleep without nightmares himself for a few days. The pure, undulated terror that pierced the night had probably caused the neighbours some panic, too.

Sighing, he swung his legs over the edge of the bed, wincing when his knee twinged. He'd ignored the pain for the last two days, but he couldn't any longer and limped into the bathroom for ibuprofen. Swallowing two tablets dry, he splashed water over his face and returned to his room without checking out his appearance. He knew he looked like death warmed over, but there was nothing he could do about it.

Throwing on some clothes—again, not caring what—he shuffled down the hallway to Miki's room, knocking softly. When Miki's tired voice called out, he stuck his head around the door.

"I'm heading to get some food. Do you want anything?"

He tried to ignore the gaunt, startling appearance before him, but it was hard. The memory of Miki when he first joined their team floated through his mind. The twenty-four-year-old beefed-up kid who wanted to play in the majors was a far cry from the slender man in front of him.

"Can you pick up some lemonade? It helps with my scratchy throat," he croaked.

That scratchy throat was the result of endless screaming. Kenzo cleared his throat. "Sure. I'll be back soon."

The fresh air, however brisk, was a balm to Kenzo's body, both inside and out. The sun, hiding behind the dark clouds, was almost too bright, and the outside noises, almost too loud, which was surprising when comparing it to what he'd witnessed recently. He concentrated on putting one foot in front of the other and collecting what they needed to last the day, and then he stumbled to pay before heading back home.

The ringing of the phone greeted him when he entered the apartment, and he frowned, glancing around for the location of the sound. He found his phone in the kitchen, vibrating across the table and caught it before it dropped to the floor. The music cut off, and he glanced at the screen after he placed the bags on the table. He hadn't realised he'd left his phone at home; that was how tired he was.

His eyebrows rose when he saw he had eighteen missed calls and fifty-six messages. Checking through the log, he realised the calls were mainly from Drake. The messages were a mixture of senders but finished with a few more worried-toned ones from Drake. His phone rang again, startling him.

"Hey, Drake."

"Oh, thank god! Where the fuck have you been, man? I've been calling for hours, days even."

"Yeah, sorry. I didn't realise I'd left my phone on silent." He apologised with a half-truth, knowing, although Miki had spoken to Drake about the episodes, he had never experienced one, and Kenzo had not had the chance for the talk they'd spoken about.

"Fuck, Kenzo."

He heard deep breathing as if Drake had been running and out of breath. "Everything all right, Drake?"

"Yeah. I was..." He cleared his throat. "I was worried. I've not heard from Miki for a couple of days, and I was concerned, especially when I came round, and there was no answer."

Kenzo's eyebrows rose. He didn't remember hearing anyone at the door, and he was sure if Drake had heard Miki's screams, he would've broken down the door to find out what was happening. It must've been during one of their infrequent periods of sleep. "We've had a rough couple of days." He wasn't going to explain any further. It was something else he needed to discuss with Miki before broaching anything with Drake. "Well, I'll see you at the gym, probably tomorrow." He tried to deflect the conversation, hoping Drake would go with it.

There was silence before a heavy sigh. "Yeah, sure. Tell Miki to call me when he has a minute."

He bit off the comment about not being his message service and agreed, signing off the call. Dropping the phone onto the table, he set about putting away the shopping, his movements dragging. As he shut the fridge, he noticed a note on the front, reminding him of an appointment he had at the Veteran Centre. He turned away, paused and turned back, focusing on the date, then cursed forcefully as he realised he would be late. Checking his watch, he quickly put the perishables away, grabbed the lemonade and stalked to Miki's room.

Knocking, he entered immediately, taking the bottle over to him and explaining, "I have to go out for an hour or so. Will you be all right?"

Miki nodded slowly, eyes focused blearily on the quiet TV. "I'll be fine."

"Ring me if you need me." Kenzo walked away, throwing over his shoulder, "And message Drake, for god's sake, before he busts up my phone!"

The clothes he'd thrown on for the grocery visit would not be suitable for the veteran appointment, so he quickly changed, grabbed his things and left. Luckily, he didn't live too far away and made it quickly.

"Kenzo!" Sarah said, smiling at him.

"Sorry I'm late."

She came around the desk and rested a hand on his shoulder, looking at him with a frown. "Are you okay? You look a little worn down."

He took a deep breath and smiled. "I'm good. I lost track of time."

She waved away his concern. "It's all good. You know how informal these things are anyway. They're probably having a coffee and a chat. Go on down."

He smiled again and headed down the corridor to the therapist's room. Knocking on the door, he waited until he was given permission to enter, then strode straight over to the two men who sat waiting.

"Sorry for the delay. I didn't realise the time."

The therapist, David Pick, rose with a smile and held out his hand. "Not a problem, Mr Langley. Thank you for being here."

"Hi, Mason."

"Hey, Kenzo." Mason's voice was deep and slow, tiredness bleeding into his movements, like Kenzo's own.

Kenzo had never attended one of these specialised counselling sessions before, and he didn't know what to expect. The Veteran Centre had brought on several therapists who were willing to work outside the usual constraints of therapy—basically, they tried new things and worked on a more personalised scale for each individual. He had no clue what this was going to be about, but he refused to let it scare him off. Mason had asked him to join them for this first session because he felt calmer with Kenzo there—Mason's own words.

While he was glad to be of help, his lack of sleep

wouldn't be a good thing. He'd have to wait and see what the therapist suggested.

After an hour, Kenzo left once Mason had been collected by a nurse, who helped him back to his room. The man appeared more unsteady on his feet than usual, and Kenzo wondered whether he'd been given any medication to help him relax.

The session had been eye-opening. David Pick had asked Mason how he wanted the sessions to work and what he wanted from them. To begin with, Mason baulked at the idea, saying he had no idea what he needed to do to feel better and that he *shouldn't* feel better when he was the only person still living. Kenzo's heart broke for the man, but once they'd started chatting and suggesting different things, Mason happily butted in and vetoed certain ideas, making his own therapy schedule without realising it.

It was enlightening to find people who were willing to work with others without having to stick within a strict regime—they must do this, reach this milestone before moving onto this, this and this. It was similar to kids when they were younger. Teachers were always striving to get them to reach targets because that was what the government had told them to do. Some teachers happily went with it and became flustered when it didn't happen, whereas others were willing to think outside the box and help the child as an individual.

It was a shame to think of all those people who needed help and weren't getting it. His mind wandered to Miki. Maybe his therapist wasn't the best choice for him. David Pick had seemed on board with this new technique. Maybe Kenzo could speak to Miki and explain, without losing the confidentiality, about the session and see if he wanted to give it a try. It certainly wouldn't hurt, even if nothing came of it.

He dropped onto his sofa, having not remembered any of the car journey home, despite having driven himself. He needed to sleep but knew he needed food first and groaned when he remembered the grocery shopping he'd left on the table in the kitchen. At least he'd put the perishables away, but he needed to do the other stuff, too.

When he dragged himself upright, and to the kitchen, he was surprised to find everything put away already. Miki must have done it. Kenzo opened the fridge, grabbed a yoghurt, a banana, the milk and some cereal, quickly made himself some food and took it all to his room.

As he demolished his meal, barely tasting a thing, he thought about Zak. His mind had wandered that way several times throughout the last few days, but he kept pushing it away. Zak had made it clear he didn't want to continue seeing him, but his mind wasn't as eager to forget about the man who made him want more than he ever thought he would.

He laid down, more than ready to crash and burn now that he'd eaten, but his brain was too active. Grabbing his phone from where he'd plugged it in, he brought up Zak's information, debating whether to contact him or not. In the end, he decided to send a quick message.

I hope you and Dane are doing okay. Let me know if you need anything.

He considered adding his name or something more but decided to leave it be. Resting the phone back on his bedside table, he stripped off his clothes, forgoing his usual before bed shower, and crawled under the covers.

The next thing he knew, the sun was streaming through the open curtains of his room, blinding his retinas, even hidden behind his eyelids as they were. He pulled the pillow over his head and groaned. The steady thrum of an ache in his head told him he'd slept hard and deep, and he'd need some ibuprofen before he'd be able to manage the day ahead of him.

Removing the pillow, he repeatedly blinked to let his eyes adjust to the light, all the while listening for sounds coming from the rest of the apartment. Everything was silent.

When his eyes could focus, he checked his phone, surprised to see it was after ten o'clock. He hardly ever slept that late, although two days of limited sleep would do that, he supposed. The silence from the apartment meant either Miki was still sleeping himself, or he was locked up in his office already working. Miki never gave himself time to recuperate after the episodes, but it was his choice and his way of coping. There wasn't much Kenzo could do about it.

He saw his phone had several notifications and flipped to his back, unlocking it. Yawning, he put the emails to one side to sort out later. The first message was from Drake, thanking him for getting Miki to message him. The second message was from Zak. He paused before opening it, wondering what he was going to find as a reply.

We're all right, thanks. We've been at a wedding and have just arrived home. Dane is wiped out after having danced with every eligible and ineligible girl and boy at the party. He's a right charmer. How are you?

Kenzo smiled softly as he imagined little Dane giggling and babbling with others, basking them in the same glow he'd showered over him. His heart thudded. He wished he'd been there with them so he could see Dane in all his glory. And Zak. A suit would look fantastic on his body...actually, anything would look good on him.

Pushing upright, he made a note to reply later and shuffled to the bathroom, ready to soak in the bath and, hopefully, ease his knee a little.

Kenzo sat outside the bakery on the metal chairs, despite the chill in the air, and enjoyed the heat on his hands from his coffee. Closing his eyes, he lifted his face to the heavens, allowing the sun to bathe his face. The sky was startlingly blue, and the windows on his car had been iced over that morning. He should've known better than to leave the cover off when a clear, cold night was forecast.

Being right next to the road meant the noise of the cars drowned out most other noises; therefore, other than a conversation to his right and some music from the shop next door, which was only heard when the wind blew in his direction, he couldn't make out any other noise. He was startled, his eyes snapping open when someone scraped a chair and bumped his leg.

A smile crept across his face when Zak sat down, tucking the pushchair next to him to keep the path clear.

"Good morning," Zak said with a grin. "You looked

so serene sitting here, I thought we would come and annoy you."

"Gee, thanks." Kenzo couldn't keep his happiness contained, and he itched to reach for him. "What's brings you here on this beautiful sunny morning?"

"Dane woke up early, even with the late night. I thought I'd take him for a walk to lull him to sleep again." He yawned behind his hand. "Trust me, a grumpy Dane is a handful."

"I can imagine."

"I had planned to keep walking until I was too tired to continue, but I saw you sitting here looking far too mellow." He smirked.

"And you thought you'd be a pain in the ass."

"Yep." The bakery door opened, and several people exited, bringing with them the waft of sweet and savoury smells. "God, it always smells so fantastic here. I'd love to live here."

Kenzo couldn't keep the grin from his face. "Would you like a drink?"

"I need coffee, but I'll get it," Zak said, rising.

He waved Zak down. "No, you look like you'll fall if you try. I'll be back in a minute." Entering Sweet Tooth, he gave his order to Audrey and was reminded it was Valentine's Day for those who indulged in the celebration. It wasn't his sort of thing but to each their own. When Theo handed him a tray with two drinks, a bottle of water and a plate with three cakes with hearts on them, Kenzo raised his eyebrows at him.

Theo ducked his head and mumbled, "I saw Zak sit down. I thought you might like something to go with your drinks."

Kenzo winked at him. "Thanks. I appreciate it, and I know Dane will when he wakes up. Besides, Zak nearly broke the door down when the scent of the goodies hit him." He laughed when Theo's cheeks flushed with pleasure.

Returning to the table, he laid the tray down.

"You didn't have to get all that!" Zak protested.

"I didn't. Theo sent the cakes." He noticed Zak hadn't mentioned the hearts or the celebration; therefore, neither did Kenzo.

Zak peered through the window of the bakery and waved at someone before returning his attention to the table. "Hmm, Theo makes the best cakes ever. I have no doubt these will be amazing."

Kenzo shared the cakes onto separate plates and placed the coffee in front of Zak, moving the tray to the vacant seat next to him, out of the way.

"I hear the wedding was a blast." Kenzo chuckled.

Zak joined him. "Yeah. It was amazing. Crush was closed to the public for the reception party, and they redecorated the place with lots of twinkly lights and balloons and loads of other stuff. Three were so many people there. Max and Trent have been—oh, do you know Max or Trent?"

He shook his head. "No."

"Okay. Well, you know Luke, right?" At Kenzo's nod, Zak continued, his hands gesturing wildly with his explanation, "Trent is Luke's brother, and he met Max, who is one of my best friends, a year or so ago…I can't remember now, but anyway, Trent was straight." At Kenzo's raised eyebrows, Zak laughed. "Yep. But apparently, all Trent needed was Max. They were smitten and got together pretty quickly, but they're definitely soul mates. They're a fantastic match."

"If they met last year, they married quickly."

Zak nodded, taking a bite of cake and moaning. "This is good. I knew it would be," he mumbled with his mouth full. When he finished sending crazy thoughts and images through Kenzo's mind, he said, "Yes, it was quick, but as I said, they were meant for each other. They didn't see the point in waiting."

Kenzo thought about that. He would've loved to have a relationship like that—where there was no second-guessing what the other person's intentions were. They were…soulmates, like Zak said. It wasn't possible for him. He had too many people depending on him.

"Dane enjoyed himself, then." Kenzo flicked his gaze to the sleeping child, so innocent in his slumber.

"God, he was the centre of attention, along with

little Janie. They're a terrible twosome when they want to be, even with the age difference. I'm sure once Kayleigh gets a little older, she will join in." Zak chuckled.

"Janie? Kayleigh?"

"Oh, Sean and Asher's daughter and Tom and Ginny's daughter…and you have no idea who they are." Zak gave a self-deprecating laugh and sipped his coffee. "Sorry, I assume everyone I talk to knows the same people I do. I need to stop doing that."

"It's all good. So, Sean and Asher?"

"Sean is another one of my best friends. He got together with Asher a couple of years ago. I did some woodwork for Asher before they met. Small world." He rolled his eyes with a grin. "And Tom and Ginny, well, Tom is the manager of Crush and Ginny is his girl-friend. Janie is seven, and Kayleigh turned one before Christmas."

"Wow. You know a lot of people. Dane has plenty of kids to play with." Kenzo loved the playfulness and openness Zak was showing that day. Before, he had always been a little withdrawn, holding himself back. It was nice to see a different side of him.

"Yeah. And the circle is growing every day, too." He finished his cake with a hum of delight, washing it down with another sip of coffee. "What about you? Who do you know in this town?" He sat back, wrapping his hands around the cup, and tilted his head as he stared at Kenzo.

"Before I answer, do you want to go inside? It must be cold for the little guy?"

Zak shook his head, scrunching up his nose adorably as he looked at his son. "Nah, we're okay. He runs warm when he sleeps anyway, but I'll see how he is when he wakes up." His focus returned to Kenzo, eyebrows raised. "Now, spill."

Kenzo didn't have much to tell him, but he was happy to answer any questions Zak had if it meant he'd stay in his presence for longer. Zak was like a drug to him. Kenzo couldn't get enough.

CHAPTER ELEVEN

ZAK

He didn't know where the playfulness was coming from, but Zak was high on life. After seeing Max and Trent so happy, along with some of his friends, he couldn't help but believe life was improving. Their wedding was a bittersweet ceremony, and it lit something inside Zak. Something he'd believed he didn't need: someone who was as dedicated to him and Dane as Zak was to them. He struggled with the revelation, however much he wanted it to be true.

Dane was his life. How could he add someone into their little unit without messing up the dynamics? How could he put Dane through the possibility of Zak having a relationship without it causing irreparable damage to his life? Short of hiding his relationship from prying eyes until he could decide whether the guy was worth their time, he couldn't see it working. He refused to let Dane's life become what his had become when his mother had paraded her boyfriends through their house throughout his childhood. As he'd told Noah, why get attached when they'd only leave after a short time?

"To be honest, I don't have a wide social circle," Kenzo answered Zak's question, lifting the mug to his lips, pulling Zak back to the conversation.

"You must have friends." He knew where the need to know more about Kenzo was coming from, but he couldn't help himself, even when he told himself he shouldn't be inviting more interaction. In fact, he shouldn't have sat down at Kenzo's table in the first place.

"I do." Kenzo quirked his mouth. "Do you know Drake who owns the gym?" Zak nodded. "He was on a different team to me and my roommate, Miki."

"I didn't realise Drake had been in the Army." Now he thought about it, Drake did have the military demeanour.

"He doesn't advertise the fact."

Zak took the hint Kenzo's tone made and redirected the conversation despite wanting to know more. "What had you looking so serene when I arrived?"

The peacefulness on Kenzo's face as he lifted it to the sky had been a rope pulling Zak in. He hadn't been able to help himself, and before he knew it, he had made himself at home next to him. There was something about Kenzo that drew him like no one else ever had, not even Ashley.

"I was enjoying the calm before the storm," Kenzo admitted with a rueful laugh, barely heard over the traffic.

"You're expecting choppy waters?"

Kenzo sighed, his attention on the distance. Zak watched as his eyebrows drew together and his lips pursed, tension bleeding into his posture. Already regretting his question, he opened his mouth to change the subject again when Kenzo answered.

"There are always storm clouds on the horizon, but lately…" He sighed again, blinking before turning back to Zak. "Life is what it is. We work with what we have, don't we?" He gave a small smile.

Zak felt his heart break for the sheer…defeat in Kenzo's expression, and he wanted nothing more than to wrap his arms around the guy and protect him from whatever was causing him pain. Never having had that reaction to someone before, he didn't quite know what to do with it, but he knew he couldn't act on it. He was sure Kenzo wouldn't appreciate it. Zak was lucky Kenzo had said anything to him.

"We do," Zak agreed quietly. "But we don't have to settle for something that's not good for us." He pointed to himself. "Case and point."

They were quiet for the time it took to finish their drinks, and as Zak was about to excuse themselves and leave Kenzo alone, Dane woke, scrambling to sit upright from where Zak reclined him in the pushchair.

"Hey, buddy. It's okay." Zak unclicked the belt holding Dane in the seat, and lifted him to his knee, keeping his arm around him while the boy got his bearings. Dane rested his head against Zak's chest, his hand fisted in his shirt. Zak rocked him side to side and returned his gaze to Kenzo, whose focus was on Dane with a small smile on his face.

A siren began in the distance, and Zak felt Dane's body go rigid. The little boy loved all the emergency service vehicles, having several at home that he played with. It reminded Zak he had planned to speak with Logan about visiting the police station to see the cars. The noise became louder, and Zak had a feeling they were about to be deafened. Dane lifted his head and pulled himself to standing, his shoes digging into Zak's thighs as he made himself taller.

Zak couldn't help but smile when his son began babbling and pointing when an ambulance came into view, roaring past and making Dane bounce happily. Wincing against the bruises undoubtedly forming on his legs, he flicked his gaze to Kenzo. The blinding grin on his face was beautiful, and Zak sucked in a breath, desire coursing through his body.

Kenzo caught his eye, his mouth losing some of the joy but heating instead, a flicker of arousal sparking in his eyes.

Dane interrupted the moment by gripping Zak's hair and pulling hard. "Hey, now, buddy. No pulling." Zak pried his son's fingers from his hair and sat him back down on his knee. "Cake?" he asked, showing Dane the plate and laughing when he kicked his legs and bounced. "Okay, back in your pushchair, and you can have cake."

Once he was safely secured again with the back in an upright position, Zak broke the cake into smaller pieces and passed them over to Dane, watching as he smushed them into his mouth, the evidence around his lips.

"He knows what he wants, doesn't he?" Kenzo said quietly.

Zak glanced over. "That he does."

"Hey, Zak!"

With difficulty, he tore his gaze away and settled on the man standing next to him. "Hey, Sean." He stood and hugged him, slapping him on the back before turning to Asher and repeating the action. Refocusing his attention on the not-so-little girl with them, he greeted her, "Hello, Princess Janie." He pressed a kiss to the back of the seven-year-old's hand.

"Hi, Uncle Zak. Dane!" She pulled her hand away and skipped over to the pushchair, her dark brown curls bouncing with the movement. Those two were thick as thieves, and Janie was an absolute gem with Dane.

"How are you both?" Zak asked.

"We're good. We needed some fresh air after the late night last night." Sean stifled a yawn, and Asher laughed. Sean's usually neat sandy brown hair was mussed like he'd just rolled out of bed, and his bright blue eyes, while sharp, looked tired.

"He needed stronger coffee than what we had at home," Asher explained. His own appearance was a little more relaxed than usual, although his brown hair was so short it would never look untidy. His golden-coloured gaze flicked to Zak's table, reminding him of Kenzo's presence.

"Oh, sorry. Guys, this is Kenzo. Kenzo, this is Sean, Asher and Janie."

Kenzo stood, holding out his hand. "Your reputation precedes you," he said with a grin.

Sean narrowed his eyes at Zak. "Have you been telling tales, Mr King?" He paused, then chuckled as he shook hands. "They're probably all true."

"The ones about you, yes," Asher quipped, shaking Kenzo's hand.

"Would you like to join us?" Kenzo asked.

Sean waved a hand. "No, we don't want to interrupt. We'll go find a table inside."

"Honestly, it's absolutely fine. You're welcome to if you want." Zak returned to his seat as Sean and Asher had a quick, silent conversation between them. Zak had always marvelled at the fact they could do that. With a mere look, they seemed to be able to know what the other wanted or was feeling.

"Sure. If you don't mind us butting in," Asher finally agreed.

"Not at all." Kenzo sat back down and flicked his gaze over to him, raising his eyebrows.

"It's fine with me." Zak wasn't sure how to feel about having Kenzo interacting with his friends, and when the thought crossed his mind, he mentally slapped himself for being an asshole. Kenzo had said he didn't have much of a social circle. Why should Zak refuse him the chance to meet new people?

They pulled over a couple more chairs, and Sean settled himself down as Asher went to grab some drinks. Janie was still playing with Dane, pulling faces and tickling him; she was an absolute star with little kids. It must've rubbed off from Asher.

"I didn't think you'd be up yet, Zak. With the amount of dancing Dane did last night, I expected him to still be asleep," Sean said.

"Yeah, me too, but he was up at the crack of dawn, unfortunately. I know I could've done with several more hours." Zak rolled his eyes. "What about you? You look like you could sleep now."

"Definitely. I feel like I've hardly had any, but it was a fantastic night. Max can't wait to get to Greece."

"I bet."

"Greece is a lovely place to visit. Where exactly are they going?" Kenzo asked.

"Zakynthos," Sean said, smirking at Zak.

"Shut up! Just because it shares part of my name!" Zak huffed and turned to Kenzo. "They think it's hilarious the island has 'Zak' in it. Why I have no idea. I don't think it's particularly funny, do you?"

Sean chuckled. "You have to admit it's funny when Max only chose it because of that reason."

Zak threw his arms up. "He only did it because if he hates it, he can, apparently, blame me for it."

Kenzo rolled his lips inwards as he stared at Zak, his eyes twinkling. "It's a good plan. Which groom would ever willingly blame the other when it comes to their honeymoon destination? If they blame it on you, they're both in the clear."

Zak was saved from answering by Asher returning with a tray full of drinks and snacks. "Janie, sweetheart? Can you sit down for me, please? I got you a treat." Asher glanced at him. "I didn't get one for Dane as I saw he'd enjoyed something chocolate earlier, but I did get some fruit pieces if he wants them instead."

"Thanks. You didn't have to."

"I know."

"So, Kenzo, how do you two know each other?" Sean asked, wrapping his hands around his mug and blowing across the top.

"We met at the gym. I told him off for not having

the correct posture when he was lifting." Kenzo tilted his head at Zak, eyelids lowered.

"Naughty boy, Zak. I didn't realise you were still going." Sean looked a little sheepish. "I thought you would've given up before now."

Zak picked up a napkin, rolled it into a ball and threw it across the table before huffing. "To be honest, I thought the same thing. Surprisingly, I'm enjoying it. Most of the time, my mind clears, and I can focus on the movements I need to make instead of everything else going on." He shrugged and ducked his head, embarrassed.

"It's exactly the same for me," Kenzo said. "There's something about it that lets every bit of stress leech from your body. Nothing beats it."

Sean nudged Asher. "Maybe you should try it. The kids drive you nuts most days."

"That they do. As much as I love them, they do push more boundaries than ever." Asher smiled across at Kenzo. "I'm a childminder, and I look after anywhere up to twelve children every weekday. I'm a glutton for punishment, so I'm told."

"Ah." Kenzo's eyes widened as he nodded.

"How long have you two been together? You kept that quiet, Zak," Asher said.

"Oh, we're not...I'm...we..." Zak didn't know how to answer the question without sounding like an asshole.

"We're friends," Kenzo answered smoothly.

"Yeah, friends," Zak echoed.

Sean raised his eyebrows at him and hid what Zak knew was a smirk in his cup, and Zak briefly closed his eyes. He was never going to hear the end of it.

"Right. I'm going to have to leave you guys to it." Kenzo stood, tucking his chair back under the table.

"Thanks for the drink," Zak said, his eyes caressing Kenzo's chest and neck before resting on his eyes.

"You're welcome. I'll see you soon." Kenzo leaned forward and pressed a kiss to his cheek, ruffled the boy's hair before heading off down the street.

Zak watched his uneven gait as he walked away with his hands stuffed into his pockets. Kenzo was a handsome man, and if Zak could have confirmation that a relationship with him would work out, he wouldn't hesitate to start one with him, but he couldn't do it. There was no guessing what the future held, and Kenzo wasn't exactly forthcoming with information about his personal life.

"Friends, my ass," Sean muttered.

Zak snapped his head around to Sean and glared. "It was one..." He cleared his throat. "It was two nights, and that was it. Forget about it. We're friends." He picked up his newly filled mug and sipped, trying to avoid their gaze.

"Uh-huh. Wait...*two* nights? You told me you would

never spend more than one night with someone. Why did he manage to get two?"

Zak gritted his teeth against the slip and focused on the swirls in his drink. The air seemed to be warming because his hands weren't as cold, but it could also be to do with the coffee. He would be bouncing all the way home with how much caffeine he'd had in such a short amount of time. He usually switched to tea or hot chocolate by now.

"He seems nice," Asher said, no doubt trying to keep the peace.

Zak glanced at Sean, seeing him returning the gaze, eyebrows lowered and a crease between them. Zak slumped, knowing he couldn't ignore them.

"I don't know what it is about him. He's nice. It doesn't bother him that I have Dane, and Dane seems fine around him. But I'm not bringing anyone into our lives at the moment. It's barely been a month since I got custody of Dane. I can't fuck it up because of a guy who may or may not stick around."

Sean's expression softened. "Life is full of surprises, Zak. You can't live expecting disappointment because you'd never love at all."

"I love Dane. He's all I need." Zak stood. He hated being on bad terms with them, but he wasn't going to sit there and listen to them preach that being in love was the best thing. He shook his head, internally slapping himself upside the head again—it was becoming a habit—for thinking such a thing about them. Sean and Asher meant well, but he didn't need their advice. He needed to concentrate on taking care of Dane. "I have to get back. I have plenty of work to get done."

"Zak, wait—"

"I'll see you soon. Bye, Janie." He managed to wave and smile at the little girl before spinning the pushchair around and heading down the street.

His words had been a bit cutting, but he wouldn't take them back. His mother had shown him enough times that love was fleeting, and he refused to build his life around something that may not survive. It was an easy way to lose everything, including Dane.

Ashley had been absent and silent since the final court hearing. He was both surprised and not surprised. She didn't seem interested in caring for Dane, but at the same time, she fought to gain custody. The reason behind the decision was a mystery. Having no communication with her was a good thing as far as he was concerned, but it did worry him a little. She could easily turn up one day and cause trouble.

Dane was cranky again by the time they returned home, so Zak changed and cleaned him and settled him for another nap. Zak had plenty of work he could get on with, but he rarely worked when Dane was asleep and there was no one else in the house, even if he had a monitor to hear him. He refused to take any chances. Tomorrow, Emily would be babysitting him while Zak worked, but he needed to find a more permanent solution. It wasn't fair on Emily to keep taking her time away from her work, even if she said she didn't mind.

Slapping his palm against his forehead, he sighed. He should've spoken to Asher about it while they were at Sweet Tooth. He pulled out his phone and opened their message thread.

Hey. Sorry about today. I am trying to sort things out about Dane. Do you have any space for him at all?

He fumbled, trying to decide whether he needed to add any more to his apology, but realised they would know what he meant. When he next saw them, he'd apologise properly.

Unable to sit still, he knew he needed to do something, or he would be pacing around and getting wound up, so he nipped into his workshop to grab some smaller tools and wood and took them to the kitchen table to do some whittling. It had been a long time since he'd last done it. It would be more Colton's job now, but Zak still enjoyed it every now and then. He'd been snowed under with furniture orders and hadn't had the time to focus on smaller things.

Spreading a few sheets of old paper over the top of the table, he chose a piece of wood and a knife and began to shave away at the material. There was never a plan when it came to whittling for him; he let his hands do the work, and, eventually, something would come from it. The last thing he made had been some building blocks for Dane, sanded until they were as smooth as glass before letting him have them. That was over a year ago.

The minutes went by, and he lost himself to the rhythm. When he heard Dane stir, he blinked repeatedly and refocused on the wood, eyes widening. There in front of him sat the beginnings of a miniature tennis racket.

Even when he wasn't consciously focusing on Kenzo, his brain was.

CHAPTER TWELVE

KENZO

There is a triple birthday party at Crush on Saturday. Would you like to come? Zak.

Kenzo stared at the message he'd received that afternoon. He didn't know quite how to take it. Was Zak asking him on a date? Or was it a friendly get to know people thing? How could he ask what it was without sounding stupid? Or should he see what happened if he decided to go? So many questions.

Shaking his head, he pocketed his phone, deciding to think some more before replying. He enjoyed Zak's company—a lot more than he thought he would—but he didn't know where their future lay. He would've liked to see something grow between them, but with everything he had going on, and with all the difficulties

Zak had been through, he couldn't see it happening any time soon.

A knock at the door brought him from his thoughts, and he ambled towards it, his knee still twinging from the workout he'd given it that morning. Opening the door, he froze, staring at the two people he didn't think he'd ever see again.

"Sorry to show up unannounced. We weren't sure if you'd see us if we asked permission."

His breathing came in short pants, and he felt the sweat drip down his back. Not saying a word, he opened the door wider, allowing Pete's parents to enter. Closing the door behind them, he rested back against it, hoping it would keep him upright, and watched as they wandered closer to the sofa.

When they turned to face him, he could see the strain on their features. Even two years after the incident, they were still paying the emotional price for their son's actions.

"I know you probably don't want to hear from us, but we wanted to check on you. You were such a big part of our lives before...this happened. We care about you," Miranda said quietly.

Kenzo's breath shuddered from his lungs, and he closed his eyes briefly, trying to recall those years when he would be at their house as much as his own. "I know you do. And I care about you, too." He pushed off the door and shuffled closer to them, glancing towards the hallway. He hoped Miki hadn't heard the door and stayed in his office instead. He wasn't sure how he'd react to seeing them or whether it would set off an episode.

"How are you doing?" Robin stared at him as if Kenzo held all the answers to the universe.

"I'm all right." He indicated for them to sit down, then sat in one of the leather armchairs that had been left by the previous owners and Kenzo had claimed as his. "I've been doing some tennis coaching at the gym recently—only covering for the coach while he was ill, but it reminded me how much I enjoyed it."

"That's great! Are you thinking of continuing with it?" Miranda scooted closer to the edge of the seat, linking her fingers as she rested her forearms on her knees.

"I don't know. There's a lot of things going on. I don't know if I should add anything else into the mix yet."

"You were so good at it. You'd have so much to share with people."

Kenzo huffed, "It was years ago, Miranda. I've probably forgotten half of what I'd learned."

"Yeah, but I bet the half you remember is still pure gold to those students," Robin argued with a smile.

"Maybe. How are you?" He switched his gaze between them both, seeing some of the tension seep back into their bodies.

"Some days are easier than others."

"That they are," he agreed.

"We've been considering starting a foundation for those in similar situations to you, but we don't know if our association with…our son would make things more difficult for the charity or not. What do you think?" Robin wrung his hands together.

Kenzo paused. He'd been about to give his usual "You'll be fine" speech but stopped to consider the possible implications before replying. "In all honesty, I don't know. We…" He swallowed hard against the lump in his throat, his stomach churning. "We struggle when we think about…him. I can honestly tell you I don't know the answer. You'd be better speaking with someone else about it. I'm too close."

"We just want to help—"

A gasp brought Kenzo's attention to the hallway, seeing Miki stood there, the blood draining from his face, and him swaying on his feet. Kenzo shot out of the seat and ran to Miki, catching him in a crouch before he hit the floor. Miki gripped his hair and began rocking back and forth, a keening sound tearing from his throat.

Kenzo kept his arms wrapped around him and glanced towards Pete's parents. "I need you to leave."

"Is he okay?" Robin took a step closer.

Firming his voice, Kenzo said, "You need to leave. Now."

Miranda pulled at Robin's biceps, leading him towards the door. "Can we call?"

"I'll call you." He wasn't sure if it was the truth, but he needed to tell them something if just to get them out of the apartment.

He could see they weren't sure if they believed him, but they left, closing the door firmly behind them. Kenzo closed his eyes and rested his head on Miki's, murmuring words of reassurance and reminders of the present rather than the past. Never knowing what would help at any given time, Kenzo had learned different ways of talking to Miki to ground him in the present instead of leaving him in the past. Sometimes, they worked quickly, and Miki returned to him after a few hours; sometimes, they didn't, and it would be days before Miki was himself again.

Staring at the front door, he clenched his jaw. Pete's parents should've stayed away.

Kenzo finally replied to Zak two days later, saying he would love to go to the party. He offered to pick Zak up, but he declined, much to Kenzo's disappointment. It had nothing to do with him not liking the idea of turning up at Crush without knowing anyone. Much.

Still, he got himself ready. After making sure Miki was doing all right, he left the apartment with several presents and climbed into the waiting taxi. It would be strange meeting Zak on *his* turf, so to speak. Kenzo had been to Crush before but not during the busiest times. Miki would've never been able to manage, but Kenzo would be fine. He hoped.

Entering the bar, he glanced around, seeing birthday banners and balloons all over the inside. There was a guy with a clipboard near the end of the bar, who drifted over to him when he saw him.

"Are you here for the party?" the guy asked.

"Yes."

"Name, please."

"Kenzo."

"Perfect. If you follow down that way, you'll come to some tables enclosed by rope barriers. That is where the party is. There are other partygoers there already. Enjoy."

"Thanks."

He followed the instructions and found the tables the guy had mentioned; the red rope hanging between the wooden support columns, surrounding several that were already filled, others that were empty. The doors to the Garden Bar were open, letting in a slight chill, but not enough to make someone freeze their ass off.

"Kenzo!"

He whipped his gaze towards where his name came from, scanning for the owner because it definitely wasn't Zak. Sean waved from one of the chairs, and Kenzo smiled and wandered over.

"Hey! Glad you could make it." They shook hands.

"So, who are the birthday people? I have gifts, but I don't know whether they're suitable."

"Oh, god. You didn't have to do that!"

"I know, but I wanted to."

Asher leaned forward. "Well, the first birthday boy is right here." He pointed to Sean. "His birthday is tomorrow."

Kenzo reached into the bag and pulled out the three presents he'd meticulously wrapped, checking for the code he'd written on the outside, so he knew what was in each one. He pulled one from the stack and handed it to Sean. "Happy birthday."

Sean's cheeks flushed as he accepted the offering. "Thanks."

"The other corruptors are Charlie, who has just turned twenty-one and is a bartender here if you didn't know, and a belated birthday for Max, as he was on his honeymoon during his birthday."

"Ah, okay. The remaining gifts should work fine, then."

"Have a seat. I'll point out the birthday boys when I see them." Sean dropped back into his seat next to

Asher and picked up a glass. Before he raised it to his mouth, he said, "Oh, and drinks are on the house. Gemma and Analise will be around to top us up and grab us more throughout the evening."

"I'll pay for my drinks. It's only fair."

"No, no. Honestly. Tom, who manages the bar, does this for everyone's birthdays. He says it's better than trying to choose a birthday present." They all laughed.

"What's so funny?"

The silky-smooth tone slid down Kenzo's spine, and he refrained from shivering but only just. He glanced over his shoulder to see Zak in dark blue jeans with a black shirt, which was open at the throat, showcasing his amazing skin. Kenzo felt the need to bury his head in Zak's neck and shoulder and inhale the scent he knew was unique to Zak.

"Explaining about Tom."

"Ah." Zak pulled out a chair between Sean and Kenzo, settling himself down. "Hi," Zak said, a small smile playing on his lips. "I'm glad you could make it."

"Zak, are you having a party here as well?" Sean asked, a slight quirk to his lips as he glanced between the two of them.

"Oh, is it your birthday soon?" Kenzo noticed the darkening of Zak's cheeks as the man narrowed his gaze at Sean.

"Um...yeah, in three weeks."

Kenzo noticed Zak hadn't told him the exact date

and mentally made a note to grab another gift to give to him around that time.

"And I'm not planning on doing anything. There's enough of us now to celebrate without throwing mine in, too."

"But it's Dane's birthday soon as well!"

"That's different. Of course, we'll celebrate Dane's. It's not every day he turns three." Zak chuckled, rolling his eyes.

"Well, as of next week, you'll be able to work a bit longer. Dane will have great fun with us," Asher said with a smile on his face.

"Yeah, that will be handy. I have loads of orders that need completing, but I've explained to the customers there may be a delay, and they've been great about it, thankfully." Zak glanced over at him. "I've arranged for Dane to go to Asher's during the week. Did I tell you he's a childminder?"

"Yeah."

"Well, he had space for him, and I need to get back to working full-time."

Kenzo placed his hand on top of Zak's and gave a squeeze. "You don't need to explain your choices."

Zak exhaled and smiled. "Thanks. It's difficult. I'm so used to having to explain away everything I do. It's hard to get out of the habit."

"Who made you do that?"

"Ashley."

Kenzo felt the need to rage at her but refused to in her absence. From what he'd gathered from their conversations, Ashley wasn't a nice person, and he was glad Zak seemed to be free of her. Dane, too.

"Anyway, it will be nice to get back into some sort of routine."

"I bet."

"All right, guys. What drinks are we needing?"

A firm, hoarse voice sounded from next to him, making him flinch. He breathed deeply, settling his heart. It was only after he looked up, he realised he still had hold of Zak's hand, and he'd felt Kenzo flinch. Concern etched on Zak's face, but Kenzo plastered a smile on his face.

"Do you have any brown ale?" he asked.

"Sure." The woman wrote down the order on her pad, her long blonde hair dropping forward as she did.

"Two Kronenburg and a Stella, please, Analise. I know these two want more," Zak said, grinning at Sean and then Asher.

"No doubt about it," Analise replied. "Do any of you want any food at the moment?"

"Not yet, thanks." After each of them declined, she winked and left as three other people joined them.

"Ah, here we are, another birthday boy!" Sean exclaimed, standing and throwing his arms around a good-looking, dark-haired guy who had his fingers linked with another man.

"That's Max."

The whisper in his ear had Kenzo shivering in response and tilting his head closer. "Thanks."

"His husband is called Trent. They're the ones who recently married."

He nodded distractedly. Kenzo would do anything to keep Zak as close as he was. He wasn't paying attention to the people around him anymore, just on the sensation of Zak pressed against his biceps and his hot breath against his ear. Kenzo's cock decided to perk up at the thoughts running rampant, and he tried to shift without being obvious.

Zak moved his hand in front of Kenzo's face, pointing towards another man heading in their direction. "And that's Charlie, the other birthday boy."

Kenzo focused more on Zak's strong but slender fingers rather than the guy he was referring to, feeling a loss when the hand dropped away from sight. Clearing his throat, he refocused on the people around him. There were mainly men with a few women, one heavily pregnant, all within the cordoned-off area. Apart from at the gym, he hadn't been around so many strangers in a long time.

"How is…Miki? Is that right? Your roommate?" Zak asked, lifting his newly delivered beer to his lips.

Kenzo inclined his head, impressed Zak had remembered such a fleeting mention of him. "Well remembered. He's fine. Busy as always."

"What does he do?"

He downed some of the ale the woman had brought for him. "He's a computer engineer. A bloody genius if you ask me. He'll quite happily go off explaining everything to me, and it mostly goes over my head." Huffing, he shook his head. "He doesn't get out much—" Kenzo halted, not wanting to give out too much information. "How's it going at the gym?"

A fleeting tightening of Zak's face before he softened again showed the change of subject had not gone unnoticed. "It's good. I'm feeling stronger, and my arms don't ache as much when I'm finished. I assume that means I'm getting used to it. I—"

"God, there are so many of us now, and we have so many birthdays, we may as well live here!" The man—or boy really, he didn't look that old—named Charlie said as he dropped into a seat opposite them.

Zak's musical laughter sparked something inside Kenzo. "*Don't* you live here?"

Charlie snorted. "I may as well. It's a good job, and I enjoy the work."

"How's the training going?"

The guy bounced in his seat, a huge grin splitting his face. "It's great! I can't wait until I can take over for Tom. He needs to be at home with Ginny, Kayleigh and the new addition, rather than working all hours under the sun."

"You'll do great. You've been here long enough to know everything anyway."

Kenzo took a drink, not wanting to interrupt while they were conversing, and gazed around the bar, taking in the laughter and camaraderie of the people surrounding them. It was a heady feeling to be part of something like this, part of something bigger. Just like being in the team. Slightly different dynamic but with a similar feel.

"Kenzo?" He glanced at Zak. "Sorry, this is Charlie. He's a bartender here and soon to be the manager. Also, he's just turned twenty-one."

Zak had given him similar information to what Sean had done, but he was glad of the reminder. "Happy birthday." Kenzo dipped into the bag he'd brought and passed a small gift over to him.

"Oh, you didn't have to do that! Thank you." Charlie said as another wide smile graced his face, cradling the gift to his chest.

"You're welcome." Kenzo turned to Zak. "I have one for Max, too."

"Max!"

Zak's shout had Kenzo wincing and regretting being so close for a moment. When Max wandered over, Kenzo proffered the gift, receiving an introduction and a shoulder squeeze in response.

As more and more people joined their group, Kenzo gazed around him in awe. He focused on the conversations close to him, namely Zak and Sean, but mainly, he people watched. He'd always loved doing it and trying to figure out what made those people tick. A fun game for passing the time.

"Come on," Zak said suddenly, gripping his forearm and tugging at him.

Kenzo glanced at him, then stood, placing his ale on the table and followed Zak into the chilly outdoor area. He'd not been there a lot, but the Garden Bar was a comfortable place. Tables dotted around the patio, a couple of wooden benches and vines intertwined on trellises enclosing the space on all sides except the one facing River Cam gave it a trendy, sheltered feel. There were four heaters placed in each corner, warding off the cold.

Zak led him to the right and stopped near the far wall of the building. He rested back against it and grabbed Kenzo's shirt, pulling him forward until there wasn't an inch of space between them. Kenzo placed his hands at Zak's hips as Zak's hands slid up to his shoulders and around his neck.

"Why can't I get enough of you?" Zak whispered before he covered Kenzo's lips with his own.

Their mouths opened immediately, tongues duelling and twining around each other while Kenzo wrapped his arms around Zak's back, tightening his grip until his hard cock was pressed against the other man. Zak made a whimpering noise, and Kenzo loosened his arms a little, giving their bodies more room to move.

Zak's hips began a gentle rhythm against Kendo's own, heightening the arousal tingling at his spine.

A loud musical burst startled him, and he pulled away from Zak, breathing heavily. The music continued, and he realised it was his phone, the vibration in his pocket making itself known now that he wasn't distracted.

Cursing, he fumbled to retrieve it one-handed, not wanting to let Zak go completely.

"What do you want, Drake?" he growled.

"Where's Miki?"

Drake's worried voice dispersed more of the fog from his brain. His heart pounded as hard as it had when Zak was in his arms.

"What do you mean, where's Miki? He's in bed where I left him."

Zak pulled away, sliding to the side to remove himself from Kenzo's embrace, and Kenzo glanced at him, furrowing his brow. Although he wanted to find out why Zak's face had gone pale, he needed to focus on the conversation at hand. He turned away and lowered his voice. He didn't want everyone to hear what was going on.

"Have you been home?" he asked.

"He's not at the apartment, and there's no answer

when I call him. The phone rings and rings, not even going to voicemail."

"I don't understand. He hardly leaves. Where would he go?"

"I should be asking you that question. You know him better than I do," Drake said with a sigh.

Kenzo heard the sadness in Drake's voice. "We will find him, Drake, and you can get to know him better. He's let you in more than anyone else I've known. Don't let it stop you from pushing him a little."

Drake blew out a loud breath. "I know. Where the hell could he be?"

"Okay. Let's think about this logically. I will call his therapist to see if he's been in contact with her. I'll also call the Veteran Centre, just in case. You try driving from the apartment down some roads and see if you can see him walking. I've had a couple of beers, so I'll have to get a taxi home, but then I'll join you."

"All right. I'll call you back in a bit."

They rang off without further conversation, and Kenzo immediately called Mrs Valatin, Miki's therapist. He had her number for emergency situations, and he thought this would count. Maybe she knew of some other places he could look.

"Hi, it's Kenzo, Miki's roommate. I'm sorry to disturb your evening, but Miki has gone missing. You don't happen to know of anywhere he might have mentioned that he would go?" he asked without preamble.

She cleared her throat, her voice hoarse as if she'd been woken, which was entirely likely at this time of night. "The only places he has mentioned are the apartment, the Veteran Centre and the office. Whenever we speak about it, he doesn't bring any other places into the conversation. That's all I can disclose."

"Damn it! Sorry, thank you."

"Please let me know what happens."

"Will do."

He ended the call and dialled the Veteran Centre, hoping someone would answer so he wouldn't have to leave a message.

"Hello, St John's Veteran Centre. Vince speaking."

"Vince! It's Kenzo. Have you seen Miki around?" Luckily, Miki had been to the Veteran Centre a couple of times, though not recently, and most people knew what he looked like.

"Hey, Kenzo. No, I've not seen him."

"Okay. Can you let me know if he turns up, please?"

"Sure thing. Is everything okay?"

"I hope so," he mumbled and said goodbye.

Staring at his phone, he blew out a breath, his heart racing at the implications. He refused to let Miki down like he'd let Pete down. He *had* to find Miki. Calling for a taxi, who said one would be there in less than five minutes, he trailed inside to offer his apologies to Zak.

Finding him sitting and nursing a beer, Kenzo said, "I have to go. Sorry."

Zak jumped, then nodded in his direction, not saying a word.

Wanting nothing more than to explain but not having the time to do so, he grabbed his coat and left.

The taxi was at the kerb waiting. Kenzo entered, giving the driver his address and proceeded to call the few people he did know to see if they'd seen Miki. No one had, which made Kenzo tenser than ever. Nausea became his companion as they worked their way through the Saturday night traffic. Drake had called again, saying he'd not seen anything yet, and Kenzo gave him a status report.

They joined forces at home, Drake driving while they both scanned the streets for anyone who looked like Miki. After two hours of searching, they headed back to the apartment to regroup.

When they arrived, they found Miki on the sofa, trembling so hard his teeth were chattering. Kenzo grabbed the blanket from the back of the sofa and draped it around Miki's shoulders while Drake made a hot drink. Kenzo stayed with his arms around Miki, mumbling the usual mundane words he always did. Inside, he was scared to death.

There would be no getting answers from Miki until he had recovered, but when he did, they needed to have a chat about where Miki had been. They needed to know where to look, should it happen again.

All three of them spent the night staring at a quietly playing movie while Kenzo and Drake alternately held Miki, who eventually fell into a troubled sleep.

That night, Drake was given his first experience of what Miki had been going through.

CHAPTER THIRTEEN

ZAK

Zak stared at the bottle he held in one hand and peeled at the label as he berated himself for thinking Kenzo was different. Yet again, Zak had taken everything Kenzo had said as true and look what happened, Zak was left standing alone as always.

"You look like you need this." Analise held another bottle in front of his face and waited until Zak took it before sitting in Kenzo's vacated seat.

Zak didn't say anything, not willing to explain what an idiot he was. "Thanks."

"You know, everybody has secrets, especially at the beginning of a relationship. Take me and Kade. He had the police following me without my knowledge, but eventually, once you gain their trust and they yours, the secrets will be shared."

Zak exhaled heavily. Their situation was different

from his, and if he was honest, he didn't think Analise should've forgiven Kade for what he did. It wasn't Kade's place to dictate what she should do. Obviously, something was working for them so far, though, because they'd been together for over a year. In fact, looking around, a lot of the couples had been together for more than a few months. He shook his head, clenching his jaw. He hated watching their relationships and knowing they wouldn't last, but it wasn't up to him to decide for them.

"People have a tendency to keep themselves to themselves, thinking no one else will ever understand what they've been through, when in fact, the people you are drawn to are usually the people who understand the most."

Zak gulped some of his beer, still silent and avoiding her gaze.

"Just because you can't see it at the moment doesn't make my words a lie." She stood, wrapped an arm around his shoulder and rubbed his upper arm before letting go. "Think about it."

Zak stared at the table, then forced his gaze away and focused on his friends. He wouldn't let what happened ruin his friends' party, though the words never left his mind all through the smiles and laughter.

He's in bed where I left him.

Zak held the electric router firmly as he pushed it into the wood, gouging a pattern within it. The vibration tingled the skin of his hands and partway up his arm, but it felt familiar, lessening the emotional weight on his shoulders.

The rich mahogany would eventually be made into a cabinet for the customer. The doors, which he was currently working on, would have a hand-chiselled pattern on the front, and once it was varnished, the deep, luxurious wood would look magnificent. He was bringing Colton in on this project, as he'd had more practise with the smaller, finicky details than Zak had, and would continue to work with him from then on. Zak was looking forward to having someone to chat with while they worked.

His thoughts tripped towards Kenzo again, making him clench his teeth as hard as he held the tool. Every time he was reminded of the way Kenzo left, he felt himself tense up again. Disappointment gave way to anger, which slowly swirled in his stomach until he felt like a match waiting to be lit. The only time the feeling eased was when he was completely focused on his work or completely focused on Dane. With Dane being looked after by Asher now, it gave Zak the opportunity to go back to work full-time, but he missed him like he missed Kenzo, although he hated it when that thought blew through his mind.

The worst thing about the whole situation was Kenzo had not been in touch since the party. Not one word. Almost three weeks since he last heard anything from the man, and that annoyed him the most. The least Kenzo could've done was send an apology text or something.

Zak stopped the router and stood, wincing as his back protested. He switched the tool off at the mains— a safety precaution—and stepped back, surveying his progress. He'd given the customer a longer completion date than necessary as he hadn't been sure if Dane would settle at Asher's or not, but he shouldn't have worried. Sometimes, Noah picked him up, like he was today, and sometimes, Zak fetched him, but either way, Dane was as happy as ever, if not happier.

"Hello?"

Zak whipped his gaze to the open garage door, seeing the man he hadn't—and had—wanted to see again, standing there with his hands deep in his pockets and a neutral expression on his face. A rictus of emotions passed through his body, and Zak carefully refrained from doing or saying anything that would give away his conflicted feelings.

"Hi," he managed through gritted teeth.

He turned his back on Kenzo and puttered around, pretending to be busy when in fact, he wasn't sure what he was doing. His body felt heavy as he moved items from one place to another, avoiding eye contact with Kenzo.

"I want to apologise for leaving so suddenly." Zak heard Kenzo clear his throat. "Miki doesn't…leave the house. Hardly ever, except for his appointments. So, when Drake called and said he couldn't find him, I panicked. I should've explained before I left."

"You do not need to explain anything," Zak said shortly.

"Yes, I do. You invited me there, and I left. It's not the done thing."

Zak clenched his jaw. "The done thing is not sleeping with someone when you already have someone *in your bed*." He threaded his fingers through his hair, forgetting he had it tied up, and it came tumbling down around him. He quickly gathered it back up, replacing the band.

"I don't—"

Glancing over his shoulder, he spat, "I don't want to hear it, Kenzo. Apparently, you want your cake, and you want to eat it, too. Isn't that the right phrase? Miki is welcome to you, although if he doesn't know about your transgressions, you really should tell him. I'm sure he'd be *overjoyed* to find out you sleep with other people while he stays at home."

Zak slammed some of the wooden pieces he'd been moving onto the counter, making the contents of the shelves rattle.

"I'm not with—"

"Save it. You're just like all the rest." Zak's voice broke on the final word, but he inhaled slowly and deeply, refusing the let any tears overflow when he pivoted to face Kenzo. He rested his hands against the counter at his hips, steadying himself as he leaned back. "I should've known better, especially after almost three weeks with no word from you."

They stared at each other, Zak trying not to crumble under the intense gaze. After nodding once and pursing his lips, Kenzo turned around and walked away. Zak watched him pull something from his pocket and disappear around the corner of the house. Exhaling heavily, he slouched against the counter, his gaze dropping to the floor, although not seeing anything.

He wanted nothing more than to run after Kenzo and stop him from leaving, but he knew from experience that it would only delay the inevitable. Besides, Zak refused to be the other man.

Wetting a cloth at the sink in the far corner of the workshop, he wiped his face free from grime and the tears he refused to acknowledge, then sighed and returned to work. The orders wouldn't make themselves.

Several hours later, he heard a car horn and smiled.

It was Noah's way of telling him they were home without making Zak jump too much when he might have a sharp tool in his hand. That had happened a couple of times before they realised they needed to figure out some other routine before he chopped off some fingers. He replaced the tools where they lived and washed his hands in the sink, the icy water cooling his heated hands, and he ran a damp cloth over his face again before locking up the garage and heading inside.

Entering through the creaky back door as he always did, he found Dane already fastened in his chair, munching on some cheesy animal biscuits and drawing his finger through the crumbs on his tray.

"Hey, buddy! How was your day!" Zak crouched next to him and rested his hand on his back. The scent of cheese mixed with Dane's unique baby scent was a balm to him, and he felt his shoulders drop and his muscles relax.

"Dada, bikit," Dane babbled, spraying more crumbs and holding up his biscuit.

Zak laughed. "Thank you for the offer, but you eat it. I missed you, too." He pressed a kiss to the boy's forehead and stood, turning to Noah. "Hey, thanks for picking him up."

"You're welcome. I love spending time with this little guy." Noah grabbed some plates from the cupboard above him and walked them over to the table where a large bag rested. "I bought a takeaway. I thought you might be hungry."

As soon as the words were spoken, Zak's stomach groaned so loudly, it was physically painful, which reminded Zak he hadn't stopped for lunch.

"I'll take it as a yes." Noah laughed.

"Thanks."

"Did you manage to get much done?" Noah asked, sitting opposite Dane, allowing Zak the seat next to his son. He reached into the carrier bag, rustling around until he picked out one of the cartons before repeating it with the others until five boxes sat on the table.

"What did you buy!" Zak gaped at the amount of food sitting before them.

"Leftovers are always welcome." Noah grinned. "I am living alone, after all."

They were silent as they chose from the options, then Zak answered Noah's question, "I did actually." He conveniently ignored the slight break he had when Kenzo arrived. "The doors for the cabinet are done apart from the pattern. Colton will be coming tomorrow to start that. All I need to do now is finish the side panels, and it can be fitted together."

"You're ahead of schedule." Noah raised his eyebrows. Although Noah wasn't part of the business, Zak always told him when pieces were due and other information to keep him in the loop.

Zak nodded, his mouth full of spicy chicken. Once he'd swallowed, he said, "Yeah, but let's not jinx me."

Noah rolled his eyes. Comfortable silence reigned—apart from Dane's chatter—as they dug into their dinner until Noah made a sound. As Zak looked over at him, Noah's eyes widened, and he tried to mumble something from behind his hand before standing and dashing into the hallway. Zak frowned, peering around the table at what could've caused such a reaction but couldn't identify anything.

His brother came back with a large, gift-wrapped parcel, complete with a bow on the top. The gold and blue wrapping paper glittered under the kitchen lights.

"What's this for?" Zak asked with a bemused smile, wiping his hands on a paper towel before taking it.

"I've no idea. I found it on the porch. I only just remembered. There was no label or anything on it, but as it was resting against your door, I assumed it was for you." Noah's cutlery clinked against his plate as he tucked back into his food.

Zak, on the other hand, stared at the present. Where had it come from? His birthday was on Friday, but why would someone leave it against his—Kenzo. Swallowing against his now dry throat, he held the gift, wondering what to do with it.

"Aren't you going to open it?"

Should he? Or should he give it back, especially with how they left things? Maybe Kenzo had put it there before he'd sought Zak out and had meant to take it back. "Yeah," he mumbled, unable to resist the lure.

Pushing his seat further back, he rested it on his knee as his fingers found the edge of the smooth paper. The deeper sounding crinkle belied the cost of the wrapping, and Zak was spellbound, watching as more of the inner gift was revealed. A plain cardboard box was his first view, and when he opened the end of that, a small piece of paper was revealed.

I know this is something you could've probably made yourself, but it reminded me of you and Dane. I hope you like it. Kenzo.

Zak's brow furrowed as he placed the paper on the table and held onto the top of the wooden item. Slowly, he inched it out of the cardboard, revealing a heavy, bubble-wrapped item. By the weight of it and remembering Kenzo's written words, Zak assumed it was wooden. When he unwrapped the protective layer, he revealed a large figure—or rather, two figures. Roughly twelve inches in height, the larger figure was shaped like a man and was carrying a small child in his arms, whose head was on the man's shoulder. The positions of the figures were so reminiscent of the way he carried Dane that tears pricked at his eyes.

Sliding his hands along the rosewood, he felt no roughness, only a sleek, smooth, glass-like finish. He stared at the gift, his emotions rioting inside him. He rubbed a hand over his scruff, unable to form a coherent thought as he remembered the words he'd thrown at Kenzo earlier that day.

"It looks like you and Dane," Noah remarked.

"I told him to leave me alone," Zak whispered. "Why would he…?"

"When?"

"Today. He came by earlier and apologised for leaving the party early the other week. I was angry and lashed out." Zak placed the figures on the table and rested his forehead in his hands. "Have I got it wrong? Or is this another way to make me believe the lie?"

Noah said nothing but rested his hand on Zak's shoulder. "Why don't you go for a shower? I'll keep Dane amused for a little while, and when Dane's asleep, we can talk it through. I have nowhere to be tonight."

Zak nodded numbly and, pressing a kiss to Dane's head, headed upstairs. His movements were mechanical, muscle memory from having done the same actions many times before, but once he stood underneath the hot spray, he began to tremble and rested against the cold tiles, making sure to lock his knees to stop himself from falling. Tears overflowed. He had no idea what they were for or why, but he couldn't stop them.

As they began to slow, he stood upright again and washed his hair, removing the wood shavings and dust particles that had undoubtedly covered him throughout the day. Once he was clean, he dried off and threw on some joggers and a t-shirt before walking barefoot, enjoying the soft fibres of the carpet in the hallway and the slight chill of the wooden floor once he reached the downstairs.

He found them both on the floor in the living room: Noah on his stomach building a tower of wooden bricks, and Dane knocking them over with enthusiastic giggling. Zak couldn't help except grin, the little cheeky laughter always brightening his day.

Zak joined them on the floor for a short time. They had half an hour or so until it would be the start of Dane's bedtime routine. At one point, Dane clambered onto Noah's back and bounced up and down. By the expression on Noah's face, he wished he hadn't eaten so much food. Saving his brother, Zak grabbed Dane and tickled him, earning those infectious giggles.

Tired but content, Zak lifted Dane from the floor and threw him into the air, catching him again. "Right, mister. It's time for bath and bed." The musical laughter surrounded them again.

Once he was bathed, changed and sat on Zak's knee, Dane drank milk through his sippy cup while Zak read a story, his little eyes already blinking sleepily. Zak carried the tired boy to his cot, laying him down and covering him with his small blue blanket. He left a small kiss on his forehead and crept out of the room, closing the door tightly behind him. Detouring to his room to fetch the monitor first, Zak went downstairs and found Noah flicking through the channels with a bottle of water in his hand. A second bottle was waiting on the side table for him, he presumed.

Picking it up, the cold of the condensation coating his hand, he took a long gulp and sat heavily on the opposite end of the sofa to Noah.

Lifting the water in cheers, he said, "Thanks for today."

"You know it's no problem. I have no set time for when I need to work. I can work around everyone else."

"Yeah, but you shouldn't have to."

"But I want to. Anyway, how else would I see my nephew?" Noah grinned at him.

Zak switched the bottle to his opposite hand and flicked his fingers towards Noah, sending water droplets of condensation through the air.

"Oi!"

Zak chuckled before sobering when he saw a new addition to the fireplace mantelpiece. He stared at the wooden figures.

"I saw the note that came with it," Noah said quietly. "It was nice of him."

Zak bobbed his head, his gaze transfixed by the gift. His feelings were all over the place, and he couldn't seem to grasp any particular one to hold onto.

"What happened earlier?"

Noah's voice brought him back from the edge of insanity, and Zak inhaled and blew out a long heavy breath. "I thought I knew the truth, and that was all that mattered to me."

"Tunnel vision." Zak saw Noah shaking his head from the corner of his eye. "You have a tendency to see black and white when there are many shades of grey."

"Some things *are* black and white."

"But not everything. What happened?" Noah repeated.

Zak rambled through Kenzo's visit and his own words, although he couldn't remember everything he'd thrown at the man. When he finished, he placed his feet flat on the floor and rested his forearms on his knees, staring at the floor.

"I think you're wrong," Noah said quietly.

Zak scoffed, "About what?"

"Miki being his partner. Doesn't sound that way to me. If anything, it sounds like maybe he's looking after him. If they were on the same team, they're going to be close, but I'd be surprised if Miki would stand by and knowingly allow Kenzo to cheat on him if they were together. I don't know Miki, mind, but you know, from what you've said."

He felt the sofa move, and Noah leaned their shoulders together, Zak squeezing his eyes shut at the familiar, comforting action.

"You are not Mum, Zak. You're too careful with Dane to allow him to go through what she put you through."

"Me through? You went through it, too!" Zak stood, flinging his arms wide. "I don't know why you keep pretending it didn't affect you as well."

Noah shrugged, gazing at the empty bottle in his hand. "I'm not pretending, Zak. I'm fed up with using so much energy to fight with her. Nothing will change what happened, but we're stronger. That's why *you* fight so hard. Me? I want an easy life."

"Life is far from easy."

"Ain't that the truth."

CHAPTER FOURTEEN

KENZO

"What's up, kid? You're looking all melancholy over there."

Kenzo glanced over at Jack with a small smile. "I'm good. A little tired today, I suppose."

"You can't bullshit a bullshitter, kid."

He rubbed his face, feeling and hearing the scratch of his scruff from not having shaved for several days. Every loud noise or bright light sent spears of pain through to his already pounding head. Slumping further down in the armchair he was currently inhabiting, he blew out a breath.

"Miki's not in a good place, but we're managing."

"Seems like it." The sarcasm in those words was difficult to miss.

Resting his chin on his fist, Kenzo studied the older man. "Fuck it," he mumbled. "He's not good at all, and things seem to be getting worse. I'm scared to leave him alone too long, and a few weeks ago, he went AWOL. It took me and Drake two hours to find him."

"Scary stuff."

"I just can't…" He shook his head, wincing when the spikes pierced harder.

"You need to step back, Kenzo. Let someone else deal with it for a while. You can't take all of this on your shoulders alone. You wouldn't have done that as a team, and you shouldn't do it now."

"But teammates help each other. That's what we've been taught."

"And you are helping him, but sometimes you need to bring in a specialist from another team to get the job done right."

He stared at the man, noticing the lines on his face seemed to have deepened without Kenzo realising. The words Jack had spoken—in the language Kenzo understood—made him see what he'd done was hinder Miki instead of help. By protecting him from others, he'd ensconced Miki in the apartment like a dirty little secret, not understanding it was taking its toll on Miki's mental and emotional health.

"Fuck," Kenzo whispered. "I need to find someone else to talk to him. I don't think his current therapist is helping at all, although it seemed to in the beginning."

"Why not David? He's managed to help Mason a little in the few weeks he's been here. Not a huge amount, but with how much that man is carrying, it will take longer than that to sort through it all."

"That might be a good idea. I wonder if he makes house calls."

"No time like the present to ask. I know he's in the office."

Kenzo sat upright, dropping his feet with a clunk to the tiled floor, and winced when the brain diggers went back to work. "Thanks, Jack. I'll see what he says and let you know." He rested his hand on the man's shoulder. "And you, take it easy. I've heard rumours you're chasing skirts in here. No wonder you're looking a little tired." Kenzo winked and quirked the corner of his mouth as he stood.

"I'll never tell," Jack crooned.

Jack's laughter followed him down the corridor, his footsteps echoing in the empty space. When Kenzo reached the office that all of the therapists used, he knocked, waited for the okay to enter and stepped inside.

David Pick appeared to be around the same age and build as him but had more hair. He wore black, thick-rimmed glasses through which hazel eyes shone, the crow's feet making him seem kind and gentle despite his size.

"Mr Langley, to what do I owe the pleasure?" The man rose from his chair and held out his hand.

"Kenzo, please." After David nodded in agreement, he carried on, "Do you make house calls?"

David raised his eyebrows and nodded. "I do for some patients. Usually, those who are house-bound for some reason or other."

"Is there any way you would be able to help me out by visiting my roommate? Long story short, he's suffering from PTSD, and although he has a therapist, I don't see any improvement. If anything, he's getting worse. I've...made mistakes with him that I need to rectify, and I can't see any other option."

"Normally, I would have to speak with the patient's current therapist, but if you're saying they're not doing what they're supposed to do, I can avoid doing that." He tilted his head. "Unfortunately, the one thing I can't do is speak to someone without their permission."

Kenzo's heart raced as his hopes came crashing down. "Can't you come around and see if he'll agree? Do you have to have his permission over the phone before you meet him?" He was clutching at straws, but he needed this to happen.

David tapped a pen Kenzo hadn't seen him holding against his other hand as he visibly pondered Kenzo's questions. Kenzo held his breath.

"It's a very thin loophole, Kenzo, but I might be able to get away with it." He turned to his desk, flicking open a small spiral-bound diary. "I can fit you in tomorrow at eleven."

"Perfect. Thank you so much."

"I would suggest making sure you have one or two other people around at the same time, in case he disagrees, and it sets something off."

"I'll call Drake. That's Miki's...partner? Lover?" Kenzo huffed a laugh. "I'm not sure if they've labelled it yet."

"Good." David sighed. "This might not work, Kenzo, but I'll help as much as I can, even if it doesn't."

"I appreciate it. I really do. I don't know what else to try."

David cupped his shoulder. "You need to take care of yourself, too. Remember that."

"I know. And I will as soon as I help Miki."

He stayed and gave David all the information he needed to find them in the morning, then strode back down the corridor. He popped his head into the Hub but couldn't see Jack or anyone else who needed him. Signing out at reception and waving goodbye to Sarah, he left and headed to his car.

The first place he needed to stop was the gym to see if Drake was there. Kenzo had a lot of explaining to do.

Kenzo was bricking it. The phrase had never been so true to form as it was at that moment. Miki had no idea what was going to happen in…he checked his watch… fifteen minutes, busy as Miki was with his work in his office. Kenzo knew, and he was pacing a hole in the carpet by the front door. Drake should arrive at any time.

His stomach rolled as he thought about Miki's reaction. He'd moved a few things out of reach in case Miki raged and threw punches, but he thought the main thing would be words that were thrown, not objects.

The quiet knock at the door made him jump even though he'd been expecting it. Checking over his shoulder to make sure Miki didn't come out, he opened it and let Drake slip in.

"How is he?" Drake murmured.

When Kenzo had finally come completely clean about the situation the day before, Drake had screamed at him so much, the receptionist had come back from the front of the gym to tell them to keep it down or leave despite having no seniority over Drake. Drake, it seemed, didn't care about the tone and strode out of the building, shouting for Kenzo to follow. They'd gone to Drake's house in Drake's car where they'd discussed it like the stereotypical military man was seen to—with alcohol and yelling.

Kenzo had apologised several times, and Drake eventually waved them away. They both knew Kenzo had been in the wrong, even if he was doing what Miki had requested, but he was trying to fix it. Explaining the plan hadn't been easy either, especially with how Drake felt about Miki, which Kenzo was surprised to find out was a lot. Drake had flushed when he admitted he was in love with Miki and had been for years.

Drake's initial response was to disagree with him and tell him it wasn't fair to spring it on Miki, but once Kenzo explained his motives, Drake eventually came around.

"He's in fine form today. I even heard him whistling."

"Won't be doing that for much longer," Drake mumbled, walking over to the sofa and dropping onto it, the creak of the leather against his clothes loud in the quiet. He rested his head against the back, staring at the ceiling. "I have a bad feeling about this."

"At the end of the day, if Miki is adamant he doesn't want this, we'll listen. We can't make him do anything."

"Agreed."

Kenzo returned to pacing, going through all the possible scenarios like he had done when he was the leader of their team. He cracked his knuckles as the time ticked closer to eleven. Sweat dripped down his spine, and his mouth was as dry as a desert.

Another knock sounded, and Kenzo's breath stuttered before he swallowed and opened the door. David stood there with a grim expression on his face, but he nodded as he entered.

"Are we ready to try this?" David asked, placing his briefcase by the front door.

"Yep," Kenzo answered hoarsely.

"Try what?"

Kenzo's eyes widened when he spun around and saw Miki standing at the entrance to the living area. He knew Miki needed to be here, but he truly expected to have to go and fetch him, giving himself a little more time to work up to it. Instead, here he was, right in front of him.

Kenzo cleared his throat. "Um...I brought David here to talk to you if you're up for it?" He inwardly slapped himself for giving Miki a choice, but he knew that was what David needed to see.

"What?" Miki's voice had lowered, his eyebrows pinching together while he glanced around the room. "Drake? Kenzo? What's going on?"

Kenzo sighed, refusing to let anyone else take the blame for the situation. "You need more help than what I can give you, Miki. I can't..." His voice broke, and he swallowed against the lump in his throat. "I can't do this alone anymore. Your therapist isn't helping, and I asked David to come and speak to you. He's a therapist at the Veteran Centre."

"No! You promised me, Kenzo! You told me we'd do

this together. That we wouldn't need anyone else to know." Miki gripped at his hair and sank into a crouch.

"Miki, nobody outside of these walls will know what goes on today or any other day. The ball's in your court now. You can refuse to get help. That's your prerogative, but I hope you'll give me a chance." David took a step closer, the carpet muffling his advance.

"A chance to do what? Tear me apart? Rip out my insides? It's the only way these nightmares will go." Miki slapped at the wall beside him and stood.

"That's not true, Miki. We can work together and find the best solution for you. I work in a different way than most therapists. I can try to help you, but you need to meet me halfway."

"Why should I?"

"Miki, please." Drake's voice broke, and Kenzo glanced at him, seeing tears trailing down his cheeks. "I don't want you to suffer alone. I want to help you, too. Please, Miki. Please get help. I can't do this without you."

Kenzo had never seen Drake so open, so vulnerable, so emotional. It took a brave man to throw it all out there and hope the other person caught the rope.

Zak.

After they got through this situation, he needed to do the same with Zak. He needed to take a leap of faith and hope Zak caught him.

"Drake, don't—" Miki cut off with a cry of pure emotional upheaval.

Kenzo stood tall. "As your best friend and partner in crime," he added with a hint of a smile, "I think you need this as much as we do. Try. Please, Miki. Even if it's one session. See what you can do with it. Come back to us."

Miki burst into tears, and Drake stumbled over to him, wrapping him in his arms and taking them to the ground with a thump.

No one said a thing until Miki lifted his tear-stained face from Drake's neck. "Okay," he croaked.

The relief was palpable and almost had Kenzo's knees buckling. "Thank you." A weight lifted from his shoulders, and he trudged over the armchair, sinking into it with a sigh. His head dropped into his trembling hands, and his breathing was ragged. Without caring who saw, he let the tears track down his cheeks—one less ball for him to try and keep up in the air for the moment.

"Right. Where's the coffee? I think we all need some," David said, puttering into the kitchen.

Several hours later, despite being exhausted, Kenzo couldn't help but concentrate on the muted voices of Drake and Miki as he stared at the dark ceiling from his bed. He couldn't hear what they were saying, but he could hear the tone, and both appeared calm and quiet, which was more than Kenzo could've asked for after springing this on Miki as he had.

Kenzo deserved more than the forgiving Miki had given him, at least as far as he was concerned. He shouldn't be forgiven for pushing Miki into something he hadn't wanted to do, even if it was the best thing for him. Hopefully, he'd be able to forgive himself for letting Miki down. Eventually.

The music playing through his earbuds masked any noise from the apartment. As he lay on his bed, arms behind his head, Kenzo tried not to move around too much, not wanting to alert the others to the fact he was in the apartment at all. After the fiasco from six days ago, he'd been doing everything possible to avoid Miki and Drake, and David, who was becoming a regular visitor since Miki had agreed to see him.

He closed his eyes against a new wave of tears that had been his constant companion. It was the worst feeling in the world to see how he'd let down his team-mates, his friends. Nothing could make up for what he'd done.

Sleep was never far away, but it was also never for

long. Dark circles under his eyes were reflected back at him every time he stared in the mirror, and he knew he looked exhausted. His eyes were constantly gritty and dry, and the lump in his throat didn't want to move.

Jack had called him out when he'd visited the Veteran Centre the previous day, saying he looked worse than he had the day they'd spoken about the potential intervention. Kenzo laughed it off and changed the subject. The Veteran Centre, the gym and home had been the only places he'd been, always at times he knew the others would be busy.

His phone beeped, and he reluctantly lifted a hand to swipe it from the bedside table where it was plugged in. Rolling to his side when he saw the message was from Zak, he hesitated, wasting time by tucking the duvet in around him before pressing to open it.

It's Dane's birthday party today at 1pm if you would like to come and join us and some friends. It's at my house. Zak.

After almost two weeks of no contact, he hadn't thought Zak would reach out, let alone ask him to such a personal event. He frowned, not knowing how to respond. He wanted to see Zak, and if he was honest, he wanted to see Dane, too—the kid was more than cute—but Kenzo didn't know if it was the right course of action. His instincts were numbed, and he was unsure for probably the hundredth time that week.

But if he could spend a fraction of time in the company of people who were happy and loved and wanted, it might bring him out of his funk.

Thank you for the invite. If you're sure, I'd love to come.

He held the phone in both hands, watching the screen, waiting for words to show up again. Every time the screen went dark because of inactivity, he lit it up again. After seven minutes exactly—he'd been watching the clock as well—a new message popped up.

I wouldn't have asked if I wasn't sure. See you later.

He blew out a harsh breath as he read the words, tears overflowing once again. Burying his head in his pillow, he let the fabric soak them up while he tried to calm down. When he had, he replaced the phone on the table and rolled over to his opposite side. His eyes were no doubt red and swollen now as well as gritty, but a shower should help a little. He'd do that and spruce himself up enough to not scare anyone away; he had five hours before he had to be there.

When he finally turned up at Zak's house purposefully late at ten past one, he heard the music and laughter before he turned his engine off. There was a large arrow taped to the front door with the words 'Party around the back' on it.

Picking up the gift from the passenger seat, he climbed out of his car and headed around the side of the house, the same steps he'd taken when he'd come to bring Zak his present and ended up on the end of a volley of anger instead. He hoped Zak liked the present he'd left, but there was no guarantee he hadn't thrown the thing away.

The back garden had a small dinosaur bouncy castle and an inflatable obstacle course, which Kenzo assumed was for the numerous adults milling around. The smell of wood and trees could be overwhelming for some people, but for him, it settled something. His shoulders lowered, and his face relaxed marginally.

His gaze scanned over the occupants of the large grassy area until he settled on the one he wanted to see. Zak's focus was already on him, and Kenzo saw him say something to the person he was with, then move towards him. With every step closer, Kenzo's heart pounded, and he had to lick his dry lips.

"Hey. I'm glad you could come." Zak's voice was low, but Kenzo could hear the truth in them despite the hesitation.

Kenzo gave a small smile. "Where's the birthday boy?" He shook the wrapped box he still held.

Zak chuckled. "The birthday boy has already had too much cake and is dozing in his bed in the shade over there." He pointed to the fenced part of the garden where Kenzo could see the edge of what he assumed was a cot.

"I don't blame him. It's surprisingly sunny today. I don't believe a word of the 'April's showers bring May's flowers' phrase on days like this." Kenzo was babbling, but he couldn't help himself. He wanted to prolong their conversation as much as possible.

Zak smiled, then sobered. "Thank you for my gift," he said. "It's amazing."

Kenzo blinked and swallowed hard against the emotion welling up. Everything he was feeling was right at the surface, and he struggled as he had never struggled before with keeping them hidden. "You're welcome. I'm glad you liked it."

"Come on. Let's get you a drink."

Zak whirled and headed for a table near the back of the house where several ice boxes full of beer and soft drinks as well as all the items needed for hot drinks were sat.

Kenzo placed the gift on a separate table housing other presents and grabbed a soft drink. "It's a fantastic space you have here."

"Yeah. We're lucky. I found the place at a time when the housing prices had lowered around this area. Not many people wanted the work of looking after such a large piece of land, but it suited my needs perfectly, and it was difficult to turn it down."

"Are there boundaries around the outskirts, or is it open for anyone?" Kenzo squinted to look in the distance at the large trees, having no idea what type they were, but they were too far away to see if there were any fences behind them.

"Yes. Wooden fences are surrounding the whole property. It's only the front that is completely open, although it might change soon." Kenzo raised his eyebrows in question. "As Dane gets older, he's going to want to be out and about more. I need to make sure he'll be safe, so I will be enclosing the front garden and blocking access to the back soon. I need to check out the legal aspects as this is a conservation area."

"Oh, I didn't know that."

"Luckily, I knew that when I bought the house, and it wasn't a surprise. It makes things a little trickier when I want to change things."

"I can imagine. Having to jump through hoops all the time must be a pain."

"Sometimes, but it's worth it. I do, after all, work with wood." Zak chuckled. "I think when I first bought the house, the council was worried I was going to chop the trees down when they found out what I did as a job."

Kenzo snorted. "I bet they panicked."

"I'm sure they did. They didn't expect me to love living trees as much as the wood I work on." Zak held up his hand to someone. "I have to go talk to someone. Will you be okay?"

No. "Yeah, I'll be fine."

"Great. Help yourself to food and drink. You know some of the people here. Don't be afraid to approach them. They don't bite. At least not while there is still alcohol flowing." Zak winked and jogged over to a woman with long black hair tied in a large plait.

Kenzo glanced around and saw some chairs dotted around the place. Moving over to one, he sat, stretching his legs out in front of him and clicked open his can. As the fizzy liquid soothed his parched throat, he studied the people around him. He remembered names pretty well and saw Sean, Asher, Max and Trent, who he'd been introduced to at the previous party; he recognised the little curly-haired angel bouncing on the castle, Janie; and he received a nod from Zak's brother, Noah. There was one guy he thought he recognised, but for the life of him couldn't figure out from where.

Although Zak had said he could approach them, Kenzo didn't feel right doing so; therefore, he stayed in his seat, watching the interactions, seeing happy smiling faces and hearing laughter and conversation.

When the memories of the mess he'd made of everyone's lives slid to the forefront of his mind, he rubbed at his chin as nausea battled within him. How could he think about trying for more with Zak when he ruined everyone in his life: Miki, Drake, Pete, Miranda, Robin, and undoubtedly the other teammates who he'd not spoken to for a while.

The scent of the trees was no longer comforting but a reminder of what he couldn't have. Breathing deeply to hold back the tears, he stood, dropping his half-empty drink into one of the bins, and weaved his way back towards the front of the house and his car, making his escape.

As the tears dripped down his face once more, he berated himself for believing he could be good for someone.

CHAPTER FIFTEEN

ZAK

"Kenzo!" Zak called after the man's retreating figure. He had no idea where he was going.

"Zak." Sean jogged up to him. "Go after him."

"I can't. It's Dane's party." Zak frowned as Kenzo disappeared around the front of the house.

"We can keep an eye on Dane and the guests, though they are more than capable of looking after themselves," Asher added.

"But—"

"He looked devastated, Zak. Something's going on there. You need to go after him."

"But—"

"I know you care about him despite not wanting to. Go!" Sean urged, peeling Zak's drink from his hand.

Zak didn't waste another minute. Running towards

the front, he saw Kenzo reversing, ready to leave. "Fuck!" He stumbled up the steps to the house, opening the front door to grab his car keys from the table inside, and slammed the door shut again, wincing when the loud noise reverberated through the whole house.

He ran to his car, climbing in and driving off. There was only one exit from where he lived, and he hoped he caught up with Kenzo by then. He would be able to follow him to wherever he stopped from there.

Gripping the steering wheel tightly, he tapped his thumb against the smooth surface as he wondered where Kenzo's final destination was. After around ten minutes, although it seemed like a lot longer, he followed the black car into the Riverside car park. Zak pulled in next to Kenzo and climbed out, slamming his door shut. He wasn't angry as such, but he was a little annoyed Kenzo had left without saying anything. Stalking to Kenzo's driver's door, he whipped it open, startling the man.

"What are you playing at, Kenzo? Were you not going to say goodbye?"

He watched Kenzo curl in on himself, and a tear drop down his cheek. Zak crouched beside him. "Tell me what's wrong?" he whispered. "You're not the bubbly, confident person I first met. What happened?"

Kenzo exhaled. "Can we take a walk?"

"Sure." He stood and stepped out of the way to allow Kenzo to get out, and they both locked their cars. Zak waited for Kenzo to lead the way, and they walked in silence for a while, under a bridge with the noise of traffic bustling overhead.

They crossed to the path that ran alongside the River Cam and, with their hands deep in their pockets, continued on. The slight breeze blowing from across the water brought the chill towards them, but he didn't acknowledge it because the sun was warm on his face. He removed the band from his hair, then pulled it into a ponytail and tied it again tighter to keep it from flying around him.

Zak watched a couple of people power down the water, the rowing blades slicing through it quickly. People on bikes passed them, sometimes alone, sometimes in groups. The gentle lap of the water against the concrete brought back memories of his childhood when his mother brought them down here to run around and leave her in peace. He'd forgotten about it.

Shaking the reminders away, he focused on the man beside him, a mere shadow of the one he'd met. "Kenzo?" he whispered.

Kenzo cleared his throat. "Miki suffers from PTSD. He has since…we came here. Although he does speak to a therapist twice a week, I've been managing his episodes when they crop up. Sometimes, it lasts a few hours. More often than not, it's days."

Zak closed his eyes as the meaning sank in. "Those days I didn't see you, you were helping Miki."

Kenzo nodded slowly. "Unfortunately, things have been getting steadily worse, and while I thought I was doing the right thing—what Miki wanted, keeping things quiet—I realised Miki needed more than I could do."

"You're only one person, Kenzo."

He sighed and stared out towards the river, their steps slow but even. "Someone said I should get another therapist to speak with Miki, but I knew if I suggested it, he'd baulk at the idea and lock himself away, even from me this time. So, I had someone turn up at the apartment. Drake was there for support as well. But—" His voice broke, and more tears escaped.

Zak knew he couldn't touch Kenzo, not when the man was so emotionally fragile, but he wanted nothing more.

"Miki broke down. I've never seen him like that. It was completely different from the PTSD episodes. I should've done it from the beginning, instead of listening to him. Nothing is more important than him feeling better."

"You're just as important."

"When Miki looked at me…the hurt…the betrayal I saw on his face, it cut me like nothing else."

"What happened since?"

"Miki's been seeing the therapist for the past week,

and I've stayed away. I've let so many people down..." He shook his head.

"You've not let him down! You were trying to do the best you could to keep true to his wishes. But his wishes weren't helping him; they were making things worse. You are a good friend to push for him to do something else." Zak stopped them, chancing a hand on Kenzo's biceps as he turned him to face him. "You did the right thing."

Kenzo wouldn't look at him. "Then why does it feel like I've lost everyone?" He walked off, continuing down the path, and Zak let his hand drop back to his side. He stared at the water rippling and causing the moored boats to bob up and down. An idea popped into his head, and as much as he hated the idea of bearing his soul, he jogged to catch up.

When he was once again at Kenzo's side, Zak began, "I was nine and Noah was four when our parents fought over custody of us. When nothing could be agreed upon without a court decision, they suggested splitting us up: Noah would go with Mum, and I would go with Dad. Luckily, Social Services got involved as well as the courts and decreed it a bad idea." He had been so young, but he still remembered the relief that went through him when he realised Noah would be staying with him. "Courts lean towards the mother when it comes to custody arrangements, and we ended up staying with Mum."

Zak's heart pounded painfully, and he rubbed the back of his neck. "Life carried on as normal for a short time before Mum brought home her boyfriend. Gary was a nice guy. Huh, I can't believe I remembered his name. He helped us with our homework and chores; he talked *to* us instead of down to us. But after a few months, he left and never came back. Within days, a new man had replaced him. Over the years, I lost count of how many men were apparently 'the one.'"

This part was the hardest to admit—to anyone, not just Kenzo. "I had my heart broken over and over again during those years. The joy of someone taking an interest in us before the disappointment of when they left again without any warning. I began to hate Mum for dangling the possibility of a real family in front of us. It took years for me to realise that love is fleeting. It's easy to say the words, but to mean them…it's a whole other ballpark."

"What about Dane?" Kenzo asked. "You love him."

Zak smiled. "Yeah, I do. He's everything to me. It's a different kind of love with Dane. I know I will never put Dane through what I went through. It was why I stayed with Ashley when we found out she was pregnant. We'd agreed not to have kids originally, but we both refused to think about termination when we found out. I probably would've divorced Ashley sooner had it not been for Dane. I was trying to give him a solid foundation." He snorted. "Look how that worked out."

"He's loved, Zak. He couldn't ask for more."

"Oh, I know. It's also the reason I finally went through with the divorce and custody case. Dane is still young; I'm hoping the issues will be forgotten by the time he grows up. This is the time to make sure he has stability and security, instead of the wishy-washy life I had."

They strolled in silence for a moment, only the ducks making their presence known. Zak was overcome by how much he'd shared, but he still needed to explain. He blew out a breath.

"The reason I shared this is because I've been let down my whole life. I've learned not to rely on anything other than myself. I know what it feels like to be on the receiving end." He stopped, turning to face Kenzo again. "You have not let your friends down. If you did, they wouldn't still be around, waiting for you to go back to them."

"They're not—"

"Have they moved away? Have they barged in on you screaming and shouting, telling you to get lost?" Zak paused. "Then they're giving you time to grieve. They're giving you time to realise you don't need to be everything for everyone. You need to be *you*."

The keening sound that came from Kenzo broke Zak's heart, and he steered him towards a nearby bench. Once they were sitting, he wrapped his arms around the giant of a man and held him as he broke. Zak's eyes watered at the pain he could feel and hear from Kenzo. When he'd first met the guy, he'd thought Kenzo was so confident, so sure, so solid, but he was as vulnerable as everyone else.

Zak's own words reverberated through his mind. He'd spoken from his heart and acknowledged some things he'd never realised, but he filed them away to think about later.

When Kenzo pulled away some time later, the sun had gone behind some clouds, and it was becoming colder. Zak stood, holding out his hand. "Come on. I hear there's a party going on."

Kenzo wanted to go home instead of back to the party, but Zak persuaded him to come, citing the need for relaxation before facing his friends. He agreed, eventually, and Zak led the way home. As they pulled into his driveaway, Zak slammed on his brakes and exited the car as fast as he could.

"Ashley!"

"Ah, the prodigy daddy returns."

"What do you want?"

"What I want is to see my son. These assholes here won't let me past." She stood with her hands on her hips, chewing gum noisily.

Zak glanced past her to see Max, Trent, Ethan, Eric, Luke, Casey and Samuel all standing, forming a line to prevent her from moving further than the edge of the house. He nodded at them in thanks.

"The reason you're not allowed to see him is that you're drunk, Ashley," Max said.

Zak's emotions were already so close to the surface but to know she tried to get to Dane while she was drunk... That irked him. They had never been drunk when they had to care for Dane. It would always be one or the other who drank, so at least one of them was in the right frame of mind in case of emergencies.

"What the fuck! You haven't bothered to see him in three months! Why do you think you could waltz in now and see him without checking with me first? Your visits need to be supervised, Ashley. You know that."

"The courts said I could see him whenever I wanted."

"With my permission, Ashley, and with someone from Social Services here, too. Jesus!"

"What's the point in trying to get permission, Zak. You know you'd never give it to me."

"Actually, you're wrong. I would've, just not when you're drunk."

"I don't know why they gave him to you. You're always working, and I bet you hardly ever see him anyway. Probably palming him off on that bitch friend of yours."

The words cut Zak, mainly because he knew there was some truth to it. He clenched his fists and jaw.

"What? You gonna use those fists on me? Again?" Ashley smirked.

"Stop with that shit, Ashley. We all know you're full of crap. Zak has never laid a hand on you and never would!" Trent shouted.

She whipped around. "How the fuck would you know? You've all got your heads so far in the clouds with your fuck buddies, the only thing you *can* find is your ass. Stay the fuck out of it."

Trent took a step forward, but Max held him back with a hand on his arm.

Zak needed to calm down a bit. He knew how to deal with her, for the most part, and she was certainly digging herself a hole, especially with Samuel here as a witness. He'd never been more grateful to have invited his lawyer to the party.

"Ashley, go home. Sleep it off. If you want to see Dane, ring me first. If we don't already have plans, it will be fine."

"Why not let me have my son back, Zak? It would make your life easier." Zak felt more than saw Kenzo step up behind him and press a palm to his lower back.

She sneered, "Jesus. It didn't take you long to find someone to warm your bed." She spat out the chewing gum towards his line of friends.

"It would make my life easier, Ashley. You're right. But I would rather have a hard life than let Dane go with an alcoholic, abusive person like you."

"Abusive? What are you going on about?"

"Would you like me to catalogue every scar I have that came from you throwing something at me? Or from where your nails gouged at my skin? You're lucky I left that out from the court case."

He watched with satisfaction as her face paled, and her hands trembled as she linked them together. Raising his eyebrows, he tilted his head. "Well?"

She straightened up, eyes burning fire. "Keep the little shit then. I only wanted him because I'd get more money if I had him with me. I'll find another way."

Zak's heart skipped. He wasn't sure if her last words were a threat to find another way to get Dane or meant as another way to get money. Ashley wobbled on her heels as she made her way across the grass and stones and into her car, peeling out of the driveway as soon as the engine was running. He shouldn't let her drive when he knew she'd been drinking, but he couldn't...

Hands cupped his shoulders, and he trembled, his knees locking to avoid collapsing to the ground. Those same hands turned him around and surrounded him, and Zak let himself sink into Kenzo's embrace, his hands covering his face.

"Fuck. Fuck. Fuck," he whispered.

"Dane's safe, Zak. He was safe inside with Sean, Asher, Tom and Emily. He's safe. No one will get to him."

The low-toned words registered after several minutes, and he became aware of a hand resting against his neck and one rubbing up and down his spine. He inhaled and exhaled before pulling away and gazing up.

"Thank you."

Kenzo smiled. "No problem."

Zak heard squealing and looked over his shoulder, seeing the kids on the bouncy castle with huge grins on their faces. He chuckled. "The innocence of childhood."

"You shouldn't be so hard on yourself, Zak. You were a child, too. Your mother was in the wrong, not you. Children believe what their parents tell them. You knew no better. It wasn't your fault; she let you down."

Zak's tears flowed again as he watched the three children bounce with adults close by in case of accidents. Kenzo rested one arm around his shoulders as they walked slowly towards the fun. The vision of so many people around who loved his son had him halting in his tracks.

"What's wrong?"

Zak stared at the ground, not seeing the grass but following his train of thought. These people here loved

Dane, and they loved *him*. He'd been fighting for years to ensure someone never got too close that they could leave and hurt them, when in fact, he had plenty of friends who could do the same, and he'd never realised it. He hadn't thought about their relationship other than as friends, but he never hesitated to leave Dane in the care of any one of them.

It wasn't just a relationship that could crush his heart. If any one of these people here, and others, left, never to return, he'd be devastated.

Fear and hope warred inside, and he trembled once more.

"Come on. Let's get you sat down before you fall. You need some sugar inside you."

He felt himself being steered towards a chair and dropped into it, the relief of having something cradling him short-lived when the heat of Kenzo left. His hand automatically reached out, clasping at Kenzo's arm. Staring at him through watery eyes, he whispered, "Stay with me."

"Okay." A hand covered his, and Kenzo sat next to him, replacing his arm around Zak's shoulders.

A cup was pushed into his hands, and the heat began thawing the cold. It seemed fear had won for now. He sipped at the hot chocolate, focus still on the ground, watching the blades of grass sway in the gentle breeze. The cup was removed from his hands in time for a small voice to say, "Dada, Dada!"

Zak smiled as the little bundle of joy crashed into his legs and tried to climb up. He slid his hands under Dane's arms and lifted him to his knee. "Hey, buddy. You having fun?"

"Up, dow, up, dow! Dada!" Dane began to babble and drool as he clapped his hands together and pointed. Zak held him close, breathing in his baby smell, and the fear receded, hope taking its place.

He turned to Kenzo. His gaze roamed the handsome features that had starred in more than one dream, and although he had some new stress lines, he looked perfect to Zak. "Thank you, Kenzo."

"For what?" Kenzo's forehead creased.

"For helping me realise I don't have to turn out like my mother."

Kenzo pressed a kiss to Zak's forehead and gathered them both close.

"Enno! Enno!"

Zak raised his eyebrows at Dane. "Say what?"

Dane scrambled from his lap and launched himself across the arms of the seats to land in Kenzo's lap. With Kenzo's help, he stood on his firm thighs and slapped his hands repeatedly on Kenzo's cheeks with a huge smile. "Enno! Enno! Enno!"

Zak laughed through his tears. "Yeah, buddy. That's Kenzo."

Kenzo had looked perplexed until he heard Zak's

words, and then his eyes widened. "Is that what he's saying?"

Nodding, he wiped his cheeks. "Yeah. He picks up words quickly now." He watched as Kenzo's gaze returned to Dane, a small smile gracing his face.

"Hey, Dane. Are you having fun?"

Dane bounced on Kenzo's thighs. "Bow, bow, bow."

"Have you been bouncing, Dane?" Eric said as he came over. "Want to do some more?" He held out his hand.

"Ah, you've been roped into it now, have you, Eric?" Zak chuckled.

"Yeah, Emily and Ethan are worn out."

"Wait! You're Eric Clarke!" Kenzo said loudly and flushed as laughter broke out around them.

Eric grinned. "Yeah."

"Holy sh—moly. I didn't know you were from around here."

"Born and bred."

Kenzo blew out a breath, and Zak couldn't hold back his laughter. "I think you've blown his mind, Eric."

"Sorry. It's not every day you meet a celebrity at a three-year-old's birthday party."

"Let me get this one bouncing, and I'll come and chat to you later on, yeah." Eric winked and let Dane pull him over to the bouncy castle.

"Am I being dropped for a celebrity now?" Zak said,

only half teasing. The fear hadn't completely left, apparently.

Kenzo peered at him under his eyelashes. "Not if you want me."

There was a whole heap of meaning in those few words, but Zak couldn't help but respond.

"I want you."

CHAPTER SIXTEEN

KENZO

The scent of Zak followed Kenzo up the stairs to the apartment, and he surreptitiously sniffed at his jacket, smiling when the smell wafted from it. As he approached the black door, his hands fumbled with the keys, shaking as he tried to insert the key in the lock. When it finally clicked open, he inhaled and prayed for no one to be in the living room while he entered. It would give him a few moments to get his bearings before he spoke to Miki.

His wish was granted, and he shoved the keys into his jeans pocket and shucked his jacket, hanging it on the wooden coat rack by the door. He removed his boots, sliding them to the side, and took a deep breath. Nothing could prepare him for this meeting.

"Miki!" he called, wanting to get it done.

A bump and a curse, and Miki's door flew open and

loud, fast footsteps came towards him before Miki became visible. "What's wrong? Is everything okay?"

Kenzo held out his hands in a calming gesture. "Chill. I just wanted to talk to you, that's all."

"Jesus Christ, Kenzo. You scared the shit outta me."

"Why? I usually call to say I'm back."

Miki raised his eyebrows. "Not for the past week you haven't."

Kenzo opened his mouth to deny the accusation but realised it was true. He'd been avoiding him, and whenever he arrived home, he slunk in with his tail between his legs and went straight to his room like a teenager.

"Sorry."

"What did you want to talk about?" Miki asked, walking into the kitchen area and opening the fridge. As usual, he stared into it for several seconds before deciding what he wanted, leaking cold air into the room. He grabbed two bottles of ale and moved to the cutlery drawer, removing the bottle opener. The clink and pop of the lids being removed and the thunk of them hitting the bin preceded Miki's return to the living room.

"One of them for me?" Kenzo asked.

"Depends."

"On what?"

"On if you're going to stop moping around and start talking to me again." Miki swigged from a bottle.

"I'm talking to you now." Kenzo sounded petulant even to his own ears.

"Not about the things that matter."

Kenzo exhaled. "I came back because I need to clear a few things up. I can't go on like this, and obviously, you aren't comfortable with it either."

Miki narrowed his eyes. "As long as the next words out of your mouth aren't that you are moving out, we're good."

"Definitely not moving out unless you kick me out."

"That's up for debate and dependent on your conversational skills." Miki held out the other bottle, which Kenzo gratefully took, gulping down the cold brew.

"Come on."

They moved to the sofa, both dropping into their usual seats on the sofa, the creak of the leather sounding like a homecoming. Kenzo didn't know where to start with his story, but Zak's voice in his head told him to start near the beginning.

"I'm used to explaining my actions—it was part and parcel of being in the Army after all—but I'm not used to my words having such meaning behind them." He sighed. "I feel like I've let everyone down." He held up his hand when Miki tried to speak. "Let me. Everyone in my life, except for my parents, have leaned on me for something or other. I have no issues with that, but I realised I can't do everything myself."

He took another swig of ale, wiping his hands over his face. "Most of what I've been struggling with was things I'd taken on myself when I didn't necessarily need to."

"Like me," Miki said.

Kenzo glanced across at him. "In some ways. Although with you, I wanted to help. The tennis lessons at the gym I did because I felt I had to; Drake called in a favour, after all." He wet his lips. "I let Pete down by not seeing what was going on. He was my best friend, for god's sake! How could I not see it?"

"That was not your fault, Kenzo! There was no way you could have predicted Pete would do that. Even if he was visibly depressed, you still couldn't have said that was what he'd do."

"It doesn't feel that way. It's the same with his parents. Every time I face them, I'm sure they look at me like I should've known. It's why I hardly see them anymore, though they were a firm fixture in my life when I was younger."

"If they think that, they're wrong. Pete obviously had demons he never told anyone about. It wasn't just you that he didn't speak to."

"I don't want you to hate me," he whispered, staring at the blank TV.

"Fucking hell, Kenzo!" Kenzo startled and turned to see Miki pointing a finger at him. "You are a stupid asshole. How you ever got to be a lieutenant is beyond me. How the fuck could I hate you when you have done everything in your power to help me?"

"I brought David here when you specifically told me not to. How is that helping?"

"Of course, that's helping!" Miki put his bottle on the table and stood, raking his fingers through his hair. "I needed a new therapist, Kenzo, but I was too scared to ask for one. I knew I was pulling you apart every time one of my episodes happened, but I couldn't stop it. I tried, even asking Drake to take some 'shifts,'" he used his fingers as air quotes, "but every time an episode happened, you were either around or I called you automatically. If it's anyone's fault, it's mine. You had every right to find someone to take this burden from you."

"It's not a burden, Miki, but it takes a stronger person than me to be able to deal with it all the time. That sounds bloody awful, but hopefully, you understand what I'm trying to say."

Miki nodded. "I do, and I appreciate it more than you could ever know."

"I don't hear the thump of fists. I'm assuming you're working things out!" Drake called from down the hall.

Kenzo huffed. "I didn't realise he was here."

"Yeah, sorry. He may be a more permanent feature soon." Miki quirked a smile. "If it's all right with you, that is."

"The more, the merrier."

"Can I come out yet?" Drake asked.

"Get your ass in here!" Kenzo shouted.

Miki moved to Kenzo, resting a hand on his shoulder. "You did the right thing with me. I'm sorry for everything I put you through."

"How about we're both sorry and be done with it?"

"Deal."

They embraced tightly, then laughed and cursed loudly when Drake wrapped his arms around them both, declaring it a "Family hug!"

They decided to do a movie night, and while Drake and Miki were bickering over which movie it was going to be, Kenzo pulled out his phone. He knew Zak would be waiting to hear what happened, and he took a minute to message him.

All's good. Thank you for everything today. It means the world to me. x

He waited in a similar holding position as he had that morning when Zak had sent the message inviting him to Dane's party. Within seconds, a message came back.

I'm so glad it worked out. I knew it would. Speak to you tomorrow. x

Kenzo didn't reply. He knew if he did, he'd end up

texting for hours with him. There was so much about Zak he wanted to find out, but he had time. They'd arranged for him to visit Zak's workshop the following day. Zak wanted to give him a tour of the small garage space and introduce him to Colton. He couldn't wait.

Miki had lasted all of fifteen minutes before he'd asked why Kenzo was smiling and who he had texted. When he'd explained about Zak, Miki had literally squealed—Kenzo had never heard such a sound from the guy before. After that, he'd had to message Zak again because Miki had insisted on inviting Zak over the following weekend to get to know him. Zak had agreed, and it was now the night he was coming over to watch a movie and eat takeaway—or in other words, be grilled and grill in return.

As the time of Zak's arrival drew nearer, Kenzo couldn't sit still. He paced the floor, wiping his sweaty palms on his trousers, grumbling when Miki told him he had sweat patches on them, when in fact, he didn't. He wanted the night to go well, but he was scared Zak wouldn't like his friends or vice versa.

A knock drew his attention, and he grinned, opening

the door quickly enough to startle Zak on the other side.

"Sorry." Kenzo pulled Zak into his arms, just inside the apartment, and held him tightly, breathing in his unique woody scent.

Zak slid his hands around his back and up and down in a soothing motion. "I'm here."

How Zak realised he was overwhelmed, he had no idea. Forcing himself to pull back, Kenzo cupped Zak's jaw and pressed a kiss to his mouth. "Hello."

"Hey." Zak chuckled.

"Come on in." Kenzo shut the door and linked their fingers together, heading further into the open plan living area where Miki and Drake were waiting. "Zak, this is Miki and, you know, Drake," he said, pointing to each in turn. "Guys, this is Zak."

Zak let go of him and shook hands with the other men. "So, I hear you are the people to talk to for the scoop on this guy." Zak thumbed over his shoulder in Kenzo's direction.

Miki grinned. "Oh, the things we could tell you. Like the time he took a shower in the outside car park—"

"Okay, let's not." Kenzo grabbed Zak and pulled him into his arms, chest to back, resting his chin on his shoulder and pressing a kiss to his jaw. "We thought we'd decide what movie to watch when you got here. That way, these two wouldn't monopolise the TV."

"Hey! You always tell us to pick! No making us look bad in front of the new guy," Drake said in faux anger.

"I'll grab us some beers. Oh, Zak, do you want water instead if you're driving?"

A blush coloured Zak's cheeks, and the other two cackled. "Noah's looking after Dane overnight. That is if you want me to stay?"

Kenzo ignored Miki and Drake and dragged Zak to him once more, kissing the hell out of him. When he pulled back, he growled, "I'd love for you to stay."

He turned away, adjusting himself not so discreetly and headed to the fridge. Four bottles filled his hands, and he inhaled deeply before returning to the living room. Drake had Miki wrapped in his arms on the sofa, and Zak had chosen an armchair. Kenzo narrowed his eyes. It wouldn't do at all. Rounding the sofa, he passed two bottles to Miki and stood in front of Zak.

"Up," he said.

Zak frowned but stood. Kenzo dropped into the armchair, then grabbed Zak's arm, tumbling him down onto his lap. After repositioning a flushed Zak, Kenzo passed him a beer and rested his arm around his waist. The armchairs were big enough that they weren't squashed together or completely unable to move.

"Did you decide on a movie?" he asked, lifting the bottle to his mouth.

Zak squirmed on his lap, eliciting a quiet groan from Kenzo before he froze and settled.

"Well, we all wanted an action film, but none of us could decide which one." Drake rattled off the name of four films, and Kenzo chose from those.

Miki had the remote, so Kenzo didn't need to do anything except enjoy the feel of Zak on his lap.

"If you want to move, you can, but I love you being here," Kenzo mumbled into Zak's ear, a shiver transferring from Zak to him.

"It's fine," he whispered back, resting his head against Kenzo's shoulder.

The movie passed in a blur, and though comments were thrown throughout, Kenzo had no idea what was going on because he was too content with tracking every part of Zak that was pressed against him. He had been half-hard since Zak had said he could stay overnight, though he could ignore it for the moment. Zak and his friends were getting on great, which had alleviated some of the worries he'd had. Now, he had to trust Zak would stick with him.

When the movie ended, Zak's head was resting in the crook of his neck, his legs were draped over his lap, and one hand was gripping his t-shirt. Soft puffs of air were coating his neck in time with Zak's breathing. As much as he didn't want to move them from their cosy position, he wanted Zak in his bed.

Pressing a kiss to Zak's head, he whispered, "Bedtime?"

Zak sat up so fast, he nearly clocked Kenzo on the

chin. "Sorry." He rolled his lips inwards, trying not to laugh, it seemed.

"You will be." Kenzo narrowed his eyes and nudged Zak to stand before following. "Right, we're going to bed. See you tomorrow."

"Don't do anything I wouldn't do!" Drake called.

"It doesn't leave us much!" Kenzo replied with an eye roll and a chuckle from Zak. He rested his hand on Zak's lower back and steered him towards the bedroom. Safely ensconced behind a firmly closed door, he pressed Zak up against it, covering his body with his own before cupping his chin to lift his face. "I'm so glad you're here."

"Me, too."

Their lips met in a gentle nudge before Kenzo licked across the seam of Zak's lips until he opened. Kenzo inhaled deeply through his nose as his tongue invaded Zak's mouth. He didn't care about beard burn, he didn't care about air, he didn't care about anything apart from the taste, feel, scent of Zak.

Zak raked at Kenzo's back as the kiss deepened, and Kenzo pulled at the band holding Zak's hair in place, letting it free to thread his fingers through it and tug. Answering moans showed Zak loved it as much as Kenzo did. Not wanting to leave his mouth yet, Kenzo dropped his hands to Zak's jeans, unbuttoning, then unzipping and pushing them down over his ass cheeks. Kenzo slid his hands around to cup Zak's ass over his briefs, squeezing and rubbing and holding him close enough to rub his hard cock against Kenzo's jeans-covered one.

Tearing his mouth away, Zak groaned loudly, and his head thunked back against the door. Distantly, Kenzo heard laughter and shouting, but he ignored it, concentrating instead on nibbling his way down Zak's exposed neck to his collarbone. He inhaled once more, the woody scent that was pure Zak and reminded him of the tour he'd been on earlier that week. He was sure Zak would never look at his workshop the same way again.

"Fuck, Kenzo," he panted, writhing against the door.

After a brief lick to each of Zak's nipples, Kenzo dropped to his knees with a wince. He'd regret the action later, but he needed to do this.

"Wait!" Zak's words startled him out of his need to get Zak's cock in his mouth. Zak scrambled away from him, and Kenzo worried he'd done something wrong, but when he saw Zak holding his jeans up and rushing to the bed to grab a pillow, Kenzo's heart leapt. He brought it back with a sheepish grin. "I'm not going to say no to you on your knees, but you need to be careful." He dropped the pillow to the floor, and Kenzo, gratefully, lifted his knees onto the softer cushion.

"Thank you." He gazed up at the amazing man before him, knowing his life had changed for the better and hoping it would stay that way.

"It's a selfish thing, really. I *so* want whatever you wish to give me from down there." Zak grinned.

"Well, lean back and enjoy it."

Kenzo winked and refocused on the shaft begging for release from the confines of the briefs. He kissed the tip, licking at the wetness already evident, and nibbled his way down the underside as his fingers hooked into the waistband. When he reached Zak's balls, he lifted his head and pulled the briefs over Zak's cock, revealing the flushed red dick. He slid the briefs down Zak's legs, along with the jeans, and pressed his nose into the crease of his hip and groin, inhaling the musky, woody scent.

Zak helped remove his jeans and briefs, kicking them off somewhere, and Kenzo's hands returned to his skin. He smoothed his hands up Zak's thighs and under his t-shirt, bunching it up and up, all the while licking at the exposed skin.

"You're a fucking tease, Kenzo," Zak growled as he yanked his t-shirt over his head, threw it away and cupped the back of Kenzo's head. "Lick it." He pushed against Kenzo's head and ground his cock against his cheek.

Kenzo moaned, enjoying the bossiness of his partner, and lifted his gaze to Zak's eyes before licking a stripe up the underside of his cock. He watched as Zak's mouth dropped open and his eyes grew heavy, and when Kenzo sucked the tip into his mouth, air audibly rushed from Zak's lungs.

He tongued the slit, chasing every bit of fluid he could find before relaxing his jaw and moving down, maddeningly slow if Zak's curses were any indication. Kenzo wanted Zak to lose his cool. He wanted Zak to fuck his mouth, but he refused to ask him to. Kenzo wanted to see how far he could push Zak before he broke.

Every lick, every suck, every nibble, every blow of air was done carefully, methodically until Zak was a writhing mess against the door, and Kenzo had nail marks on his shoulders and head.

"Fucking hell!"

Kenzo barely had time to gloat to himself before Zak gripped the back of his head and thrust his cock forward. He kept his eyes on Zak's to allow Zak to see he was okay, and when Zak's eyes softened, Kenzo knew he understood. Kenzo relaxed his throat as Zak moved his hips faster, his cock tunnelling in and out. Zak's face was so expressive, the flush high on his cheekbones showing how aroused he was, the way his mouth dropped open further and further the closer he came, his eyes narrowing as his focus also narrowed. It was mesmerising.

"Ah!" Zak pulled away with a grunt and held the base of his dick tightly; Kenzo assumed to stave off his orgasm. "Fuck, fuck, fuck!"

Kenzo stayed on his knees as he regained his breath, his own cock hard as steel and leaking like a tap into his briefs. "Fuck me, Zak," he said hoarsely.

Eyebrows raised, Zak nodded and held out a hand to help Kenzo stand, which he did with a grimace. Even with the pillow, it had a dull ache deep inside, and not the good kind of ache.

"Blow jobs on the bed from now on. No more on your knees," Zak said with a frown, grabbing the pillow from the floor.

"I'm good."

"I know you are, but your knees are not." Zak winked.

For that, Kenzo pushed him off balance, and Zak landed on the bed with a yelp. He chuckled, undressed, then crawled onto the bed, ignoring the twinge in his knee until he lay on his stomach, resting his head on his crossed arms. Zak immediately straddled his thighs and pressed kisses all across Kenzo's back, his hands smoothing along after. Shuffling further down, Zak massage the globes of his ass before taking small nips. Nudging against Kenzo's good leg, Zak repositioned it wider, keeping the second leg between his own.

Kenzo felt Zak pull his cheeks apart and take a tentative lick on his crack. He dropped his face into the covers and groaned when Zak ate at him. He loved rimming and being rimmed, but most of his previous partners had not, so to find someone who appeared to love it as much as he did was great.

"Fuck, yes. Oh!" Kenzo's voice rose as Zak speared his tongue against his entrance, loosening him bit by bit until he was able to slide his tongue inside a little way. "Jesus! Fuck! Enough! Fuck me now."

Zak retreated, and Kenzo wasn't sure if he was pleased or not with that. He heard a drawer and the click of a tube.

"Ready?" was the only warning he got before the cold lube was spread against his ass.

His exhale was choppy and soon turned into more moaning when Zak began preparing him, one finger at a time.

"I think I'm going to fuck you like this. I like the idea of you squirming beneath me as I pound your ass." Zak took a rough bite of Kenzo's ass as his fingers thrust deeper.

With every forward motion, Kenzo's cock rubbed against the covers beneath him, heightening the tingles flowing through his body. "Now! God, please, now!"

The intrusion vanished, and he heard a wrapper, then another click before the pressure at his opening returned. He immediately bore down, wanting Zak inside him as soon as possible. Zak's fingers clenched at Kenzo's hips in time with his inward and outward movements. He pushed in, and his fingers bit into

Kenzo, then pulled out, his fingers relaxed until he was fully seated.

At that point, Zak let go of his hips and covered Kenzo's back with his body, reaching his arms underneath Kenzo's chest to cup his shoulders. He pressed several kisses to his shoulder blades while he paused. Kenzo knew it was because Zak was giving him time to relax into the feeling, and Kenzo appreciated the thought. Pressing a hand against one of Zak's on his shoulder, he cleared his throat. "I'm good to go."

"You're very good," Zak whispered with a kiss.

CHAPTER SEVENTEEN

ZAK

Plastered against Kenzo's back as he was, he could feel Kenzo's heart racing. He needed to be careful of his knee, and this position enabled him to keep the leg straight and for Zak to still be able to move without aggravating or putting pressure on it.

Knowing Kenzo was ready, Zak canted his hips, withdrawing his cock from the heat of his channel, then thrust straight back in. He did this a few times, using his grip on Kenzo's shoulders as a counter to his movements. He felt amazing. When he needed more, he kissed Kenzo's shoulder blades and lifted to his knees, being wary of Kenzo's leg. Gripping Kenzo's hips once more, Zak glided his dick in and out of that glorious ass, watching as it disappeared and reappeared.

Soon, he couldn't take the slow pace any longer—and if Kenzo's curses were any indication, neither could he—he braced himself and slammed inside, the ripples on Kenzo's ass showing how hard he was thrusting.

"Jesus, fuck!" Kenzo voiced Zak's own thoughts, gripping the covers until his knuckles were white and pressing his face into the fabric, muffling his words.

Having been on edge for a while now, Zak could feel the tingling down his spine, indicating he was close. "Kenzo, can you come with me? I'm nearly there."

In response, Kenzo released the cover and slid his hand beneath him. Zak couldn't see what he was doing, but he assumed he'd encircled his cock because a louder groan came from him.

"That's it. Come on."

Zak wet his lips, the heaving of air through his throat having dried him out. Unable to stop his orgasm, he thrust harder, the slap of skin on skin loud in the room, heightening his sense further. "I'm coming! Fuck! Ah!"

The tortured moan from beneath him and the rhythmic clenching of his channel assured Zak Kenzo was coming, even lost in the haze of his own climax as he was. He caught himself on his hands as his release poured into the condom, his forehead resting on Kenzo's sweat-slicked back.

"Fucking hell."

Zak chuckled weakly and, with a trembling hand, gripped the base of the condom and withdrew. He removed it and tied it off before dropping to his ass on the bed. Kenzo hadn't moved at all, and Zak slid a hand to his ass cheek, squeezing gently.

"You okay there?" he asked.

"In heaven," came the muffled response.

Zak snorted and stood on shaking legs, stumbling to the en-suite. He binned the condom, washed his hands —the cool water feeling great—and wet a cloth with warm water. The aftercare portion of sex had always been a favourite of his; he loved being able to care for the person who had shared their body with him. It's something he'd missed since being with Ashley because she'd always hated it and preferred to jump in the shower alone afterwards.

Brushing the thought of his ex from his mind, he returned and cleaned Kenzo up. Then he climbed onto the bed next to him and faced him, placing a hand over Kenzo's between them.

Kenzo's bright whiskey-coloured eyes pierced him when they opened. "Thank you."

Zak knew the words weren't about the sex, and he smiled in return and repeated the words back, his as fraught with dual meaning.

"Sleep now," Kenzo mumbled.

"Yes, but under the covers."

"No move."

Zak chuckled. "Yes, move." He rolled Kenzo to his side with effort, pulled the cover from beneath him and rolled him back, throwing the covers over the top. He wasn't on a pillow, but if he wanted to be, he could scoot himself up the bed. Sliding under the covers himself, he snorted when Kenzo's head slowly appeared above the covers and onto a pillow, then he snuggled in against him and slept.

The sun was shining down on the back garden, a veritable unusual occurrence on a May bank holiday weekend in the UK, but he wouldn't let that stop him from enjoying himself. Zak looked around the expanse of grass, seeing wooden picnic benches filled with friends. His social circle had definitely increased over the last few years. To begin with, there had been him, Sean and Max, then Ethan had joined the group when he started his studies. Add in Ethan's brother and sister on occasion as well as the bartenders and manager of Crush, and it was already increasing without the partners and family members of the group joining, too.

Seeing so many happy, smiling faces made Zak's heart expand further than he thought was possible. Now, throwing in Kenzo, who was currently being pinned by Luke on a mat they'd set up to showcase Luke's new business venture, and his heart felt like it would burst. At that moment, Kenzo looked up, squinting in Zak's direction and grinned.

It was all a big surprise since he'd been determined not to let anyone get too close to him in case they left. He shook his head and chuckled. He'd had no idea how many people had a claim on his heart until they were all gathered together like this. Zak gave a small wave and refocused on the rest of the partygoers.

The barbecue was sizzling away under Trent's and Logan's capable hands, the scent of cooked meat and fried onions blowing on the wind. Asher had brought some children's play tents with him, along with a few more outdoor toys, so the little ones had something to entertain themselves with while the adults caught up with each other.

The whole group had agreed to alternate babysitting duties for the afternoon. Emily, being the organiser she was, had arranged it all, making sure every adult had to spend time in "The Pen" as they were now calling the enclosed back garden. Zak had snorted his drink when Casey had piped up with that name.

Currently, it was Samuel and Tom's turn—Tom and Ginny's ten-week-old son, Joseph, in Tom's arms—and Samuel was pushing Dane on the swing.

Noah's birthday was almost always celebrated around the bank holiday, giving them two excuses to celebrate. Noah was currently wearing a top hat with a purple sash that said "Birthday Boy" on it and had his arm around his girlfriend, Sadie. Zak had been surprised when Noah had told him about Sadie a couple of weeks ago. Apparently, they'd been seeing each other for around six months, but both wanted to focus on each other before being introduced to everyone else. When Noah had mentioned bringing her to the barbecue, Zak had been stunned and a little hurt that Noah hadn't confided in him.

"Yo, Woody!" shouted Ethan from the opposite end of the bench.

Zak rolled his eyes. "You do know that nickname will never stick. It's stupid."

"I'll keep saying it until nobody has any choice but to use it," he sing-songed.

"Whatever. What do you want?" Zak sounded annoyed, but he didn't mind, honestly. Oh, he minded the nickname but not the teasing.

"When's the food going to be ready?"

Zak huffed, "What are you asking me for?"

"It's your house."

"Does it look like he's cooking?" Ginny volleyed, throwing an empty cup in Ethan's direction.

Ethan frowned. "Well, no…"

"Go ask one of those knights," Charlie interrupted, indicating Trent and Logan, who were, apparently, having a sword fight with the metal tongs. Zak laughed.

This was his life. And he loved it.

Kenzo came to sit next to him when the food was

dished out, pressing a kiss to the side of his head before settling Dane into one of the highchairs they had brought out for the kids who needed them. Zak smiled at the care and consideration Kenzo took with his son.

Conversation and laughter continued after all the food had been demolished and the kids had conked out in the shade. He was in no rush to send everyone home, especially as he lay between Kenzo's legs on the grass, sleepy and content.

A phone trilled, and Zak jumped.

"Sorry," Kenzo said with a laugh, pulling his phone from his pocket and answering it, "Hello?" The smile dropped from his face when the person on the other end started talking.

Zak couldn't hear what was being said, but he could hear the murmur of sound, and taking into account Kenzo's now rigid body, it wasn't a welcomed call.

"I can't. Not yet." His nostrils flared, and his jaw clenched. "Not yet, I said. I'll call you." He hung up the phone and shoved it back into his pocket, giving Zak a small smile. "Sorry about that." Kenzo pulled him back into his original position but wrapped his arms around him this time.

"Everything okay?" Zak asked quietly.

"Yeah. Someone not wanting to take no for an answer."

Zak didn't reply, just turned to his side and cuddled up against Kenzo's chest, his hand resting over his heart. He watched the banter and laughter, content to sit quietly, though his mind whirled with questions about the phone call.

When the time came for some of the people to pack up and leave—mainly the ones with kids—Zak regretfully stood and waved them off. As he wandered back to the rear of the house, he saw Kenzo furiously typing on his phone, forehead furrowed. He tried not to let it bother him that Kenzo wasn't opening up about the call, but it was difficult. Hopefully, Kenzo would say something once everyone had left.

The evening wore on, and Eric, who had managed to get back from abroad for a long weekend, had brought a special DVD player projector for outside. They pegged together several sheets and hung it on the side of the house—don't ask him how they managed it—and voila! An outdoor cinema.

"An action movie would be epic outside!" Ethan yelled.

"No, a space one," Josh countered. "Imagine all those stars mixing with the real ones we have tonight."

Zak glanced up from his wooden loveseat, seeing said stars shining brightly in the clear night sky. It was a shame Dane was fast asleep in his arms. He would've loved to see them. Zak inhaled deeply, scenting wood, trees, Dane's baby smell and Kenzo, who was wrapped around them both. He was in heaven.

"Noah should choose. He's the birthday boy," Logan said, dropping into a seat, holding a bottle of water.

That caused a ruckus with multiple people calling for Noah to choose their vote, ending with a shout from Eric declaring all his films off-limits. Noah shouted, "Armageddon!"

Groans and celebratory shouts combined until Eric set the film going, and everyone calmed, settling into their chairs with drinks and partners if they had them. Zak glanced around: Max and Trent, Noah and Sadie, Sean and Asher—Janie had gone home with Ginny and Tom for the evening—Casey and Luke, and Charlie and Josh. Then there was Logan, Samuel, Eric and Ethan, the only single ones left at the party.

He hoped they would find their happiness soon.

Zak's mind was all over the place. His hands were busy hand sanding an intricate design, making sure all the sharp edges were smoothed out, but his mind was not on it. Instead, it was on trying to figure out how to sand down the edges between him and Kenzo. The barbecue had gone well, and everyone had seemed to enjoy it, but ever since then, Kenzo had pulled away.

Zak couldn't understand what he'd done wrong. Maybe this was the beginning of the end already. He sighed, his hands automatically doing their job as his mind whirled.

Their relationship had been good, great even once they'd worked out their issues and Kenzo had sorted things with Miki. The difference this past week was immense. They communicated through texts, usually one or two words from Kenzo's side of the conversation, but Zak hadn't seen him since the previous weekend.

He stood, ripping the hairband out of his hair and scraping his hair back before retying it. His hands were sore from the position he'd had them in for the past however long he'd been working, and he flexed them and wiped his forehead against his arm, closing his eyes and inhaling the woody scent of his livelihood.

Resting his hands against the worktable, he stared vacantly at the pattern. The only thing he could think that had happened was the phone call Kenzo had received whilst at the party. Zak had been close enough to hear Kenzo say he wasn't talking about it and that he'd call them back, but Zak had no idea what it was about. To Zak's shame, he wasn't sure whether he wanted to know if it meant the end of their relationship. After pushing Kenzo away for so long, then finally giving in, Zak was *all* in. It was a shame it seemed like Kenzo wasn't.

"Right! That's it!"

The sharp, loud words and the thump of something being dropped onto a hard surface made Zak jump and whirl around to face Colton, his heart pounding.

"I've had enough, Zak. You have not been in this workshop all week—"

"Yes, I have. Every day!"

"—mentally, and you need to go and sort your shit out with Kenzo. I know it has something to do with him because you've been silent, teary and tired. Relationships do that to you." Colton wandered closer. "If you scrub at this pattern much longer, you will have to redo it because you will have worn the pattern away."

Zak glanced at the design, wincing when he saw Colton was right. In some areas, he might need to do a patch job anyway. He rubbed at his face, the dust particles like exfoliator on his skin as he tried to breathe deeply and not give in to the tears that had been so close to the surface for days.

"Sorry."

"You don't need to be sorry, Zak. You need to go and talk to him."

"He's probably changed his mind about us. He's allowed to do that."

"Yes, he is, but you need to know if that is what he's decided. The only way to find out is to go and see him."

"I'm scared," Zak whispered.

Colton rested both hands on Zak's shoulders and

squeezed. "I know you are. From my experience, being scared is more of a reason to find out the truth. Then you can stop being scared because you know where your future is going. Even if his answer is not what you want to hear, at least you'll know and can change your expectations."

Zak sniffed. "You're pretty wise for a woodworker."

Colton laughed. "I'm going to tell Ioan you think I'm wise. It'll give him a laugh."

"Hey, don't knock yourself. You moved across an ocean to take a chance on love. That's a wise choice as far as I'm concerned."

Colton squeezed his shoulders again and let go, stepping back over to his side of the workshop. "Go on. I'll lock up when I leave."

"Thanks."

Zak spent a few minutes tidying up what needed to be put away safely, and with a final goodbye to Colton, he strode towards the house. A quick shower and change and he was on his way to Kenzo's place.

For the whole journey, he wavered back and forth about whether he was doing the right thing, but Colton's words kept coming back to him: *At least you'll know*. It was true, and if he knew, he could change his dreams. Before he knew it, he was parking near the apartment building and heading up the stairs. He brushed his palms against his trousers as he stood in front of the door, then straightened his posture and knocked, his heart racing at what was to come.

After a minute or two, Miki opened the door and smiled. "Hey, Zak. Come on in. I've not seen you for a while. Work keeping you busy?"

Miki shut the door behind Zak once he'd tentatively stepped through it. "It is a bit busy." He gave a small smile. "Is Kenzo here?"

A slight tightening of Miki's face was all Zak saw before he said, "He's at the gym. He will be back in around," he checked the clock, "ten minutes, probably. He's been gone over an hour and a half. Would you like a drink while you wait?" Miki headed for the kitchen area.

"No, I'm good, thanks."

Zak wrung his hands together and stayed glued to the spot while listening to Miki rummage around in the cupboards. He was trembling and crossed his arms over his body, turning his gaze to the window. When a cup appeared in front of him, he jumped and glanced at Miki.

"You seem like you needed something warm." Miki sipped the steaming brew from his own mug and tilted his head at Zak. "Tell me to mind my own business, but is everything okay?"

Zak sighed, shoulders slumping as he cupped the mug tightly, the heat burning his palms. "I don't know." He shook his head. "Kenzo seems…distracted…distant, and I can't take it anymore. I need to know where we stand."

Miki nodded. "I've noticed he's been distracted, but I don't know why. He's—"

The words stopped as a key in the lock sounded, and Kenzo came walking through, looking wrecked. He paused when he saw Zak, a wince crossing his face, and Zak's heart broke. He had a feeling he knew where their conversation was going to end up. Zak put the mug down on the coffee table and turned to face him.

"We need to talk."

Miki cleared his throat. "I'm going back to work." He pivoted around and rushed down the hallway, and Zak heard the door close behind him.

"Zak…"

"No. Let me talk for a minute." He swallowed hard. "I thought things were going well between us, but obviously, I was wrong. A relationship, as far as I'm aware, doesn't involve one person ignoring the other person without good reason. I don't know if your reasons are good because you won't talk to me. I'm supposed to be someone you lean on when you're struggling, someone you talk to when you need to figure something out, someone you hold onto when you're scared. I've been none of those things, and I don't know where that leaves us."

Kenzo dropped his bag to the floor with a thump

and rubbed his hands across his head. "I don't... It's not..." He heaved a sigh.

"Talk to me, Kenzo. I will help if I can." Zak stepped forward. "Otherwise...I guess my previous beliefs were right, and love never lasts," he whispered.

CHAPTER EIGHTEEN
KENZO

Hearing the disappointment and hurt in Zak's voice was his undoing. Kenzo had thought he was doing the right thing by keeping this from Zak, but he'd hurt him more than he'd ever wanted to. Trying to find the right words was difficult.

"Can we...sit?" He indicated the sofa and was relieved when Zak nodded.

They sat on either end of the sofa, as far away as they could be on the three-seater. Kenzo had his good leg bent so he could face Zak, but his gaze stayed on his fingers as they fidgeted.

"I haven't told you the story of what happened to me. Of why I am retired. I don't know where to start with it. I'm probably going to ramble."

"I've got time."

Kenzo chanced a glance at Zak and saw nothing but

concern on his face. Staring out of the window, he began his story: when he and Pete met, how close their families were, the tennis, the Army, the team. After talking for so long, his voice was hoarse, and Zak jumped up and grabbed a glass of water for him, pressing it into his trembling hands and helping him drink it.

When the glass was empty, Zak placed it on the table and stayed close to him, holding his hands as he finished the story of the explosion and what he remembered of the hospital.

"I was so angry at Pete for not confiding in me, for hiding something so big from me. I was his best friend! He caused so much pain and suffering, but he also suffered himself, and I didn't see it. His closest friend didn't see how much he was hurting, how much he struggled with everyday life. His best friend took the laughter and socialising as meaning he was okay. His childhood friend didn't see *him*." His voice broke, and tears streamed down his face as Zak hauled him into his arms, holding him so tight he could barely breathe.

Kenzo had no concept of time after that, no idea how long they stayed that way. When he finally broke the surface again, he was lying on the sofa, wrapped in Zak's arms, the scent of the man he was in love with soothing him as nothing else had managed to do.

"Sorry," Kenzo whispered.

Zak's arms tightened briefly. "You have nothing to be sorry for, but I want you to realise one thing."

"What's that?"

"You hid as Pete did."

Zak said nothing else, but Kenzo understood. He finally realised how difficult it must have been for Pete to come to him. He hadn't wanted to seem weak in front of the person who had known him for so long. Deep down, Kenzo knew Pete would've asked for help if he realised what the end result might have been. Kenzo had hidden what was happening because he didn't want Zak to see him as fragile and cowardly.

"Pete's parents want to start a charity in his name. That's who called me at the barbecue. His mother, Miranda, has been texting and leaving voicemails all week, wanting to know if they should go ahead with it or if they should stop. They're worried people will think badly of Pete and not support the charity."

"What will the charity be for?" Zak slid his hands up and down Kenzo's back.

"Mental health of Army recruits, past and present."

"Wow. I think it's an amazing idea. Maybe, if you're feeling up to it one day, you can tell the story of Pete and who he was and how he struggled silently. If the story could only get one other person to seek help, it would be worth it."

Kenzo hummed against Zak's chest. He wasn't sure

if he'd be able to do it, but it was something to consider.

He nuzzled his cheek against Zak. "I'm sorry for everything. I should've told you."

"You just did."

The living room was getting dark, and Kenzo finally realised how much time had passed. He sat upright quickly, pausing when his head spun. "Oh, god. What about Dane?"

Zak held out his hands. "Dane's fine. I messaged Noah to get him. He'll stay with him as long as we need him to."

Kenzo dragged Zak into his arms, making him straddle his lap, and wrapped him tightly. "Thank you. I would really like to spend the evening at your house if that's okay with you."

Zak pulled back and smiled. "More than okay with me."

They lay in Zak's bed, Zak's head resting on Kenzo's naked chest, arms encircling each other. After they'd said goodbye to Miki, they drove to Zak's and relieved Noah of babysitting duties. Noah had said he didn't mind staying if they needed him to, but they declined, telling him to rest up because there was another party that weekend.

Once they had settled Dane into bed, Kenzo had opened up further to Zak, explaining about his leg and how it looked. Zak had not realised it had been weighing on Kenzo's mind. Zak had said he'd seen part of it during sex but had not thought anything of it. Whereas Kenzo had been concerned it was ugly and off-putting, Zak had been concerned about whether it hurt him. It was another show of Kenzo putting words into Zak's mouth and not asking him first. Kenzo had let Zak look at his leg fully when they'd gone to bed. Apart from a gentle kiss across the puckered skin, he hadn't appeared put off with it.

"Kenzo?"

He hummed in response.

"Did you have any therapy after the explosion?" Zak asked quietly.

He cleared his throat. "Yeah, I did. There are mandatory sessions which need to be completed after something happens."

"And what about once those sessions were finished?"

Kenzo's muscles involuntarily tensed, and Zak's hand smoothed along the skin of his stomach in a soothing gesture, something Kenzo wasn't sure Zak knew he did.

"No."

He sounded defensive even to his own ears, and he blew out a breath, trying to relax.

"I think it might be helpful. I..." The heat of Zak's exhale flowed over Kenzo's skin, tightening his nubs. "I'm considering it for me, too. I think I need to finally sort my head out about everything that happened with my parents."

Kenzo squeezed Zak's shoulder and sighed. "I think you might be right. About both of us needing it."

He lay awake for several hours after Zak's soft, even breathing indicated he was asleep. As much as he hated talking about himself and baring his soul, he needed to make sense of everything going on in his head. He hadn't realised how much blame he had put on himself for what Pete had done, and though he still believed he should've been able to see it, he knew it wasn't only his fault.

Through the monitor, Dane snuffled loudly, then quietly whimpered. Kenzo waited to see if he'd settle, but when he made the noise again, he decided to go and see if he was okay. He didn't want to wake Zak for no reason.

Sliding out from under Zak's arms, he pulled a t-shirt over his head and tiptoed to Dane's room. The door was kept ajar, and he quietly slunk into the room and over to his cot. Dane was sat up, rubbing at his tear-stained face. Kenzo's heart went out to him. He hadn't heard him crying at all, but maybe he'd been crying in his sleep.

"Hey, little guy. Are you okay?" He rested his arms on the top of the cot, looking down into those big, innocent eyes, and smiled.

"Enno." Dane's voice was thick. "Enno, up." He held out his arms.

Kenzo was unlikely to ever be able to resist the little bundle of joy and reached down, catching him under his arms, and lifted him to his chest. He paced slowly around the room as Dane rested his head against Kenzo's chest, his thumb going into his mouth. The warmth of the child seeped into Kenzo's body, and the scent of baby powder had him closing his eyes, emotional once more.

There was a rocking chair in the room, which Zak sat in to read stories to Dane. Kenzo carefully sat himself down and, using his toes, rocked them gently, his hand resting against Dane's back and one under his bum.

Losing track of time seemed to be a regular occurrence for him at the moment, and his heart jumped when he realised Zak was standing in the doorway, staring at him with a small smile on his face.

"What?" he whispered.

"Nothing." Zak came over to the rocking chair, and Kenzo paused the motion. "Let me put him back into bed. You'll end up with an ache somewhere if you hold him all night."

Reluctantly, Kenzo let Zak take him, missing Dane's heat as soon as he was gone. He watched as Zak cuddled his son close and carefully laid him down, covering him with his blanket. He indicated for them to leave, and Kenzo followed, checking the cot once more before pulling the door slightly closed.

When they were snuggled back up in bed in their previous positions, Zak said, "Thank you for that."

"What?"

"For taking care of my son. It means a lot."

"He's part of you. There's no you without him, and he's as easy to love as you are."

Kenzo froze. He hadn't planned on saying those words, even in the roundabout way he had. Not yet, anyway.

Zak chuckled. "Don't panic. We're just getting started."

The next thing he knew, it was morning, and he was alone in bed. He yawned, stretching his arms wide, and swung his legs over the edge of the bed, grimacing as his bad knee protested. He couldn't believe it was almost ten o'clock. The only time he ever slept late was after one of Miki's episodes, which, when he thought about it, he hadn't seen one of for the past few weeks. He made a mental note to ask Miki about them. It would be great if the therapy was working already, but he knew it was a pipe dream.

He jumped in the shower and dressed, then descended the stairs to the sounds of giggling and fake anger. As he stepped into the living room, he saw Zak pushing some plastic balls into the metal bars of the playpen until they stuck between them and Dane popping them out again with a laugh. Zak grumped about it and repeated the actions. Although Dane was on the inside of the playpen, the gate was open, allowing him to get out whenever he wanted. Zak had made it clear Dane's bitch of a mother, Ashley, had Dane in the playpen far too long each day.

"Enno!" Dane pulled himself to standing and toddled over to him, lifting his arms.

Kenzo laughed and picked him up. "Hey, little guy." He tickled his tummy and turned to Zak. "Good morning."

Zak stood and walked over, pressing a kiss to Kenzo's mouth. "Good morning."

They stood there for a moment, Kenzo holding Dane while his other arm was wrapped around Zak, and he felt like he was home. As emotional as he had been for the past few days or weeks, he cleared his throat, trying to beat back the tears.

Zak must've realised because he pulled away, saying, "Come on, you two. Let's make some breakfast."

"Haven't you had breakfast already?" Kenzo asked. "You didn't need to wait for me."

"Oh, we've had breakfast," Zak said, looking over his shoulder. "There is always room for more, isn't there, Dane?"

Kenzo strapped Dane into his chair as Zak poured a handful of honey hoops onto the tray in front of him. With Dane occupied, Kenzo grabbed Zak and kissed him good morning properly.

"Wow. I need to suggest breakfast every day!" Zak grinned.

Kenzo slapped his ass and headed to the bread bin. "I'm happy with some toast."

Zak slapped his hand away and pushed him to the table. "Go, sit. I'll make you scrambled eggs on toast."

As he sat watching Zak putter around the kitchen, he remembered the first breakfast he'd had there. He'd honestly thought he was going to sneak out, but Zak had surprised Kenzo, and himself it seemed. Since, things had been up and down, but he didn't regret a minute of it.

He fiddled with a coaster and coughed. "I'm going to the Veteran Centre after I've eaten. I think David will be there, so I can arrange a time to speak to him if he has space for me."

"That's great news. Would you like some company?"

Kenzo stared at him, mouth gaping. "You want to come?"

"Yeah. Well, it's a place we've never been before, and it's somewhere that means a lot to you, so, yeah. If you want us to, that is?" Zak hadn't looked at him the whole time he spoke, but if Kenzo kept silent, he knew Zak would glance over his shoulder. Which he did.

"Thank you." Zak smiled. "The guys are going to love Dane."

Once they were all fed and cleaned up, they piled into Zak's car. Kenzo couldn't believe Zak wanted to come with him, and he hoped all the guys would be on their best behaviour. Walking through the entrance, he saw Sarah behind the desk.

"Kenzo! We've not seen you for a while. How are you doing?" She glanced between him and Zak, her eyes softening when she saw Dane, whose face was hiding in Zak's neck.

"I'm all right, thanks. This is Zak, my boyfriend," and didn't he get a kick out of saying that still, "and this is Dane, his son."

"Nice to meet you. Oh, aren't you a cutie?" She dipped her head down to catch Dane's eye, but he wasn't having it. "I'm sure I'll see that gorgeous face soon."

"Is David in today?"

"Yeah. He's just had a session with Mason. He'll be in his office."

"Thanks. Is it okay if I take these two to see the Hub?"

"Go on. You know you don't have to ask." She dropped herself into her chair and chuckled.

He guided them towards the main room, hearing laughter and cursing, wincing at the latter. Grimacing at Zak, he apologised. "You don't have to go and see them if you don't want Dane picking up words."

Zak laughed. "It's fine. I think the group we're friends with say enough for Dane to come out with plenty of words he shouldn't."

Kenzo was pleased to see Jack in his usual seat, reading, his trembling hands steadying the book on his lap. "Hey, Jack."

Jack glanced up with a smile. "My favourite visitor! How are you, Kenzo?"

Kenzo's heart broke as he realised how much he had pulled away from everyone over the last week or so. He had a lot of apologising to do.

"I'm good. This here is—"

"Zak and Dane," Jack answered.

"How did you…?"

"You spoke about them enough; I'd recognise them anywhere. Nice to meet you. Have a seat."

Zak sat, settling Dane on his knee, still facing his chest. "I'm glad to meet you."

"Jack, are you okay to keep them company while I seek out David?" Kenzo raised his eyebrows at Zak, who nodded in understanding.

"Of course, I can! When the little guy gets more

comfortable, we can grab something for him to play with. We'll be fine."

Kenzo pressed a quick kiss to Zak's lips and ran a hand down Dane's back, then hurried down the corridor. He didn't want to leave Zak with a stranger for longer than he had to, even if he did trust and love Jack.

When David called for him to enter, Kenzo's palms started sweating. He opened the door and called out a greeting.

"Kenzo! Nice to see you again. Is everything okay with Miki?" Concern etched lines into David's face.

"Oh, yeah. He's doing good. Although…" He paused, thinking through what he'd been about to say. "You know what, I need to ask Miki the question."

David chuckled. "Fair enough. What can I do for you today?" He sat back in his chair.

Kenzo inhaled deeply. "I need to start therapy again."

David smiled at him, nodding. "I'm glad you've made that decision. You're carrying a lot of weight on your shoulders, Kenzo. Would you like me, or do you want someone I recommend?"

"You, if you have space, please."

"I do." He turned to his diary, picking up a pencil and using his thumb to flick through the pages. "We can start on Thursday if that's good for you. Say two o'clock?" David glanced at him for his answer.

Although Kenzo's heart pounded painfully, he

nodded in agreement. Before he turned to leave, he cleared his throat. "It's not going to be easy for me."

"It never is. Do you have someone to support you? Maybe someone other than Miki."

Kenzo smiled. "Yeah, I do."

David grinned. "I see. I'd love to meet him one day."

"He's in the Hub with Jack if you can spare a minute."

"Go on then you twisted my arm. I can grab another coffee while I'm there."

They wandered back to the large room, Kenzo pausing when he saw Zak and Dane surrounded by six or seven guys, all laughing while Dane was at Zak's feet playing with some toys. His heart expanded at the sight, and when he caught Zak's gaze, he mouthed, "Thank you."

Zak winked and returned to his conversation, watching as Dane stood and stumbled over to Jack, who quick as a flash lifted him onto his knee. The little boy was enraptured as Jack pulled faces at him.

Zak wandered over. "Everything okay?"

Kenzo pulled him close. "Yeah. Zak, this is David Pick, the therapist. My therapist," he said hesitantly, testing the idea.

Zak slid his arm around Kenzo's waist and squeezed. "Nice to meet you."

"You, too. I hear you're taking on this big guy."

Zak snorted. "Yep. He's mine."

Kenzo looked down at him with a small smile. "And you're mine."

"That I am."

They shared a kiss, and he reluctantly pulled away. As Kenzo was about to talk, Zak said, "David? Do you have any space for me as well? Or would it be a conflict of interest?"

David's eyebrows rose. "Yes, I do, actually, and it would be fine unless you'd feel more comfortable with someone who didn't know Kenzo?"

Zak glanced over at the group who were keeping an eye on Dane, and Kenzo could see the cogs whirring. "No, I don't mind at all."

"Sure, then. Let me grab a coffee, and Kenzo can keep an eye on that young lad while we set a date in my office. How about that?"

"Perfect."

CHAPTER NINETEEN

ZAK

He had not expected to come home that day with a date for his first therapy appointment, but when they'd been talking, he couldn't stop with the idea that it was the right thing to do. While they'd been in David's office, they'd had a brief discussion about his needs, but David had said they would talk more about it at their first session.

The first session had been easy enough. They'd talked about what Zak thought he might want from the sessions and began talking a little about his current situation. That had been the easy bit. By his fourth session, he'd figured out he needed to destress after each one, and the best way to do it was to work. So, when he finished with David mid-afternoon, he headed back to his workshop and started on the sanding. That was another thing they'd figured out—he couldn't use electric tools straight after a session. He would either hurt himself or break the tool. Colton had banned him from using them but held out a hand chisel and sandpaper. From then on, he'd worked out his frustration the hard way.

That day was harder than ever. They'd finally broached the subject of his mother and father. Zak had explained, devoid of emotion, how they had fought over the boys, and when his mother had gained custody, how they had been let down time after time.

The familiar unfairness of it all boiled his blood, and Zak felt himself getting worked up. What had they ever done wrong to be treated with such... disrespect? Zak had never been able to figure out the correct word to use for how he felt.

The unending carousel of men they'd be introduced to over the space of nine years had been astronomical; Zak wasn't sure he could count that high. His jaw clenched tight as his hand gripped the sandpaper tighter. The muscle memory of how to sand something had been ingrained in him for years, and he knew what he needed to do, but he pushed his muscles harder, feeling the ache beginning in his biceps and the blisters rising on his hands.

The scent of wood couldn't settle him that day.

"Hey, Zak, Colton. How're things?"

Noah's voice waded through the fog of Zak's thoughts, and he glanced over to the open garage door.

"Hey, Noah," Colton replied.

Zak saw Noah's eyebrows rise at Colton before he returned his gaze to the wood in front of him. He could feel the tension behind his eyes, turning into a full-blown headache, but he needed to settle; he needed the normality to be able to ground himself again.

Ignoring the whispered conversation behind him, he used a small brush to clean the intricate design before grabbing another piece of sandpaper.

"How are you doing, Zak?"

"Fine," he mumbled, focusing on the wood despite his back aching from being in the same position for too long.

"I wondered if I could stay for dinner? I could cook for us all?"

"Sure."

Noah sighed. "Zak—"

"Enough, Noah. I can't do this now." He bit off more words, not turning to see his brother's expression.

"I just want to—"

Zak whirled around. "You know what *I* just want? I want you to stop being so blasé about everything she put us through. I want you to get angry at her. I want you to realise how horrible she is. But every time we're around her, you act as though none of our childhood happened!"

Noah worked his jaw. "I know it happened, Zak. I was there."

"Then why are you always helping her? Why do you go and see her so often? She doesn't deserve any of it!" Zak threw the sandpaper across the workshop, pissed off when it didn't give any kind of significant thump to satisfy him. He stormed past Noah out into the fresh air but headed for the trees in the back garden. He knew he couldn't be in an enclosed space right then.

"Do you really not know why I can't hate her?" Noah's voice was quiet, but it made him jump—Zak hadn't realised he'd followed him. Zak swung around, fists clenched, although there was no way he'd *ever* hit Noah.

His dark blond hair whipped around his face, the wind picking up the strands as he stared at his younger brother, he ached for the childhood Noah never had. At least until nine years old, Zak had been able to live as a child, whereas Noah had only been able to have four years of it before it was all blown away.

Zak shook his head, answering Noah's question.

Noah took a deep breath and looked away. "Because of you."

His forehead creased, his mind unable to understand what Noah was trying to say. "What...?"

"You shielded me from most of it. You protected me every time. I remember when I was about six or seven, one of Mum's boyfriends tried to help us with our homework, you politely declined and moved us to your bedroom instead." Noah had a small smile on his face as he stared at what could only be trees—there was nothing else around in the direction he was looking. "I don't remember much of the first couple of years, but I do remember I thought it was cool to have different people around so often." He snorted. "Obviously, I was too young to understand." His gaze returned to Zak. "But as we grew older, you protected me from everything that would hurt me, either physically or emotionally."

Zak stared at him, unable to say a word. He didn't remember doing it, at least not consciously. He knew they spent a lot of time in one or the other's bedroom, but he hadn't thought any more of it than keeping them out of their mother's way.

"I always felt bad as we grew older that you took the brunt of it all. Me, I got off lightly. All because of you."

Noah's voice was thick with the unshed tears shimmering in his eyes. Zak's legs couldn't keep him upright any longer, and he sank to the ground, the dry grass and soil crumbly beneath his knees.

"I never..." He shook his head and rubbed a hand over his mouth before curling it into a fist and pressing it against his lips. Zak inhaled shakily and gazed up at Noah. "You were okay?" he whispered.

Noah nodded, the motion setting his tears overflowing.

Zak scrunched his eyes tight and leaned forward, resting his hands on the ground with his head bowed.

The band across his chest eased at the same time his shoulders relaxed. He hadn't realised until that moment he'd been angry on Noah's behalf as well as his own. To find out Noah hadn't been put through what he had was an enormous relief for him, and his body trembled from the emotion.

Arms surrounded him, and he burrowed into them, knowing his brother's scent anywhere.

"I'm sorry you were put through so much. I wish I could've helped," Noah croaked.

Zak pulled back, cupping Noah's face with his hands. "No! Don't ever wish that. I would've never wanted it for you. I'm relieved you were able to stay away from it all." He inhaled. "I don't know if I'll ever be ready to forgive her, but I'm working towards some sort of...I don't know...acceptance, maybe. That's for David to help me figure out." He gave a small huff of laughter as he pulled back, sitting on his backside, then flopping to his back. "All this emotional stuff is so exhausting!" he yelled to the sky.

Noah laughed with a second voice joining in. Zak lifted his head to see Kenzo striding towards them, a smile on his face.

"Maybe I can help out," Kenzo said, coming to a stop next to him.

"Yes, please," Zak whispered, holding out his hands.

Kenzo pulled him to standing and hooked his arm

under his knees, making Zak yelp as he was swung up into Kenzo's arms, bridal style.

"Your knee!"

"I'll be fine for the few steps to the house."

Zak wasn't sure but didn't want to move in case he overbalanced Kenzo and caused him more pain.

"I'll take a rain check on dinner!" Noah called from behind them.

"Definitely!" Kenzo shouted back. To Zak, he said, "Colton is locking the workshop up and leaving early. We have two hours to ourselves before Dane needs picking up. Let me help you."

Zak leaned his head against Kenzo's shoulder and closed his eyes. "Okay."

Kenzo helped him to his feet when they crossed the threshold, and hand in hand, they ascended the stairs to the bathroom where Kenzo sat Zak on the closed toilet seat while he turned on the shower.

As the water warmed, Kenzo pulled Zak to stand once more and divested him of his clothes, removing his own quickly afterwards. They stood under the spray, Zak's back to Kenzo's front, Zak's head resting against Kenzo's shoulder. Kenzo washed Zak's hair as he had been shown several times.

As relaxed as Zak was now feeling, he soon perked up when Kenzo's hands went roaming across his wet skin, plucking at his nipples and running a wet cloth across his cock and balls. Zak hummed and shifted his hips, feeling the hard shaft of Kenzo against his lower back.

"Fuck me hard, please, Kenzo," he whispered into his ear.

"As you asked so nicely."

Zak barely moved or opened his eyes as Kenzo's arms reached for something. Several seconds later, he felt fingers at his entrance, and he leaned forward, bracing his hands on the cold, wet tiles in front of him and thrusting his ass out.

"So eager." Kenzo's growl was more pronounced when he was aroused, and Zak shivered from it.

Zak rested his head alongside his hands when a finger breached him, quickly followed by a second and third. When the fingers were removed, he ached with the loss. He jumped when pressure began at his hole again, the loudness of the shower hiding any pertinent sounds.

Tiles were useless for gaining traction when all Zak wanted to do was grip hold of something while Kenzo pressed deeper inside him. When he was fully seated, Kenzo pressed a kiss to his shoulder and whispered, "Ready?"

Zak nodded.

After that, Kenzo set a punishing pace—hard and fast as Zak had asked for. It probably wasn't even minutes later when Zak's climax tore through him, a hoarse cry falling from his open mouth, with Kenzo following shortly after. Zak slumped against the wall, drained—for more than one reason.

Tears began to join the shower spray until it was turned off, and Zak was lifted from the shower. He barely registered anything until he was enclosed in strong, warm arms in his bed, tears still leaking.

"Go on. Let it all out."

"Sorry," he mumbled as he tried to stop the flow.

"Don't be sorry. I've been waiting for your emotional drop. I wasn't sure how long it would take you."

Zak succumbed as he remembered Kenzo's a couple of weeks before. He'd been an absolute wreck, but luckily, David had prepared them both for the possibility of it happening. Not everyone had one, but when emotions were high and bottled up for a long time, sometimes the lid blew.

Thankfully, they both had the other one to help out. And help Kenzo did, holding Zak until they needed to grab Dane. Then once the little man was in bed, he held him again. This time, all night.

A little over two months later, Zak could see the difference the therapy sessions had made in their lives.

Kenzo was a lot more open with his thoughts and feelings, and Zak had learned not to hold Dane too close as to potentially suffocate him; in other words, he had learned to lean on others. He had been doing that in the past, but always with one foot still in the door in case they couldn't cope or in case they turned into Ashley.

After Kenzo's second session, they had decided to increase to two sessions a week. Each hour wore Kenzo out, and he regularly came back and needed to decompress before he *could* talk about it with Zak, but each time Kenzo left, Zak knew he would come back.

They hadn't moved in together, but Kenzo was definitely at Zak's house more than he was at the apartment, especially now that Miki was doing a lot better and Drake was taking responsibility for the episodes. That had been hard on Kenzo, too. He'd asked Miki about not having had any setbacks, and Miki had explained about turning to Drake instead of Kenzo because he didn't want to burden Kenzo any longer. Initially, Kenzo had stormed out, but after a phone conversation with David, he'd gone back and apologised and listened to what Miki had to say.

To say their lives had been a whirlwind would have been putting it lightly, but Zak wouldn't change it for the world.

"Hey, you almost ready?" Kenzo's soft, deep voice vibrated along Zak's back as his arms came around him.

"I am. I still can't believe how many parties and things we go to now."

"Are they parties when we just sit there and drink?" Kenzo asked.

"Of course, they are. We bring presents for the birthday person, don't we? Which reminds me…"

Zak slipped out of Kenzo's arms, smiling when he grumbled about it and grabbed the gift from the bed. Eric was such a difficult person to buy for. As an award-winning celebrity, he could afford to buy practically anything; therefore, finding him a gift had taken some thinking. When he'd shown Kenzo what he'd bought, Kenzo had roared with laughter for many long minutes afterwards. He couldn't wait to see Eric's response.

Eric was also rarely home, but he'd put his foot down with the studio, according to Ethan, and demanded the time off. In a twist, the director had given him two weeks, saying he could do the other actors' scenes, but he'd made Eric promise not to take any more time during the remainder of production.

Zak thought it was a bit mean, but he didn't know the ins and outs of contracts, so he couldn't say anything. What mattered was Eric had been spending time with his family, and they were throwing him a party tonight at Crush, as usual, followed by a barbecue at Zak's house tomorrow afternoon. Most of the people were hoping the barbecue food would soak up the immense amount of alcohol they were likely to consume that night.

"Come on. Let's go."

As they descended the stairs, they saw Dane walking towards them, holding Jocelyn's hand. Jocelyn was Trent's daughter from his first marriage and had been looking after Janie and Dane whenever the group went out, giving Emily some much needed time off. They were on their way to Jocelyn's car. When she had first started looking after Dane, Zak had dropped Dane off at Asher's house—which was where everyone had agreed was the best place to use as a babysitting base due to all the childminding safety stuff he had—but once he'd stopped fretting so much, thanks to David, he'd allowed Jocelyn to collect him.

Zak picked Dane up, giving him a tight hug and a kiss on his head before passing him over to Kenzo, who did the same. Jocelyn left, then the two of them gathered their final things and followed in their wake.

As Kenzo drove, fingers linked with his, Zak thought back to the disastrous first time they'd tried to spend the evening together with the group. Zak had believed that had been the end of them, but he was glad to be wrong.

"What are you thinking about so hard over there?"

Zak rolled his head on the headrest to see Kenzo. "About how far we've come."

Kenzo squeezed his hand but didn't reply. Zak knew

he struggled with believing he was doing better, but he didn't see himself as Zak saw him. He would, one day.

The party was already in full swing when they got there. Charlie—who had finally taken over managing Crush when Tom's little boy had been born and after the shocking discovery that Tom actually owned the bar and didn't just manage it—had shut the bar to anyone who wasn't part of the party group. None of the usual bartenders were working tonight because Charlie and Tom had decreed they would try out two new staff and see how they went. They had also hired external caterers for the night. It worked well because it was their usual crew who would weigh in if the staff were no good.

Crush was becoming a hub of activity lately. Tom had bought Romano's next door after Old Joe had died last year, and there were huge projects in the works. Zak, Sean, Max and Ethan, plus several others, had been hired to create something unique. If it all went to plan, the place would be amazing when it was finished.

"Where's Eric?" he asked Sean.

"He's in the Garden Bar talking to someone, I think."

"We need to make sure he opens this in front of everyone, all right," Zak said with a grin.

Sean raised his eyebrows. "All right," he said hesitantly.

"It's nothing dirty, unfortunately, just hilarious," Kenzo added.

"How are you anyway? I've not seen you for all of a week!" Zak joked with Sean, sitting down beside him. Sean had recently left where he'd worked and started his own architect business, using the work they were getting from Tom as his first official jobs. It had been Tom's idea, and everyone had chipped in their positive thoughts on it. If things kept going as they were, he could see a few of them joining forces to create a whole host of services within one business. It was something that had been whirling around in Zak's brain for the last few weeks but needed a lot more thought and discussion before anything was said about it.

"Good. I'm getting all the little bits sorted for the business. I'll be up and running within a few weeks, I think."

"That's great news."

"What's great news?" Eric asked, dropping onto the seat opposite them.

Zak half-stood and leaned over the table to hug him. "Happy birthday! How does it feel to be twenty-four?"

"Thanks. Um…not much different to twenty-three?"

"That's a good thing. It means you're not getting old."

They laughed, and more people joined them. Zak marvelled at how many had joined their ranks since it had only been the four of them a little under three years ago. Despite having wanted to keep a distance before, he'd begun to realise these people were as much his family as Noah was.

Now that there was a larger audience, Zak passed over the gift to Eric. "You can open it now." He was dying to see his response.

Kenzo wrapped his arm around his shoulders and chuckled in his ear. "You are crazy."

Zak grinned.

"Why am I suddenly worried?" Eric said, his gaze flicking behind them before returning to the present again. He chuckled along with the crowd, then ripped off the paper. Holding it up, he stared, eyes wide, mouth open. "What the hell?"

CHAPTER TWENTY

KENZO

Zak bounced on the seat next to him, unable to withhold his excitement. "It's an award statue moulded after you."

The room cracked up, and Eric shook his head bemused. "I never realised something like this was possible. It's uncanny. It can go on my mantelpiece with the other two." He smirked.

Everyone jeered him, knowing, although, yes, he did have two real award statues as he'd been told by Zak, Eric would never truly be anything more than one of them. Zak had quickly confirmed Kenzo was in that category now, too, which had made him a little emotional—apparently his usual state now.

"I don't know what you're talking about. It looks nothing like you. The nose needs to be bigger," Ethan said, laughing when his brother shoved him off his chair.

Kenzo winced at the thump he made as he landed, but Ethan cracked up more when he couldn't get up because he was laughing so hard. Looking around the room, Kenzo was reminded of the barbecue they'd had several months ago. Everyone had been in fine spirits that day, too. It reminded him of the camaraderie he felt when he was amongst his teammates when they were on location or at home. The tight-knit family feeling. He had never thought he'd feel it with any other group of people, but here he was with a group of men and women who welcomed newcomers with open arms. He appreciated the sense of belonging they provided, especially after being so isolated with only Miki and Drake to call friends.

Thinking of his friends, he leaned into Zak's ear. "I was thinking of calling Miki and Drake to see if they wanted to join us. Do you think it would be okay with Eric?"

Zak smiled. "Of course, it would. Everyone would love to meet them."

"Miki might say no. It depends on how he's feeling."

"Well, if they can't make it today, there are always other opportunities."

"All right. I'll be back in a minute." He kissed the side of Zak's head and stood, heading for the double doors leading to outdoors. The music, while still being piped through to the speakers out there, was a lot more subdued, as was the conversation due to the small number of people congregating near the doors. Pulling his phone from his pocket, he dialled Miki, stepping slowly closer to the river until he could hear the little laps as the water hit the bank.

"Hey, Kenzo. I thought you were out tonight?"

"Hey. Yeah, I am. I wondered whether you and Drake wanted to join us. There's more than enough alcohol for you both, and it's free," he said, grinning into the twilight. He knew how to wind Miki up.

"Oi! I'm no alcoholic, but free beer. It's mighty hard to pass up."

"Then don't. I'd like you to meet the group. They're a good bunch."

Miki was silent for a moment, then Kenzo heard him call for Drake. A murmured conversation followed with Kenzo only catching a few words, and Miki came back on, "Yeah, all right. We'll be down in half an hour or so."

"Great. See you soon."

"Don't drink all the ale before we get there," Drake shouted.

"No guarantees," Kenzo joked.

When he hung up, he stayed staring into the sky, watching the streaks of orange and yellow merge with the muted blue as the sun set behind the buildings. He'd seen sunsets in deserts, over water and from the sky, but nothing beat viewing one from a place he called home.

Two hands slid along his sides and around to link against his stomach as a head rested between his shoulder blades. "Everything okay?"

Kenzo closed his eyes briefly, resting a hand over the top of Zak's, sinking into this feeling of being loved. "Yeah. Miki and Drake will be here soon."

Zak squeezed him. "That's great. I bet they'll get on well with everyone, but especially Max and Trent. They seem to have a similar dynamic and sense of humour."

Kenzo turned in Zak's embrace to wrap his arms around his boyfriend. "I'm sure they *will* get on with everyone. Your friends are amazing."

"*Our* friends." Zak rested his chin on Kenzo's chest and looked up at him. "Our friends are amazing."

Nodding, Kenzo dipped down and brushed a kiss across his lips. "Our friends," he agreed.

David helped him to recognise there were plenty of people around him who would help Kenzo if he needed it, but it was still difficult to acknowledge it when Zak was around because they were his friends first. He knew it didn't work that way, but it's how he felt. He was getting over it slowly.

"Come on. Let's go join them again. We don't want to be absent when Miki and Drake get here." Zak grabbed his hand and tugged him towards the bar.

Upon entering, they realised someone had brought

out a karaoke machine, and Emily and Analise were busy singing their love for the same man. Kenzo was a people watcher. He always had been, and he loved there was such a variety of personalities in the same group of people. Sitting again, he rested his arm on the back of Zak's chair and listened as he spoke to Luke about the gym. Kenzo realised Luke and Drake knew each other. It would be one common ground they'd have.

"There's going to be an extension soon." The voice came from close behind Kenzo, and for a split second, he froze, then he relaxed when he realised it was Drake.

"Is there?" Luke asked, eyes widening.

Kenzo was glad the two of them had parted on good terms. When Luke had left the gym to start his own business, Drake had grumbled about it for a while, but it wasn't because he didn't want Luke to go, well, not only that. He didn't, but Drake hated the idea of hiring people. He had told Kenzo more than once he would've preferred to give the responsibility to someone else, but on the other hand, he couldn't permit himself to hire someone without having met and interviewed them himself. It was a quandary where there was no way out.

"Yeah," Drake said, pulling up chairs for them both. "I'm trying to figure out the best way to do it but finding reputable architects is proving difficult."

Zak laughed. "I wish you'd said something earlier." He turned towards the dance floor and yelled, "Sean! Come here!"

Sean nodded, and after saying something to Asher, weaved his way through the crowd to their table, dropping onto a seat opposite with a sigh. "What's up?" He lifted his bottle and gulped several times.

Zak nodded towards Drake. "This is Drake and Miki. Drake owns the gym where Luke used to work, and he's looking for an architect."

Sean's eyebrows rose. "Seriously?"

Drake nodded. "Do you know someone?"

"Yeah, me." Sean snorted. "Ethan isn't qualified yet, but he's got a good head on his shoulders."

"That's great. Do you think we could arrange to meet up and discuss if what I want is possible or not?"

Sean nodded. "Sure. I have a big project beginning shortly, but depending on what you want, I know a few people who might be able to help out, too." He winked in Zak's direction.

Zak laughed. "Drake, Miki, meet Sean, an architect; Max, over there, is an interior designer; Craig, there, is a website designer; Emily is an accountant, and Otto is in advertising." He blew out a breath. "I think that's everyone who might have some skills to help a business out. There's probably more, but pfft," he waved his hand in dismissal, "you'll find out soon enough. There are plenty of occupations that can help around here."

Everyone around the table laughed.

"Yeah, I'll say." Drake punched Kenzo's shoulder.

"You kept all these helpful people to yourself until now."

"Jesus, Drake. I don't know what everyone does. I don't think I've met everyone myself yet."

"You'll be getting more and more visits from this group at the gym now, Drake. There's no hope for you," Luke said.

"Bring it on! If anyone has any classes or anything they want to see, let me know. Ever since *someone* deserted the ship, I have some free time on my schedule." He gave Luke a side glance and threw a straw wrapper in his direction with a grin. "You know I'm only messing. How's business?"

"It's going well. I'm only one person, so I'm not providing lots of classes, but yeah. I'm enjoying it."

"Glad to hear it."

While they conversed, Kenzo leaned forward. "How are you doing, Miki?" His voice was low enough for only Miki's ears.

"I'm doing good. I hadn't been sure if I'd manage the crowds and noise, but it's fine at the minute." Miki stared at him. "How are you doing with it all?"

Kenzo grinned. "Really well. These people are..." He sighed when he couldn't think of the best word to describe them, finishing with, "They support everyone, not just themselves. As you saw with Drake a moment ago. It seems like once you're in their periphery, you are part of them, and they help you with whatever they can."

"Kind of like a team, then?" Miki said.

Kenzo nodded slowly. "Even better. A family."

When the word family came out of his mouth the previous night, Kenzo had immediately thought of Pete. As David had taught him, he didn't immediately brush the thoughts away. Turning them over in his mind as he sat on the sofa, his head resting on his palm and his focus somewhere beyond the window, he realised thinking about Pete didn't hurt as much as it had done before.

As for his parents, he hadn't spoken to them in months, which wasn't unusual. When he'd called them that morning and explained some things, he'd expected some sort of reaction from them, although why he didn't know. He didn't need them now. He had his own family.

"Are you okay?" Zak asked, cuddling up to his side.

Kenzo pulled him close, kissing the top of his head. "Yeah. I'm thinking about Pete."

"What about him?"

He sighed and returned his gaze to the window. "It wasn't his fault, and it wasn't mine either. The second is harder to believe, but I'm beginning to. I knew Pete. He was my best friend. There's no way he would've done it if he had realised the outcome. The only thing I can figure as to why it happened at all is that the meeting time had changed. Maybe Pete didn't realise and expected an empty barracks."

"As much as it pains me to say this to you, but you'll never know the truth. From what you've told me about Pete, though, I think you're right. He wouldn't have done it knowing there would be such consequences for those he loved."

Kenzo sniffed. "I need to call Miranda and Robin."

"Okay. I'll leave you to it." Zak pulled away.

"No!" He gripped hold of his arm. "Will you stay?" Kenzo asked.

"Of course. For as long as you need me to." Zak snuggled back into him, his arm across Kenzo's stomach.

Kenzo cleared his throat as he dialled Miranda's number, putting it on speakerphone.

"Kenzo?" she asked hesitantly.

"Yeah. I'm sorry, Miranda. Things have been difficult here. I wasn't in the right frame of mind to try and deal with what you were asking. I didn't mean to upset you."

"Oh, Kenzo." Miranda's voice cracked. "I wasn't upset with you. I didn't want you pulling away from us. I'm sorry if I made you do just that, but I didn't want to lose someone I considered as important as my son. We always considered you our adopted son, Kenzo. You know that."

Kenzo closed his eyes as tears dripped steadily down his cheeks, and he inhaled deeply. "You won't lose me. I'm here."

They were silent for a moment until she asked, "How are you?"

"I've been struggling, but I'm back in therapy, which is helping a lot. Also," he gazed at Zak, who was wrapped around him like a monkey, "I have a boyfriend, Zak, and he has a little boy named Dane."

He heard sniffles on the other end of the phone. "That's wonderful news," came the watery reply. "I'm so happy for you."

Kenzo got to the main reason for his call. "I want to be part of the charity, Miranda."

"Really? That would be wonderful. We had decided against going ahead with it because we were still unsure about the connection to Pete, but if you think it would be a good idea, then we'll carry on."

"It might be difficult in the beginning because people will only see what's on the outside, what they've been told. I want to be one of the spokespeople for the charity. I think if I talk about Pete, what he was like before and the complexities of mental health, we can win people around."

"Pete would've loved the idea."

A lump got stuck in his throat, but he managed to say, "Yes, he would've."

"Do you remember…" She hesitated as if she didn't know whether to continue.

"Remember what?"

"When Pete got stuck up the tree, and you attempted to rescue him, ending up with you both getting stuck. You were there for over an hour before anyone came to find you."

Kenzo chuckled. "We were better at climbing after that. You have to admit it."

"Yeah, you were. You were both so fearless. Nothing fazed either one of you. Not even a pre-Wimbledon tennis championship."

Kenzo could hear Miranda's smile. "Why be scared? You're there to do—"

"—a job. I know. That phrase was yours and Pete's favourite." She paused again. "I was always worried about you both signing up for the Army, but you were adamant. I'm glad you had that. I'm glad you were both able to do what you wanted to do, what you felt so strongly about."

"In some ways…" Kenzo held Zak tighter, but he moved, straddling Kenzo's lap, and wrapped his arms around him, tucking his head under Kenzo's chin. "In some ways, I'm glad I was hurt because I don't know if I would've been able to continue on the team without him."

"He wouldn't have wanted you hurt, Kenzo. He would've wanted you to carry on with your life as you are doing."

"I know, but it would've hurt just as much had I carried on in the team without him being there with me."

They were silent for a moment, hitching breaths heard from both sides. Kenzo pictured Pete in his head, his cocky smile and his careful hands. He knew...he *knew* Pete hadn't meant to hurt anyone. It had taken him a while to remember the Pete he'd known, rather than the Pete everyone told him about.

He closed his eyes, tears leaking regardless, and rested his head against the back of the sofa.

"Miranda, it's Zak."

"Hi, Zak."

"We're going to have a brainstorming session about the charity soon. I'm going to ask our friends for their ideas, too. We need to head off for the moment, but can we call you back in a few days?"

"Of course, you can, Zak. Thank you. Any ideas would be more than welcome."

"We also have a variety of occupations amongst us all. No doubt someone could be of assistance."

"That's great. Talk to you soon, and take care of him, Zak."

"And I'll take care of Zak," Kenzo added hoarsely.

"Definitely. Love to all three of you."

They hung up, but Kenzo kept his arms around Zak, allowing the tears to flow freely. It hadn't been an easy phone call, but it had been a cathartic one.

"What things did Pete like to do?" Zak asked into the silence.

"In what way?"

"Well, I know he liked tennis, as you did. Maybe we could raise some money doing some tennis lessons or something tennis related, but what else did he enjoy? Maybe we could create an event around some of his interests. People will be able to get to know him through the activities and through you."

Clearing his throat did nothing to move the lump residing there. "Um… he loved planes of all types. Well, anything that could fly: helicopters, gliders, anything that kept someone up in the air. And he *loved* Christmas."

"Maybe we could get people to make model aeroplanes or offer flying lessons or a hot air balloon ride at an auction, something like that."

"They're good ideas."

"I bet, once we get our friends onto it, they will come up with some brilliant ideas," Zak said.

Kenzo was completely overwhelmed and broke.

When he finally became aware of his surroundings again, he found himself wrapped in Zak's arms and legs as they lay on the sofa. Zak was stroking his hair, which was longer than it had been in a while, and pressing kisses to his forehead. Kenzo's breath was still hitching, and his stomach and chest were aching—he assumed from the force of his cries.

His mind felt clearer, less cluttered, and he tried to remember the last time he felt like that. It had been before Pete had died, no question.

"Sorry," he croaked.

"Don't you ever be sorry for needing to cry," Zak said forcefully. "Everyone needs to on occasion. Today was your day. Tomorrow it may be mine. We'll see. Hell, it might be Dane's day." Kenzo snorted. "How are you feeling?"

"Better. I feel like a weight has been lifted from my shoulders."

"Good."

"I'm missing one thing, though."

Zak pulled back a little to look at him with a crease between his eyebrows. "What?"

"The little guy." Kenzo smiled.

Zak rolled his eyes. "We'll go get him, and you two can cause mischief while I cook dinner. How does that sound?"

"But it's my turn."

"You can cook tomorrow."

Kenzo leaned forward and pressed a kiss to Zak's lips. "I love you, you know."

"I know you do. I love you, too."

Zak stared at him for a moment. "Would you like to move in?"

Kenzo smiled slowly. "Yeah, I really would."

FIFTEEN MONTHS LATER

ZAK

They'd left several people at the Whittaker Hotel to take care of the final preparations for the night so Zak and Kenzo could get changed and ready for the event. The hotel manager had been amazing about it and had offered the use of their main banquet hall for the evening. The room was huge, easily big enough to house two hundred or so guests.

As Zak had mentioned to Miranda during their first and subsequent phone calls, his friends had been a huge help, offering their services for free. Max had gone to town with the interior design of the hall, and as they were leaving, he had almost finished. Luke's best friend, Otto, had helped with advertising; Tom had provided drinks, both alcoholic and non-alcoholic; Craig had created a website for the charity with so many bells and whistles, Zak hadn't been able to keep up when he was explaining it; and Emily had offered to help with the accounting side of things, which Miranda had almost snapped her hand off at.

Emily and Otto were being brought on as permanent members of staff as soon as the event had finished, and Craig had offered to do the upkeep on the website for free, although it had been declined initially. Miranda and Robin had demanded to pay him, and they'd eventually agreed on a half-price fee.

Kenzo, of course, would be the spokesperson for the charity because Miranda and Robin both felt they should be behind the scenes rather than upfront and centre. Despite multiple people saying they didn't need to hide, they refused, citing they would be happier arranging everything instead.

Seeing Kenzo telling people what to do gave Zak a chance to see what he would've been like as an Army lieutenant. He took people's abilities and gave them jobs that would see them succeed, rather than giving it to someone who would have to learn something new. Not everyone would take the time to do that. They'd delegate to whoever was there.

As soon as Kenzo had decided to be part of the charity—aptly named Pete's Foundation—he had been determined to make a success of it. It hadn't been all sunshine and flowers, but they had each other to hold onto when things got difficult.

Zak's mother had surprised them all when her relationship with Clive lasted. More so when she declared she was moving away, having decided to go and live with Clive in London rather than staying here. He couldn't blame her, but he knew she wouldn't see Dane often, if at all. He no longer hated his mother, but he also wasn't sure he liked her. He loved her, of course, he did, but even with working through his issues with David, he still couldn't shake the dislike of her from his thoughts. But David had said it was okay to feel that way as long as he was feeling it for the right reasons.

He walked over to Kenzo, seeing him fussing with his tie. "How are you doing?"

"I can't get this stupid bowtie to look right."

Zak turned Kenzo towards him. "Come on, let me do it." He undid the knot and retied it, pulling it tight when it was done. "There you go, handsome."

Kenzo smiled, though it was a small one. Zak knew he was worried about his speech. He'd worked tirelessly on it for months, and Zak knew how much he wanted people to understand who Pete was, rather than see him for what he'd done.

As far as Zak was concerned, the speech was perfect, but Kenzo wouldn't accept that until it was over and he'd stood in front of a room full of strangers and laid out his heart. Zak could do nothing except be there for him. He'd tried to get him to relax by having a long bath together and giving him a back massage before they'd needed to start getting into their tuxedos.

"You ready?" he asked.

"Yeah."

Zak threaded their fingers together and headed to the door, where Noah was waiting to take them to the hotel. When Kenzo went to get his keys and phone, Zak pulled Noah aside.

"I don't want you to feel like a chauffeur, but I need to sit with Kenzo. He's so nervous."

Noah waved him away. "It's fine. Help him out. It's a big night for him."

"He'll be fine as soon as the speech is done."

"Good job it's part of the first section, then."

"That's why we did it. I don't think he would've managed to enjoy the event if we didn't get the speech out of the way first."

Kenzo came towards them, and they finished getting their coats on and climbed in the car. Zak held Kenzo's hand, feeling the trembling despite how tight they were clasped together.

When Noah pulled up at the hotel, Zak had him leave the keys and go inside without them. He turned to Kenzo.

"The people who are joining us tonight know all about Pete. The heart-warming story you wrote on the website is enough for people to understand he wasn't a bad person. If they believed he was, they wouldn't be here."

"I know. It's important to me they understand—" His voice broke, and he stopped.

"They do. When you get up there, all you will be doing is reminding them about who he was: the joker, the Christmas angel, your best friend."

"Thank you for everything."

"You are very welcome, my love. Come on, let's do this."

They entered the hotel and strode towards the banquet hall. The event was supposed to start in half an hour, and they were to greet the first few people, then mingle until it was time for everyone to be seated and for Kenzo to take to the podium. Once his speech was finished, dinner would be served and some dancing after. After that, an auction would begin for some amazing items the community, near and far, had provided for them. All proceeds of the auction would be going into the charity to help those who needed it.

As they stepped into the hall, applause began, and he glanced around to see all his friends and family surrounding them, smiles and tears on their faces.

Kenzo clenched his hand harder, and Zak turned his gaze to him, seeing him fighting to keep the tears at bay.

"Thank you, everyone," Kenzo finally said. "We couldn't have made this happen without each and every one of you. I really do appreciate it."

"Now, get back to work, slackers," Zak shouted to break the seriousness of the atmosphere.

Everyone laughed as they dispersed. Zak led Kenzo over to the entryway, where they would need to be to greet the guests, and held both his hands, squeezing gently.

"Doing okay?" Zak asked, raising his eyebrows.

"Yeah, actually. That helped," Kenzo said, indicating their welcome party. He gazed around the hall. "I can't believe this place. Pete would've loved it."

Zak surveyed the room. It was decorated in blues and whites to go with the Christmas-themed event. A white dancefloor with a snowflake light show projected on it was located to the back of the room, currently with a podium on it where Kenzo and the auctioneer would speak from. Round tables, seating ten people each, were covered with white tablecloths and blue table runners, the chairs having the same treatment but with blue covers and a white bow tied to the back of them.

Eight white square planters were situated in the corners of the room with white frosted winter trees and surrounded by green foliage and white and blue baubles. At the side of the room, there were several lightboxes from floor to ceiling, giving an extra glow in the chandelier-lit room.

All in all, Max had done an amazing job making it into a winter wonderland—Pete's favourite time of year.

Zak was about to say something when the first guests appeared, and they hurried to their positions, greeting those who had given up their evening to support a wonderful charity.

KENZO

As he stood at the podium, he exhaled roughly, the noise catching through the microphone and going out through the speakers. The guests chuckled.

"As you can probably hear, I'm nervous, so please, bear with me." Kenzo glanced around the room again, marvelling at the decorations. "Christmastime was Pete's favourite time of year. No other celebration would ever beat it, according to him, not even birthdays, much to his parents' sorrow, who loved birthdays more." A few more chuckles. "Pete believed in the magic of Christmas. When we were kids, he would always save some of his pocket money each week of the year. I never knew why, and he never told me. I don't think I ever told Miranda and Robin, Pete's parents, about this because it wasn't my place to say. But every year, the money he saved was used to buy as many gifts as he could afford for those who were unlikely to get a present. When I finally realised what he was doing, and I don't know exactly when he started doing it, I followed suit. Every year from then on, and I was ten at the time, we managed to gift at least ten children with a present from Santa."

Kenzo swallowed hard, focusing on the snowflakes on the floor. He took a few breaths. "No one ever realised who those presents were from, or if they did, no one said anything. Even in his last year, we were still doing the same thing, only using our own money, not pocket money." More laughter. "I calculated this would mean approximately three hundred and twenty children received gifts who would have never received anything otherwise." He stopped as applause started. He held out his hand, waiting until they stopped. "I'm not telling you this to get recognition for me. I'm doing it because since the accident—and it was an accident, which I will explain in a few minutes—I'd forgotten how unselfish Pete had been."

He had to pause again to get his breathing under control, taking a few sips from his glass of water. "When Pete took his own life, I wholeheartedly believed what I'd been told, that he hadn't cared about anyone in his last moments. Because of that, it skewed my memories of the kind, selfless, amazing man for several years. I lost the spirit of Christmas.

"Thankfully, with help from several people, I

managed to remember what Pete stood for. He stood for those who couldn't stand for themselves. I know, from the very bottom of my heart, Pete never meant to hurt anyone that day. I knew him better than anyone, and even struggling with his mental health, he would not have wanted anyone to get hurt from his actions."

Wiping at his cheeks, he tried to continue but couldn't for a moment. Zak came up to him and gripped his hand, wrapping his other around his waist. Looking to the podium, he began to speak, reading from Kenzo's speech.

"Mental health is not mentioned a lot within any areas of life. People seem to believe it's a subject that should be spoken about behind closed doors. Well, Pete wouldn't have wanted that. He would've climbed to the rafters and shouted at the top of this voice if he had realised how much of an issue it was. Mental health can change your perceptions of all the things around you, and every person will view things differently. No two people will have the same experience. Similar, yes, but not exactly the same."

Kenzo picked up from where Zak finished, "Pete would not want people to suffer who did not need to. It is with this in mind that we created this foundation. The money raised by this charity will be used to help military personnel, both past and present, get the mental health help they need. Our goal is to help as many people as possible but to also bring awareness to the issue. In future years, our plans would like to include *anyone* with mental health needs, but, for now, that remains a dream for the future.

"What happened to Pete was a loss for everyone, but especially those children who will no longer benefit from his selflessness at Christmas. I will continue his work as best I can and hope it is enough for the doubt I felt for even a moment."

"Thank you for joining us tonight," Zak said. "It means a lot. Please enjoy dinner and dancing, and the auction will start in a couple of hours."

Zak pulled him to a table in the corner where they had been seated and pushed him down, pressing a handkerchief into his hand. He pressed it against the corners of his eyes, trying to stem the tears. After a few deep breaths, and he was back in control.

"You did it," Zak said, smiling.

"I love you so much. Do you know that?" Kenzo said, staring into those beautiful deep blue eyes.

"I do, and I love you." Zak pressed a kiss to his lips and wrapped his arms around him. "I'm so proud of you."

"I have a feeling there will be many more children with presents this year," said a voice from behind him.

Kenzo turned around, seeing Emily stood there with tears in her eyes. He hugged her, then pulled back. "What do you mean?"

"People have been asking me how to donate to the

children's Christmas present fund. We need to have a separate account set up and soon."

Kenzo stared at her. "I didn't tell the story so people would do that. The idea was to support the foundation."

"No! This is on top of what they're donating to the foundation. The charity won't suffer for your story, Kenzo. The children will benefit as well as the foundation."

He sat back in his seat, rubbing a hand over his mouth and staring at the floor. When he had chosen that story from the many he could remember, he had never believed Pete's name could live on through other means as well.

Unaware of how long he'd been contemplating the future, he felt Zak's hands on his and slowly came back to the room. The conversation was light, and laughter sounded throughout the room as the guests enjoyed the food.

"Come on, sweetheart. Let's eat," Zak said, pulling him to his feet.

He shuffled towards the table a bit more and sat back in the chair Zak had moved closer. His plate was filled with all the Christmas dinner trimmings, and the aroma was divine. His stomach grumbled, and he realised how long it had been since he'd eaten.

Leaning forward to Zak, he kissed him, uncaring of who saw. "I love you."

"I love you."

Would you like to read more about Crush? Order Love Scene now.

Sign up for my newsletter to get a free **BONUS SCENE** from Covert Strength and the Crush prequel short story, Love Conquers.

If you have a moment, would you write a review for Covert Strength please? Reviews help other readers decide whether they would like to read the book, and therefore, are also important for authors.

LOVE SCENE

CRUSH SERIES BOOK 8

A stressed lawyer finds relief in the form of a Daddy and little relationship, but not the ordinary kind. A low angst MM romance.

Can a younger daddy persuade an older boy to love and trust?

Eric can have anything and everything he wants, but what he truly wants is hard to come by: trust and love. The only people he believes in are his siblings and the clubs he visits, which are bound by their confidentiality. He doesn't need his Daddy status plastered over the media. Although he finds himself willing to go to great lengths when he finds his ideal little in an older man.

Samuel is living his worst nightmare: his ex-husband cheated on him with a colleague. The stress of his job takes him to breaking point until Eric shows him what life could be like. Samuel finds the transition to being a little easier than he'd expected, but he can't cope when he's left alone.

Will love win?

⁂

ORDER HERE:
https://readerlinks.com/l/1766668

ABOUT ELOUISE EAST

I am a bestselling author of contemporary MM romance. I write a variety of themes: sweet and fluffy to high angst to taboo, but there is a huge nod in the direction of friendships being integral to each character's experience. I write books that are emotionally realistic, even if liberties are taken with other aspects of my stories.

Reading and writing have always been a part of my life, although my debut book wasn't published until July 2019, when I was 36 years old. My experience has come from reading thousands of books over the years and being a perfectionist when it comes to trying to make things right. I live in the centre of the UK with my two children, who make life worth living, keep me (in)sane and make me laugh.

STALK ME HERE… ;-)

WEBSITE: https://elouiseeast.com/
NEWSLETTER: https://elouiseeast.com/newsletter
LINKTREE: https://linktr.ee/elouiseeastauthor

BOOKS BY ELOUISE EAST

<u>CRUSH</u>

First Kiss

Instant Desire

Primary Seduction

Deep Down

A Crush for Christmas

Life Support

Covert Strength

Love Scene

Lawful Attraction

<u>JUST A LITTLE CRUSH</u>

Star-Crossed

He's Behind You

A Special Love (newsletter story)

<u>DADDY</u>

Love Me, Daddy

Soothe Me, Daddy

Spoil Me, Daddy

DARK & DIVERGENT

A Biker Make Three

Forbidden Temptation

Too Many Secrets

CHARMED

Treehouse Whispers

Rhythm Inside (Heard it in a Love Song Anthology)